# HOPEFUL HEARTS AT THE CORNISH COVE

KIM NASH

Boldwood

First published in Great Britain in 2023 by Boldwood Books Ltd.

Cover Design by Alexandra Allden

Cover photography: Shutterstock

A CIP catalogue record for this book is available from the British Library.

Paperback ISBN 978-1-80549-463-8

Large Print ISBN 978-1-80549-459-1

Harback ISBN 978-1-80549-458-4

Ebook ISBN 978-1-80549-456-0

Kindle ISBN 978-1-80549-457-7

Audio CD ISBN 978-1-80549-464-5

MP3 CD ISBN 978-1-80549-461-4

Digital audio download ISBN 978-1-80549-455-3

Boldwood Books Ltd
23 Bowerdean Street
London SW6 3TN
www.boldwoodbooks.com

*To Angela Bateman, who never realised when she sent me the RNLI Christmas card with a gorgeous lighthouse on the front illustrated by Claire Leary, that it would spark a whole new series of books set in the fictional seaside location of Driftwood Bay. Thank you for that inspiration, Angela, along with your support for my writing and for loving my books. Kim X.*

## 1

Gabby laughed loudly down the phone.

'There must be something wrong with my hearing. For a minute there, I thought you'd said you'd just bought a lighthouse.' She continued to laugh.

Silence from my end of the call stalled her laughter for a second or two and when she spoke again her voice started to wobble.

'Meredith Robinson! Please tell me you're joking.'

'Erm. I'm actually not joking. I really did buy a lighthouse.' I couldn't believe it myself, so I wasn't quite sure how my best friend would take my news and had been avoiding her calls for most of the day.

'What the f—'

'I know you'll think I'm mad but—'

We had a habit of blurting out what we were thinking at the same time. We'd done it since we met in primary school.

'I'm finishing work in an hour. I'll be straight home. I think you need to tell me what the hell is going on.'

I glanced at my wrist. If Gabby finished work in around an hour, and it took her about twenty minutes to get home, I had just a short amount of time to comprehend myself what had actually just happened, let alone with her. Just over an hour to understand why I'd just done the maddest thing I've ever done in my life and then to put that into words to explain to my bestie. That'll teach me to do evening drinking alone.

As I glanced at my phone, my hands were trembling but at the same time, there were excitable butterflies in my stomach. It was a good job Gabby had stayed over at Luke's last night, so I didn't have to face her that morning.

I took a deep breath as I walked down the hallway of her home, which had now been my home for the last twelve months, and glanced in the hall mirror which hung above a chest of drawers that I had painted in a duck-egg-blue colour last summer. As I looked at myself, I wondered who the hell was the person reflecting back at me. I gulped and the realisation of what I'd actually done began to sink in.

Oh! My! God! I really had just gone and bought a fricking lighthouse!

# 2

Russell, the estate agent, had been super helpful over the phone, telling me about some of the local places I might find handy, and I found myself daydreaming a little before I pulled into the super-market car park, which was the first thing on my list. When I say supermarket, I think Russell had been exaggerating slightly as it wasn't much bigger than the local Co-op in my hometown, but at least I should be able to get the essentials before heading on to Driftwood Bay. The removal van was due at the lighthouse at around 3 p.m. so at least I could get in early, get a pot of tea on the go and put some cakes out for the guys. It was the least I could do after they'd driven down from the Midlands. It had taken me six hours and that was with me racing mostly in the fast lane. I was tired and hungry and gagging for a cup of tea so I was sure they would be too.

There was a space really close to the front door that I had my eye on, so I drove round the one-way system to get to it and indi-cated to pull in, just as a big royal blue four-wheel-drive truck drove the wrong way down the lane, cut right across the front of me, turned and slammed their brakes on. In my parking space! Now that was just downright rude. I humphed out loud as I undid my seat belt. This driver had annoyed me big time and I decided that I was going to give them a piece of my mind. At home, I probably wouldn't have done this, but this was the new assertive me and they had done wrong. Also there surely is an unwritten law that no one should mess with a hangry woman or one of a certain age. This driver had hit the jackpot with me. The door of the truck opened, and I saw one denim-clad leg swing round. I didn't even give them chance to get out of the vehicle before I started ranting from my open window.

'Oi! I was just about to park there. Did you not see my indicator? What is wrong with you?'

Time seemed to stand still as the body that unfolded from the truck reached its full height of about 6 foot 5 inches. Blimey, trust me to pick on the biggest person in town.

'You snooze you lose, lady. Dithering about doesn't get you a parking space in this town. Have a good day now.' He slammed the door, raised two fingers to his temple in a mock salute and strode away, which made me even more furious.

Livid, I reversed into another space that had just become vacant and abandoned the car. Stomping across the car park behind him, my shorter legs were having trouble keeping up with his very long ones.

'I thought people in Cornwall were supposed to be the salt of the earth? What happened to that? This is not what I expected from a place I've never been to before,' I yelled at his incredibly broad back as I followed him in through the sliding doors.

He stood still and turned towards me.

'Oh God, are you still here? I'm really not in the mood for this today. Can you just leave me alone to get some shopping, please? I'm in a rush.'

However, I was on a roll and words just came tumbling out.

'Clearly! So much of a rush that you have no time to consider anyone else. Not the warmest welcome that I might have been expecting when I've just packed up my life and moved here.' I was so flustered my hands had started shaking which annoyed me. Why couldn't I be one of those people who were cool, calm and collected in this sort of situation instead of a blithering wreck? Come to think of it, why was I divulging my life in the middle of a supermarket?

I channelled my inner calm and remembered what my therapist told me, counted to ten which actually did make me feel slightly better. She had always tried to instil into me the fact that being angry about something only affected me. The other party would have forgotten about it by now. She taught me that it's better for my own sanity to just let things go.

After a second slow countdown I did feel better and thought perhaps it was not even worth it. I suppose taking someone's parking space isn't really the end of the world, is it?

After getting my shopping list out of my handbag and grabbing a wire basket from the stack by the door, I wasted no time zipping around the aisles and managed to get most of the things I needed despite the size of the shop. This was the largest store close to Driftwood Bay and there wasn't another for miles so at least it was well stocked.

Just as I was about to approach the till, someone zoomed in front of me and put their basket on the end of the counter. Seriously! What was it with people round here? I looked into the face of – yep, you've guessed it – the car park space stealer.

'Seriously, not you again. Are you like the rudest man in town or something?'

He turned to me and rolled his eyes. 'And are you the biggest pain in the arse that I've ever met? Wait. Oh yes. So you are.' He turned his back on me, blocking me completely.

My eyebrows rose higher than I ever thought possible. I wasn't sure why this man had riled me up so much. I wasn't normally this stressed-out person. I was the person who let people in the supermarket queue who had fewer items go in front of me. I was the person who said sorry when someone bumped into me. It must be the long drive and the need for food.

I counted to ten again as Mr Rude smiled sweetly at the till assistant and muttered something under his breath. The woman looked in my direction and smirked. I wondered what he'd said.

When it was my turn, the till assistant didn't utter a word to me apart from grunting the cost of my shopping. This must be the rudest part of the country despite all the countryside and sea. It certainly wasn't what I was expecting. Maybe I should just turn away and head for the car. Nothing good could come from this now.

I found Mr Rude again outside, where he was getting some cash from the cashpoint and my heart sank as I realised I couldn't avoid going past him as I headed for my car. He turned round and tutted loudly as I passed him. My blood very quickly reached boiling point once more.

'There's just no need. Did you get out of bed the wrong side today? Maybe you should keep your bad temper and shitty attitude to yourself. What an absolute delight you are. Not!' I walked away determined to have the last word. I felt like I couldn't help being aggressive around this man.

He grunted as he walked away, then shouted over his shoulder, 'I sincerely hope we never have the misfortune to bump into each other again. Oh, and welcome to Cornwall!'

# 3

The sight of three big burly removal men shaking their heads in unison was not what I was expecting when I drove to the end of the little dirt track that led to Driftwood Bay Lighthouse.

I'd finally managed to get myself into a much brighter mood after the episode at the supermarket by singing at the top of my voice to Gloria Gaynor's 'I Will Survive' with the volume so high I was surprised I didn't blow the speakers. That song never failed to lift my spirits and with the late spring sun shining down on me and the glimpses of turquoise blue sea which I caught over the green leafy hedgerows, I was once again ready for this new adventure. The wind whistled around my ears as I'd taken the car roof off at the supermarket, and I appreciated the smell of the salty sea air.

'Hi there. Good journey?' I slammed the car door behind me and smiled broadly at them, hoping that maybe they just needed a bright and breezy mood to save the day. My little Mini convertible looked tiny next to the removal lorry.

'Oh, Miss Robinson, we're so glad you're here. We have one hell of a problem. Well, actually *we* don't, but *you* do.'

'What on earth is the matter?' My dazzling smile disappeared.

'Well, basically, the majority of your furniture is not going to fit through that front door!'

I turned towards the lighthouse. The front door was probably not much taller than me and not the widest in the world, but surely they were wrong.

'I'm sure it will. Let's open up and see how the land lies, shall we? Positive vibes, guys!' I pasted on a cheery smile again, thinking how negative they were. I was sure we'd find a way once we got inside. Knowing what most men were like, they probably just hadn't thought of the blatantly obvious solution. I pulled the key out of my back pocket and turned it in the lock. Up closer, the door did actually look quite small, and as I chewed the inside of my cheek, I pondered what the hell I was going to do if they were right. I opened the front door and a big chunk of peeling paintwork came off into my hand. I threw it on the ground beside me.

'Shall we go in first and have a look round and then we can see what's what? Maybe have a cuppa and a cake too once I can find the kettle.'

'Sounds good, Miss Robinson. We'll follow you.'

They all had to duck down to get into the entrance hall, which was obviously a round room with a spiral metal staircase slap bang in the middle. It looked so dark and gloomy and very different to the bright and welcoming picture that Russell had sent through. I turned to look at the removal men, and all three of them raised their eyebrows at me.

I could see that there was a window at the back of the property which needed a blooming good clean. I looked through the pane of glass at the top which was the least dirty. In all the kerfuffle of my arrival, I hadn't even noticed that there was a garden and a large building to the right with huge double doors at the front. Maybe a storage shed of some type. I didn't remember seeing that in the pictures either although there weren't that many pictures – something that Gabby had great pleasure in reprimanding me about at the first opportunity. It had all happened so quickly, from agreement of purchase, which I could vaguely remember due to my sozzled state, to exchanging contracts and receiving the keys. I may have missed stuff, but now it was clear: my gorgeous, yet rather large three-piece, chocolate-brown leather suite, which had already been in storage for over twelve months, was never going to see the inside of this building.

As I closed the door behind us and approached the stairs, there wasn't a murmur from the men. When I glanced at the driver, he smiled nervously and looked away and the others just avoided catching my eye. There was a chill in the air even though the sun was shining outside. Maybe this clearly neglected old building just needed a good blast of central heating; it must have been empty for a while. Positive thoughts, Meredith. Keep them coming.

My footsteps clanked on the wrought iron staircase as I ascended each step up to the next floor which was as bare as bare could be. Not sure what this room even was. It was hard to work out when there was no furniture in it. The windows were so filthy you couldn't see out, which made the room feel really dark and I started to notice a particularly damp and musty smell. The next floor was exactly the same, and as I climbed another part of the staircase, getting nearer to the top, I was starting to wonder what the hell I had bought. This was clearly meant to be the kitchen area which the estate agent told me was part renovated but looked like it had been abandoned the minute they'd started the process. Although I could see the label for an integrated cooker on one of the boxes which was a good start. The layer of dirt on the worksurfaces, which were propped up against the side wall, was so thick I wondered how they would ever see the light of day. Again, the window was filthy. I tried to clear a spot to see out, but it was proper grime, which had been there for a while, and would take a great deal of elbow grease to shift.

I was starting to feel like I should have bought an industrial-sized pack of Marigolds from the supermarket as I was clearly going to need them.

'Were you planning to stay here tonight, Miss Robinson? Maybe a hotel might be a better option?'

The driver spoke the words that had been swimming around in my head although my version of the sentence had many more swear words in it. Maybe after the drive down, I was tired, and nothing was making sense. Was there even a hotel around here? Perhaps we should just get the furniture we could get through the door in place and see where to go from there. I looked at my watch. It was way after three o'clock. And these guys needed to get back home tonight.

There was just one more floor to go, which I approached with caution. The constant swirl of the staircases was making me feel slightly light-headed, but it all seemed worth it when I reached the top. I gasped. The first thing that hit me was a view which took my breath away.

Through the huge glass floor-to-ceiling windows, the room looked out over the most picturesque harbour I'd ever seen to one side and a small golden sandy beach on the other. The windows on this floor weren't quite as dirty as the others and there was a chair in the middle of the room. Clearly, the last time there had been life in this building had been someone admiring the view. I didn't blame them one bit. Pastel-coloured, mismatched houses of different shapes and sizes lined the harbour walls at the end of which I could see a narrow street leading up a steep hill. Boats bobbed on the water, and I could hear the metallic jangling of the masts which sounded like tuneful wind chimes. I couldn't wait to get down there to take a closer look.

Flinging open the French doors directly opposite the staircase, I breathed in the salty sea air, and discovered a narrow wrought-iron balcony which went round the whole of the top of the building and might just be wide enough to fit a small chair. The view was absolutely spectacular, and all my concerns melted away.

'Wow! Now that's a view worth traipsing up every single one of those stairs for,' the driver said, 'but I'd be making sure it was safe before I walked on that! That's one hell of a drop down.' I gulped as he scratched his head. 'It's beautiful here but I still don't know how the hell we're going to get your furniture in.'

We came back into the centre of the room, but I left the door open to try to get some fresh air in and get rid of that awful musty smell.

'Helloooo,' a voice shouted from below, only just audible. We all turned towards the footsteps which were now clip-clopping up the stairs. 'I'm Gemma. And I come bearing gifts.'

This woman named Gemma placed an insulated bag down on the chair and produced a rug, a hot water urn, five mugs and a cake. 'Baked specially for you this lunchtime. I thought you might be ready for a cuppa and some cake when you arrived, and this might save you having to search through your boxes to find the kettle, unless you were so well prepared that you packed tea-making stuff in a separate bag and put it in your car.'

Now why hadn't I thought of that?

'Welcome to Cornwall.'

Well, that was certainly a better greeting than the last time I'd heard those words. As Gemma played mum, pouring out tea and handing mugs around, she explained that she lived in the flat above her shop just around the corner, a bakery and small café. She said she'd seen the lorry pass by so gave us a few minutes before she came along to see if we needed a brew.

Right now, I needed a brandy.

'That is so incredibly kind of you,' I said, taking in her warm smile. 'I'm Meredith, and I'm the one that's moving in. We were just working out which furniture would fit through the door but we're not sure any of it will to be honest.'

I sighed as I wondered what the hell I was going to do and how irrational my decision to come here and expect it to be the perfect idyllic dream was. Had I really thought this through? Maybe being spontaneous was actually foolish rather than fun.

'I don't suppose you know if there's a hotel or B & B nearby, that might be able to put me up tonight?' I asked. 'I think I may have overestimated the fact that I might be able to move in straight away.'

'That sounds like a very good call. The whole village knew that whoever took on this building was in for a lot of hard work and to be prepared for it to be a money pit. Let me make a quick call. You might be in luck. My sister Lucy, owns the only B & B in the village. It could very well be full but if we don't ask, we'll never know, will we?'

Gemma headed outside to make the call while I drank my tea. My anxiety level moved up a notch as I wondered what the hell I was going to do if they didn't have a room free. I'd have to beg her for a sofa or even have to sleep in the car. Clearly, she felt sorry for me and that's why she'd brought us tea and cake, if the locals had been talking about it. What on earth had I done?

Gemma headed back inside nodding and thanking the person who was on the other end of the phone. 'I'm sure she'll understand. Thanks, darling. See you soon.' She grinned at me. 'It's a yes!'

Relief flooded through my body and I released the huge breath I'd been holding.

'But it's booked from the weekend, I think she said. So, you can have it for a few nights only. The trouble with being in a small seaside village like this is that the only B & B is normally full, but someone must be looking down on you because they had a cancellation this morning. At least you get a comfy bed and some meals cooked for you for a few days while you get yourself sorted.'

'I'm so grateful to you, Gemma. It's really very kind.'

'Ah, no worries. With taking on this place I reckon you could do with a bit of kindness and luck. Do you know where you're even going to start?'

She looked around and pulled a strange face. 'Jeez. What is that smell?'

'Not me, love!' laughed the driver, sniffing his armpits after handing her a mug back.

'I'm going to make a list,' I announced. I was a sucker for a list; they made me feel in control even in the worst of circumstances. At least then I'd have a plan. And breaking big tasks down into smaller ones would make them feel more manageable. I nodded to no one in particular. 'Yes. That's my first task. Room by room. That'll do it.'

Gemma tilted her head to one side and smiled sympathetically, clearly thinking that I was completely raving bonkers.

The other two removal men, who I'd forgotten were there because they were so quiet, finished their tea and cake and thanked Gemma but said it was time for them to crack on with what they could do. They heaved boxes up and down the stairs, placing them appropriately following what room was written on the side. I'd identified the second floor as where my bedroom would be, even though it was just a big empty space right now, save for a toilet in the corner.

When it came to the big stuff, they asked me what I wanted them to do. There was no way that my three-piece suite would fit in, and as my bed was one of those sleigh beds that came all in one piece with a huge headboard and footboard, that wouldn't go through the door either, let alone up the spiral staircase. I really hadn't thought this through at all.

'Well, it looks like that building there might be a storage shed. We could have a look and see if there's room to put the big stuff in.' They headed that way and I followed.

'I think most of the furniture you eventually have might need to be built inside, Miss Robinson.'

'I think you are right.'

After my divorce, I'd moved into Gabby's spare room, which was already furnished so I had been so looking forward to getting my own furniture back in a proper home again. Some of that furniture held special memories for me, although maybe starting completely afresh might be the only way forward after all.

'Ooh, I hope you've got lots of savings, Miss Robinson. I think you're going to need them.'

## 4

I looked at my phone which was vibrating in my hand. Mum. That's all I needed at that moment. I let it ring off and then it immediately started again.

'Hello, darling. Can you hear me?'

'Yes, Mum, how are you?'

'Oh, it's so fabulous here but a bugger to get a phone signal. I don't want to go home. Good job I'm here for a few more weeks yet.' Mum had been staying at a retreat in Bali for the last two months and this was the first time I'd spoken to her as apparently they don't allow phones. Something about enabling the guests to have a full digital detox and concentrate fully on their mental well-being.

'How is it then?'

'It's wonderful. Best few months of my life. Should have done it years ago, but, well, you know...'

Yes, I did know. My mother wasn't the most maternal. When she left school, her plan had been to go to university and study to be a hot-shot lawyer, but then, when she was eighteen, she'd discovered she was pregnant with me and had never completely forgiven me for mucking up her life. And she never stopped the constant digs to let me know this. My father had disappeared the minute she told him she was pregnant, and he'd apparently made it very clear that he wasn't interested in being part of our lives, and she basically was determined that nothing, or should I say no one, was going to stop her from having the time of her life and she never really gave me a second thought. That never changed and she had been using her retirement to travel the world. Her mother, my darling Nana, had moved in with us and been my main carer until I got married and left home. She passed away just over a year ago, leaving a huge hole in my life and my heart, and I missed her more than I could ever put into words. It was because of the money that she had left to me that I'd been able to afford to buy this place. And as I looked up at the building, which had seemed far more attractive in the photographs I'd seen on the internet, I wondered what she might have made of my rather rash decision to buy a property I hadn't even viewed in the flesh.

'Are you there? Can you hear me? Bloody foreign phone lines.'

'I'm here, Mum.'

'I wanted to talk to you about the change-of-address email that you sent and make some arrangements. Peter and I are going through a bit of a rough patch at the moment, so I'm keeping out of the way. I saw that you were moving to Cornwall and thought that even though leaving David was foolish and irrational, which quite frankly is what I would have expected from you, you've shown this rash behaviour again. However, it would be perfect for me to come and visit when I leave here. You said it had two bedrooms so you can make up the spare for me. Wonderful. So, I'll be there in around six weeks. I'm going to have to go now, darling.'

'But, Mum...'

'Sorry, darling, the line is breaking up. I'll text you my flight details when I have them so that you can meet me at the airport.'

'But, Mum...'

'Bye, darling.'

The line went dead. That was my mother all over. Telling me what she was doing rather than asking if it was OK. She'd done this to me all my life and always made me feel on edge, constantly pointing out my faults and how she would have done things differently. I didn't want her to come and stay and criticise my decisions. I was nearly fifty for goodness's sake, yet she had this ability to make me feel like a little girl again.

As for her saying that I was foolish and irrational, she knew nothing about me. I was meticulous about planning everything in my life so much so that Gabby always used to rib me about making plans and the fact that I really found it difficult to do anything spontaneous. That's why she really struggled with this spur of the moment decision of mine to do something that was so completely out of character for me as I was probably one of the most rational people she knew.

When I told her that I'd got drunk and was poking around on the internet, and after seeing Driftwood Bay Lighthouse, pressed the 'click to buy' button in a fit of bravado and madness, her flabber was completely gasted.

Where was my mother going to stay? This place was never going to be ready for me by the date she'd given, let alone for a visitor. Looking up at this shabby, unloved building, I wondered what on earth was I going to do. Maybe the B & B would have some availability. She could stay there instead.

The phone vibrated again in my hand and Gabby's name flashed up on a video call. Speaking to her would make me feel better. It normally did.

'Hello, you nutter. How the devil are you and Cornwall and your gorgeous new home?'

I looked up at the lighthouse, which was quite honestly looking particularly grim even though the sun was shining behind the huge light beacon at the top.

'Erm, it's OK. Maybe "gorgeous new home" is a bit of an over-exaggeration.'

'Show me, show me! I want a guided video tour.'

'Well, it's not really ready for that at the moment.'

'What on earth do you mean? I don't really care what state it's in, I demand that you show me around right now.'

I laughed. This lady who had been my friend for as long as I could remember always had the ability to make me smile. She was bossy and annoying and also completely fabulous, and I loved the very bones of her. She'd supported me all my life, and never more than in the last year or so. There was always light with her even in the very darkest of days.

'Are you sure you're ready for this? It's not quite what I expected to be totally honest.'

'Oh, get on with it, you old slapper.'

I giggled again. I spun the camera round on the screen so that it got the front view and showed her around.

'Oh, look at that blue sky and the sea. It's gorgeous. What a beautiful sight. And those cottages on the hill opposite. How pretty. Now take me inside.'

'Are you sure? It might not be what you are expecting.'

'Do it right now, you tart!'

I heard the odd 'oh' as I walked around showing her the rooms.

'To be honest, there's not much to show. The main furniture won't fit so I'm not sure what I'm going to do about that. I suppose I'll have to buy new, and it just needs a really good clean. It's cold and it's been empty for a while. But let me show you the best bit.'

I was out of breath by the time I'd got to the top of the building for the third time in about fifteen minutes. If nothing else, this place was going to help me improve my fitness levels.

'Wow! Look at that view! Worth all the hard work you are going to have to go through for that alone. So, it's dirty, you can clean it. So, you need new furniture, you can buy it. Maybe there's someone local who could help you by building some stuff. A local handyman maybe. There must be someone like that around.'

'I'll ask Gemma when I see her next.'

'Gemma? Who is Gemma?'

'Well, I think she might be my fairy godmother. She turned up within minutes of my arrival with tea and cake and has already managed to sort me out with a bed for the night at the local B & B.'

'Sounds like a right nosy old cow if you ask me.'

'Well, it's a good job I didn't ask you then. She's actually really nice. Kind, thoughtful and sweet.'

'Hope you're not going to replace me, Mere. I've already got a complex that you've moved three hundred miles away. Now I find out the minute you arrive, you've got a new BFF.'

I laughed.

'No one will ever take your spot. But times are changing for us both and especially for you with you meeting Luke and getting serious with him – and I love that for you by the way. You deserve to be with someone as lovely as he is, and you are absolutely perfect for each other. And I need a change too. I can't keep being the third wheel in yours and Luke's relationship. You need some time away from me, to spend quality time together. You can't do that when you have your best friend living in your house and coming out with you every time you go somewhere.'

'He doesn't mind at all, you know.'

'I know he doesn't, and I love him so much for it. But it's the right thing for us both. It's not fair for Luke to have to live with me as well, you know. You need to be able to shag in every room in the house if you want to and you can't do that with me sat on the sofa, dampening your desire.'

'I'm nearly fifty, Mere. I don't think there's going to be much of that going on. It'll be more like TV and cocoa on the sofa.'

'Hey, fifty is the new thirty, you know. Who knows what surprises we have in store? It's time, Gabs.' I breathed in deeply. 'It'll never change how I feel about you. You'll always be my bestie. Although, you know, Gemma could be a very good contender...'

'Enough, I hate her already.' We laughed through our sadness. 'I hope you know how much I love you and am going to miss you too.'

'I do. I love you right back.'

I really did. Platonic relationships are really underrated and undervalued in my opinion. The society around us puts so much emphasis on finding and having a romantic love in your life. But without the never-ending love and support of Gabby, I would be absolutely nothing. Best friends rock and if you have someone in your life like I have in mine, with support and tenacity, then anything is possible.

After sharing my plans to stay at the B & B for a few days, Gabby agreed that it was the best idea under the circumstances. She offered to come and help just as soon as she was able to take some time off.

'I also think you should be ringing that estate agent. Sounds like he told you a pack of lies. I think he might have been a bit handy in the Photoshop department too if you don't mind me saying. The photos you showed me look nothing like what I've just seen.'

'Yep. I've tried a couple of times but can't get through. Don't worry though. It's on my list.'

'You and your lists!'

'I know. I know.'

Just talking to her made me feel a little more energised. She had always supported me in my life. Made me believe that I could do anything I set my mind to. I was lucky to have her as a friend. She'd rang just at the right time. Maybe I could do this after all.

# 5

The B & B wasn't far, and I didn't need to take much with me apart from a change of clothes, my washbag and my Mary Poppins handbag, so I decided to walk and leave the car at the lighthouse. It was a lovely evening, the balmy weather and salty sea air soothing my soul. There didn't seem to be a soul around, although I did pass a middle-aged man walking a golden Labrador but when I smiled and said hello to him, he looked straight through me. Maybe he had something on his mind.

Gemma's directions were perfect, and I opened the wrought iron gate and walked towards the front door, which was surrounded by a lush clematis just about to bloom into bright pink flowers. Against the cream-rendered frontage, the vibrant colour made the cottage look chocolate-box pretty. There was an old-fashioned brass bell to the right of the front door which I tried not to clang too loudly, and I straightened my posture as I heard footsteps approach from the other side of the door.

'Hiya. You must be Meredith. Welcome to Cornwall, my dear. Come in, come in.' She beamed at me. The likeness between her and Gemma was uncanny even though Gemma had said earlier that her sister was four years older. 'Do you want to see your room first, have a cup of tea and fifteen minutes to relax, or have some dinner straight away? Entirely up to you.'

A loud grumble came from my tummy and we both laughed.

'It's so lovely of you to have me stay. I'm so glad you had a room free.'

'Meant to be. I had a cancellation just this morning, so maybe the universe is looking after you. Or someone else. Maybe you have a guardian angel.' She looked upwards.

I smiled back at her. 'I am hungry, as you heard, but I would absolutely love a cup of tea and a sit-down to be honest. I'm shattered and haven't even had a chance to have a look round at the area yet. It's been a long day already.'

'Don't you worry about that. There's plenty of time for exploring, I'm sure. I'm excited to hear your plans. Why don't I show you your room and you can pop your bag in, and when you are ready to come down, I'll bring you a menu. You can choose what you want while I make us a cuppa. My husband is on cooking duty this evening, so if you fancy some company maybe I could join you and you can tell me a little about yourself and how you've ended up here. Only if I'm not imposing though. You can tell me to bugger off if you want to be alone. I'm not easily offended.'

'That would be perfect. Thank you.' I was sure that Gabby, again, would think this was someone being nosy but after a day of having to make some big decisions on my own, I felt a bit emotional at the kindness offered to me – a total stranger – by both Gemma and Lucy today. I swallowed a lump in my throat.

Three hundred miles from home seemed like a mighty long way from all the things that were familiar to me, and I was exhausted from the long drive and the constant thinking about what I would do. I knew that I needed some direction in my life and a plan as to what steps came next, but everything had happened so quickly that now I was actually here, it was quite overwhelming. I was so grateful for the fact that I could have this time away from the lighthouse to try to think straight.

I thought back to when I locked up for the night and how I'd felt when I left. I'd cranked up the huge boiler that was in a cupboard by the ground floor entrance and left the heating on, hoping it would feel warmer when I returned the following day. I was sure that leaving it on with some of the windows open was counter-productive, but I needed to get rid of the musty smell too.

It wasn't what I was expecting at all. I was starting to think Russell the estate agent may have done me over. He'd told me that it was habitable straight away but there was no way that was possible. When I tried to call the mobile number I had for him, it kept going to a voicemail which said it was full and couldn't receive any more messages.

Could I really do this? Was I mad to try and start over in a new place? I had no real renovating experience. Yes, I'd dabbled with interior design in the past and had been told that I had a good eye to make things look aesthetically pleasing and knew how to make furnishings, but renovations of this scale. Really. Whatever was I thinking?

\* \* \*

I woke to the sounds of seagulls squawking and the unmistakable drone of a lawnmower in the distance and thought of the night before. It had been so nice, to sit and chat with Lucy and Gemma, who had popped over for what was meant to be a cuppa after dinner but turned out to be a rather large glass of wine instead. I looked around the room, which felt cosy yet fresh, with white-wood-washed floorboards and furniture along with Cath Kidston pale blue and pink flowery bedlinen and matching curtains that framed a huge window.

The salty air hit my nostrils as I sat up and looked out of the window. Admiring the view, which overlooked the beach, lifted my spirits greatly. The sun sparkled off the turquoise blue sea and the pale golden sand looked glorious. Looking towards the harbour, I could see the lighthouse in the distance. From here it looked picturesque and imposing. You couldn't see the paint peeling off the window frames. You couldn't smell those patches of damp that I'd tried not to notice in the corners of a couple of the rooms. You couldn't see how tired it was and you certainly couldn't feel how unloved it was like you could when you were in it. I hoped more than anything that I hadn't made a huge mistake by taking on this project.

The clock on the bedside table said it was nine o'clock. Blimey! I never slept in till this time. At home, even at the weekends I was awake at around six. I suppose your body clock gets used to waking up at the same time every day. Yesterday had been a huge day in my life, a long journey to discover a whole dollop of disappointment.

After a quick shower and getting dressed, applying just a slick of mascara, a sweep of blusher and a tinted lip balm, I felt – and I hoped I looked – a little more respectable.

'Morning, sleepyhead. Hope you slept well.'

'Like a log. Couldn't believe it when I saw the time.'

'That's the sea air for you. Combined with a busy old day.' Lucy smiled at me. 'Full English?'

'Lucy, I think you are my dream woman. Will you marry me?'

'Well, I think James might have something to say about that, but if he ever leaves me and I decide to bat for the other side, which is probably the better side to be honest, I'll bear you in mind.' She grinned back.

After a while, she plonked a delicious looking plateful of bacon, eggs, sausage, black pudding, hash brown and beans on the table, with a pot of coffee and some toast.

'I'll never get through all of that, although I do like a challenge.'

'So you do, honey, so you do. And that's why you've bought our local lighthouse. In fact, I've been thinking. Maybe Clem can help you.'

'Clem?'

'Yes, Clem, short for Clement. A good old Cornish name if ever I've heard one. He's a carpenter by trade but is generally blooming amazing at anything he turns his hand to. He might be the perfect person to do any work that you can't do yourself. I know you can do the cleaning and furnishings and stuff like that, but if you need any labouring or building work doing, he might be worth considering. Makes some incredible furniture. Very good with his hands I've heard. Easy on the eye too.' She winked as she walked away, leaving me to write his name in my notebook and then demolish the feast before me.

I'd always dreamed of living by the sea but never thought I'd actually be doing it. The sea filled my soul; just sitting beside the water replenished my body in some way. Like a happiness battery filling up with joy if that didn't sound too bonkers. I couldn't believe that my dream had come true.

'Thought you weren't going to manage all of that.' Lucy took my empty plate away.

'Well, it felt rude to leave any after you'd gone to the trouble of cooking it. I only just managed to stop myself licking the plate and, believe me, that took some strength.' We'd fallen into an easy, familiar relationship already and I hoped that we would become friends. She and Gemma were so similar, and I had enjoyed their company last night, although Lucy's husband, James, had commented as he walked past us that they were only after the low-down on the newcomer at which we all laughed. I also remembered what Gabby had said about them being nosy and hoped that it wasn't just that.

'Much as I'm comfy, I can't sit here all day. I have a lighthouse to sort out.'

'Good luck, lovely. Will we see you for dinner later?'

'Just try and stop me. I think maybe I should just move in here permanently instead. That would solve all my problems.'

'But wouldn't be half as much fun. Have a great day, Meredith. Happy new home.'

# 6

At the back of the golden sandy beach, I sat down on a perfectly flat rock which I had decided would make me a fabulous perch. I slipped off my trainers and felt the soft sand trickle between my toes. It was a gorgeous day and even at ten thirty in the morning I could feel the heat of the sun beating down on my neck. I made a mental note to remember to buy some suntan lotion. I plonked my handbag on the rock next to me and got out my notebook, but I was mesmerised by the sea and found myself hypnotised by the gentle lapping of each wave. I sighed deeply, filling my lungs with air, and stretched my neck from side to side breaking the spell.

In no particular order, I scribbled the jobs I could immediately think of that needed doing sooner rather than later, along with reasons why I should do them. This was a habit, a bit like daily journaling to get all my thoughts out of my head, which I'd got into years ago. It helped soothe my anxious mind.

*Clean windows.*

This should let in lots of light and be simple and easy to do for no cost.

*Clean bathroom.*

At least then I could have a shower and clean up after a hard day's work. When I said bathroom, I really meant shower tray and manky old toilet, without a lid, as that was all I could find when I looked yesterday. Maybe take stock of bathroom would be a better point. Did the building even have running water? I'm sure the estate agent said it did.

*Clean kitchen.*

There was a pattern emerging here. See if anything is useable, clean what's there and then look at what needs to be done to finish the room.

*Check out garden building.*

I wondered what might be in there.

*Sell furniture that won't fit.*

No point in hanging on to things when I was trying to make a new start.

*Find new furniture – bed, chairs, wardrobes.*

Maybe hanging rails would do to start with. Now I just needed to find some.

*Get internet connected at the lighthouse.*

*Find out details of local handyman.*

Lucy had said his name was Clement something or other.

*Ring Russell.*

Russell the estate agent deserved a bollocking for not giving me the full picture.

Well, that little lot would certainly keep me busy for the time being. And sitting here staring at a little fishing boat out on the horizon wasn't going to get anything done. With a loud sigh, I stood up and headed back along the beach in the direction of the lighthouse. She didn't look the same today. The sun was at a different angle, and from a distance she looked almost pretty. The faded red and white stripes almost glittered in the sun, and as I got closer, I noticed that there was a bush outside the front door which I hadn't seen yesterday. I bent towards the one flower that had just come into bloom. It looked like a hibiscus. I only knew that because Nana had had one in her garden, and I hoped that the flower was a sign that I was welcome here. A sign of good things to come.

Smiling, I unlocked the door. The smell of must and damp hit me before I'd even stepped over the threshold. I suppose it was to be expected as the place had probably been shut up for a good while and I'm sure it would go in time.

I got my notebook back out and started to make a shopping list, adding air fresheners, room diffusers and candles. I loved nothing more than a scented candle and I'm sure that all those things along with cranking the windows open at every opportunity might go a good way to getting rid of the revolting smell. Maybe I'd wait a while before lighting the very expensive Jo Malone Pomegranate Noir candle that Gabby and Luke had bought me as a leaving present.

Typical of Gabby to say she'd try to come down in a couple of weeks when all the dirty work was out of the way. But, for now, I needed to find the box marked 'CLEANING STUFF', don a pair of rubber gloves, and get cracking on Operation Lighthouse. As I looked around me, I scratched my head – now, where to start?

The box was luckily at the front of the kitchen. I say kitchen in the lightest sense of the word, as that really implies somewhere that you could cook and there was no way that I could do that or eat anything that came out of this room without catching a disgusting disease.

The front door seemed like a good place to start. Underneath the dirt and dust, there was quite a nice duck-egg-blue-coloured paint and I hoped to keep it that colour, if I could get a reasonably close match, as it contrasted well with the outside – or at least it would when the outside was painted. I also gave the white wooden windowsills and frames a really good scrub.

As I stood back to admire my handiwork and stretched my neck from side to side to loosen up the aches, the same middle-aged man who I saw yesterday with the Labrador walked past on the top path. I shouted good morning to him but again he completely ignored me and didn't even look in my direction. There was no wind, and he wasn't that far away but maybe he had ear pods in and simply couldn't hear me. He looked sad, like he had the weight of the world on his shoulders. I'd have to remember to ask Lucy about him later or Gemma if I saw her. She did say that she'd try to pop by today if she got a chance. I really hoped that she would.

I grabbed my shopping list; I couldn't believe that I'd already worked my way through four complete bottles of bleach although I had shoved most of that down the loo – I'd noticed it was particularly revolting – along with some down the old Belfast sink in the kitchen. Thank goodness there was an outside tap, which took a little bit of coaxing to unscrew but after a little bit of willpower and using all the swear words I could muster, along with a few more that I made up, it seemed to comply. But even using the ice-cold water from that tap from there was better than traipsing up and down those blooming stairs.

A memory popped into my head of when David and I were looking for somewhere to live: 'I'm not traipsing up to the top of a three-storey house every time I want something from my room thank you very much, however nice it is.' That seemed like a whole lifetime ago now. How times had changed.

I thought it would be a good idea to put together a scrapbook so that I could show before and after images of the lighthouse, and I was glad that I'd taken a picture of the front door when I arrived yesterday. I took another in the identical spot I stood in at that point and stretched out my back with my hands on my hips. The work I'd done so far was starting to take its toll. Usually sat at a desk all day, I wasn't used to physical work like this.

Perhaps a little walk was in order. And Gemma had said that there was a little mini-market in the village centre which sold most things. I'd head off there and maybe grab a bite to eat. Strangely, even after that massive breakfast, I was ravenous again. The pub on the corner of the harbour, The Harbourside Hotel, looked cosy and inviting. Maybe I'd be brave one day and treat myself to lunch there.

Taking a meander up the cobbled, pedestrian high street was an absolute pleasure, apart from the fact that it was up a blooming big hill. I tried to keep my mind on the positive though, reminding myself that it would be much better on the way back down. The whimsical bric-a-brac shop looked particularly interesting but there was a note on the door saying, 'GONE FOR LUNCH, BACK AT 2 P.M.' I checked my watch; two o'clock was only five minutes away.

I walked through the door of the mini-market, causing a little brass bell to jingle, and I could hear busy chit-chatter from the direction of the counter, which immediately stopped as the shop-keeper and two customers clapped stern and unfriendly eyes on me.

'Good morning.'

Silence.

'I'm new to the area. I've bought the lighthouse.'

'We know who you are.' Not a smile in sight.

I swallowed and beamed. 'It's so lovely to meet you. I'm Meredith.'

'And...' The woman behind the counter crossed her arms and rested them on her rather large bosom.

'Oh. Erm. I just need some bits and pieces so I'll just have a wander round, shall I?'

'If you must...'

Gosh, I was glad I didn't come here first yesterday. The episode at the big supermarket with Mr Rude was bad enough. Perhaps they're all inbred, and I was just lucky to find Gemma and Lucy yesterday.

It was well stocked for a mini-market although I suppose in a small village it must be. I filled my basket and headed for the counter where everyone stood. They continued to talk in hushed voices as I browsed and now they looked at me like something the cat dragged in.

'I don't suppose you have any fresh bread at all, do you?' I asked with my best smile.

'No,' was all the woman said, uninterested.

'Oh, OK thanks.'

*Thanks? Why did I just thank her for that? Get a grip, Mere.*

I put my basket on the counter and asked if I could have a bag.

'Don't have none.'

I spied bags hanging from a hook behind her.

'I think there might be some behind you.' I pointed them out.

'Oh, yeah, so there is.' There was a titter from the two women on my side of the counter and the woman still made no attempt to move. 'They're twenty pence.'

Our eyes locked. I was determined not to look away. I fiddled with Nana's bracelet willing her to out-stare this woman.

She finally huffed and reached behind her, grabbing a bag and flinging it at me before ringing up the items on the till.

'Can I pay by card please?'

'Not working. Cash or nothing.'

I rooted through my purse and had just enough to pay for the shopping. It wasn't very often I had cash on me these days. I sighed and walked towards the door. 'Thanks so much,' I shouted over my shoulder, glad to be out of the place and having to fake so much kindness.

There was no response from any of them, until I walked

through the door and then I heard peals of laughter. They were laughing at me.

Tears sprung into my eyes. What had I ever done to them? Why on earth were they being so nasty? They didn't know me or anything about me.

The bric-a-brac shop door was propped open now and the bakery door too and I could see Gemma was serving behind the counter. She gave me a little wave, but I wasn't ready to face anyone. I wiped away a little tear that ran down my cheek as I scooted past and headed back down the hill, to the sanctuary of my new home.

And when I say home, I mean hovel.

## 7

Cleaning and music are two things that always make me feel better whenever I'm upset or angry. Pouring that emotional energy into a physical task has always worked for me, so I decided to tackle the makeshift bathroom next. Scrubbing the loo and the shower tray was definitely having an impact. I managed to coax the shower on and after the initial brown gunge that came out all over my nice clean shower tray – and my favourite white T-shirt which I would probably never be able to wear again – it eventually ran clear and warm but definitely not hot.

*Baby steps, Meredith. Baby steps.*

The music that was playing was definitely pulling me out of my funk. So what if the people here didn't like me just yet? I was just a stranger to them, and I was actually quite nice, so surely when they did get to know me, things would change. Maybe they were just a little set in their ways and not very welcoming to a newcomer to their village. Perhaps I should just go into the shop every morning and continue to talk to them until I turned things around.

Yes, I like that idea, I thought. That's exactly what I would do. I liked a plan and a challenge.

I moved up a floor and standing back and taking stock of the kitchen space made me realise that however much cleaning I did in here, nothing was going to improve until there was some more cupboard space. There were currently two cupboards; I'd managed to fill one with tinned goods and the other with cleaning stuff. There were still boxes of crockery, cutlery, pots and pans, which I had tidied into neater piles for now, trying to create the illusion of an organised space, but it was way beyond my capabilities. Perhaps I did need to speak to this Clem person. I would ask Lucy about him later. To make a big impact in this room in particular, I would need some help.

In the meantime, tomorrow I'd go back up the hill of doom to the mini-market and pop into the bric-a-brac shop too to see if there was anything useful that might help me out. I loved browsing around that type of shop. It calmed and grounded me, and hours could pass by in a flash. It was something I hadn't done for ages, and at the thought of getting back into this hobby something stirred within me. Was it excitement maybe?

Perhaps I could clear out the garden building and have it as a little workshop. I could set up my sewing machine in there too and make some curtains and cushions for the lighthouse. When I was younger, I wanted to be an interior designer and my friends said that I had a good eye for it, some of them even asking for my advice, but I was pushed into graphic design instead and that's how I ended up working in a graphic design company, which was OK but didn't inspire me. It just felt like a job that I needed to do to earn money.

That was until Nana and I had a chat a couple of years ago and she made me promise her that I would always try to live life to the full and find something I enjoyed doing. She knew that things weren't right with me and David, and while she tolerated him, she'd never been his biggest fan. She said that he stifled me and that I made myself a lesser person because it suited him. It was at that point that she gave me her charm bracelet. She said that she wanted to see me wear it while she was still here instead of waiting until she was gone. I'd refused, saying that I couldn't literally take it from her wrist, but she insisted. And said that every time I felt myself being dulled down, I should think of what she would say and it might inspire me to feel differently.

That's what prompted me to start my own business and one of the reasons why I could come to Cornwall was because as long as I had an internet connection, I could work anywhere. Which reminded me: Wi-Fi was on my list of immediate jobs and perhaps the most urgent one.

'Cooeee! Anyone home?'

At last, a friendly voice and one that I recognised.

'I'm up here.'

The sound of heavy footsteps carried on the metal staircase.

'You couldn't surprise anyone with this staircase, could you? Coffee and cake? Time for a break on the beach?' Gemma's happy smiling face was just what I needed.

'Oh, you absolute star. Thank you. A break on the beach sounds divine.'

We sat on a picnic blanket in companiable silence as we scoffed the mouth-wateringly delicious coffee and walnut cake that she'd brought along as today's offering. Gemma told me that one of the reasons she wanted to carry on running the bakery business was because she loved to make cakes and, my goodness, she was good at it. I wasn't a natural baker at all. While Gemma's cakes were light and fluffy, mine were heavy and ugly. I'd have to get some tips from her. Or, better still, just stay friends so she continued to bring me my daily cake.

'Between you and your sister, I'll be the size of a house before long. Both of you are cracking cooks.'

'Oh well, our mum was the most amazing baker and cook.

That's where we get it from. We're a family of feeders. And don't worry, I'm sure we'll get bored soon and leave you alone.' She grinned. I loved her easy nature and it felt as if I'd known her for years. Was it really only the day before that I'd met her? 'How's your day been?'

I sighed. 'Mixed, I suppose, after a lovely lazy start to the day. And a little different to what I experienced in the mini-market earlier. I don't think that I imagined it, but the people in there seemed to be... erm... how should I say? A bit cold towards me?'

'Oh, just try and ignore them. If she was a short dumpy redhead, that'll be Dyllis and her cronies. They're like that with anyone new that comes into the village. Almost like they're testing out people's staying skills, although to be honest it's been a while since we've had a newcomer in the village. That's why it's so exciting for Lucy and me.'

'Well, I'll just have to win her over with my scintillating personality then, won't I?'

Gemma gently nudged my shoulder. 'It'll all work out don't worry and don't let them get to you. They're really not worth it. There are a few things that you probably need to know about some of the locals. Perhaps now would be a good time to tell you.' At this point, her phone started ringing. 'Yep, I'm coming right now!' She turned towards me. 'So sorry, Meredith, but I have to go. Someone has arrived to pick up a birthday cake. See you soon.'

And just like a real fairy godmother, she'd gone.

# 8

I headed up to the top floor and flung open the French doors. The view across the bay really was incredible and quite mesmerising at times. A variety of boats bobbed about in the harbour, including some fishing boats, some little dinghies, one speedboat. The one in particular that really drew my eye was a sailing boat – it must have been around 40 feet in size. I wondered about the person who owned it. What did they do? Where did they go in it? Were they rich to have a boat like that and maybe had a millionaire mansion too? I decided that I would have a walk along the harbour later on my way back to the B & B.

The sun shimmered on the deep blue water of the harbour, whereas the sea appeared to be a completely different colour as I looked beachside to the open waters, more turquoise changing to darker shades before turning into a dark inky blue. It really was the most incredible view. I'd been on holidays here before and there had always been sea views, but to see it properly every day, in its full glory, from my own property, was a true blessing and kind of took my breath away.

I closed my eyes, drinking in the image, locking it away in my memory. And at that point I had an out-of-body moment where I could see myself sitting drinking my morning coffee on a big squashy armchair, with the French doors open, the seagulls squawking their morning call, the boat halyards imitating the tinkling of wind chimes. My heart filled with joy from the picture in my head. However, when I opened my eyes again, I realised that I was going to have to do lots more hard work to make that happen. Even though those windows were the cleanest in the whole place, they definitely still needed a scrub – the next task that I would concentrate on.

I checked my watch. It was four thirty now. Maybe another hour or so and I'd give up for the day and go for that walk.

As soon as I'd arrived I knew that renovating Driftwood Bay Lighthouse wasn't going to be easy, seeing the state of the place, and I certainly wasn't scared of hard work, but I wasn't sure that even a month of working at this rate would have any impact at all. Maybe I'd wake up one day and it would just feel better. Maybe I just had to have a bit of hope. That was the thing I was struggling to find at that moment. Especially when I felt quite alone. Perhaps I just had to trust in the universe, as Gabby always said. I would drop her a text later and see if she was up for another chat. Five minutes with her usually did the trick, making me realise that I could either feel sorry for myself or give myself a kick up the arse.

One conclusion I had come to was that I definitely needed some help and even a bit of advice. I'd been waiting to see Lucy again so I could get Clem's number or find out where he lived. Right now, I couldn't even sleep in the building. I had a mattress, wrapped in plastic, which the removal men had left on the bedroom floor. The wardrobes and chest of drawers were out in the garden building as they couldn't come up the stairs either. Buying solid wood furniture that once built would never be dismantled seemed like a great idea at the time but not so practical for when those of us decided to move into a lighthouse. Although maybe it was time I left that part of my life behind once and for all.

Once I was satisfied that there was nothing more I could do with the windows and French doors, I decided to give up for the day and head back to the B & B. I'd worked longer than I had planned, and my back had really started to ache. All this cleaning was using muscles I didn't realise I had.

A few minutes later, I was wandering around the harbour, taking in all the sights around me and the salty, fishy smells too. My walk was most pleasant although I didn't see a soul. It was around six thirty when I reached the B & B. Even though Lucy told me to come and go as I pleased, I felt like I shouldn't expect her to cook for me too late. The menu that night was limited but as soon as I saw home-cooked fish and chips, my mouth started to water.

'Caught this morning, just off the coast so you can't get much fresher than that.' Lucy put the plate down in front of me. It was the biggest piece of fish I'd ever seen, in a crispy golden batter, and was placed on top of large chunky chips covered in sea salt crystals, with a side of garden peas and a dish of tartare sauce. It looked and smelled so lush, I couldn't wait to dive in. I hadn't realised how hungry I was.

'James and I are out this evening but do feel free to sit in the lounge down here if you'd like to.'

'Oh, that's nice, although to be honest, I feel so exhausted that I might just sit in my room and read for a bit. That bedroom is one of the most relaxing rooms I've ever slept in. I'd love to replicate it at the lighthouse but am not sure it's possible. I certainly wouldn't get anywhere near the amount of light in.' I'd called it my room I realised, and it really did feel like it was mine. I had immediately felt at home and would sincerely miss it.

I wanted to make the most of the nights I had left there and try to work out what elements of it I loved and why, so I could figure out how I could incorporate it at the lighthouse. I was glad that I'd given myself a couple of weeks off work to concentrate on every-thing, maybe even a little longer if needed. I'd told all my clients that I was away, and everything was as up to date as it could be, although I knew I should probably check my emails at some point to make sure an emergency hadn't arisen. Though at that moment, I had no urge to do any such thing. Cornwall was making me feel differently about my life. It seemed such a slower pace, and just being by the sea was making me feel so much more alive. Of course, I knew that the weeks ahead were going to be tough, but it was worth it.

* * *

When I woke the next morning, I felt utterly refreshed, though when I checked the time, it was only five thirty. I decided to get up bright and early and go for a walk along the beach before anyone else was around. I crept down the stairs and jumped a mile when I saw James walking down the hall. My heart was beating like mad. I'd been in a little world of my own not expecting anyone else to be up yet. He laughed.

'Sorry to startle you. But you have to be up with the larks to beat me. I'm always up at five to get the fishing boat out. Head start on those slackers that go out later. Where are you off to creeping around at this time?'

'Thought I'd make the most of a beautiful morning and go for a stroll on the beach.'

'Well, if you're quick you might just catch the sun coming up too. Just hang on a sec, the kettle has just boiled. Let me make you a cuppa to take with you. Coffee with just milk if I remember rightly.'

I nodded and thanked him as he not only handed me a thermal cup but also a blanket as he said it might still be a little chilly. I would be forever grateful for the kindness that this family bestowed on me and realised how fortunate I was to have met them.

I frowned as another thought passed through my mind: heading up to the mini-market again. But then bravado took over. They would not get the better of me. I pushed my shoulders back and held my head high. I would win the locals over, whether they liked it or not.

The walk along the boardwalk to the beach took minutes and before long I'd arrived at the flat rock that I had sat on the other day. It was the perfect place to drink my morning coffee and watch the sunrise. Surely there could be no better way to start the day than to watch the beauty bestowed upon us by Mother Nature. The sun cast a glow all around as it emerged over the horizon, like a phoenix from the flames, creating a myriad of colours, ranging from a deep copper through to a gorgeous gold, and it warmed my soul. I don't think I'd ever done this where I lived before. Sunrise in the city wasn't quite the same when it was rising above the many rooftops.

A seagull wandered over to me, looking larger the closer he got, and I felt a bit daft when I wished him a good morning. Thank goodness there was no one else around to hear me chatting away to him. When he got up close, I noticed that he had a white heart-shaped marking on his head, and it made me smile. He looked at me expectantly so I explained that I'd got no food and apologised. I really must have been going loopy if I was chatting to the local seagulls.

It was no good though, I couldn't sit here all day drinking coffee much as it would have been nice to do so. I had a lighthouse to get shipshape. And sadly, it wouldn't clean itself.

## 9

After a good few hours scrubbing, I needed a break so decided to wander into the village. I made a note to remember to call Gabby later too. I needed to hear a familiar voice. Of course, I was glad that I'd met Gemma and Lucy but I missed Gabby being so close by and being able to see her anytime. Even when she'd been stopping at Luke's, which had been getting more and more frequent, she was just around the corner. It would be great to get a date in the diary for her to come down, but I needed to make some advancements with the lighthouse before I had any guests. I knew that Mum would have a heart attack if she saw the state it was in right now. Funny how even though I was a nearly fifty-year-old woman, who had her own business, my mother still had the capacity to make me feel like that useless child from all those years ago.

Delighted to see that the door was propped open at the bric-a-brac shop, I peered around it and my eyes lit up at the treasure trove before me.

'*Wasson shag?*'

'I beg your pardon?' I asked of the voice coming from behind the counter.

'Oh, you're not from these parts. Pardon me. I was just saying hello and asking how you were. That's what we say down here. No offence caused, m'dear.'

'Well, I did wonder what you were saying. Thought it was going to be the best offer I've had for a long time to be honest.'

The man behind the counter laughed and stood to his full height, towering over me. What do they feed the men round here? They're all giants.

'Looking for anything in particular?'

'Just having a mooch. I love a shop like this, and I've just bought a property and was looking for some bits and pieces to fit, or that I could do up.'

'Ooh, there's a lot of people buying property around here. I was only talking to the women in the mini-market this morning about the daft bint that's bought the lighthouse.'

I raised my eyebrows. So, I was the talk of the mini-market then, that's interesting.

'I'm Martin, by the way, do feel free to come in and look around, there's more in the yard out back too.'

'Pleased to meet you, Martin. I am in fact the daft bint that's bought the lighthouse. But you can call me Meredith.' I held out my hand and grinned broadly.

'Oh bollocks. My son is always telling me to think before I speak! He'd kill me if he found out I'd just said that. I'm so sorry. No offence meant. It's just a very big job. Wasn't expecting a woman either. Do you have a husband to do all the work?'

'No offence taken, Martin. I've already had short thrift from the staff at the mini-market. And no, I don't have a husband to rescue me. This princess gets to rescue herself, seeing as we're not living in the Dark Ages.'

I wasn't sure where this new-found confidence had come from, but I knew I should start as I meant to go on and show these people that I wasn't completely stupid.

'Oh lord, you're not one of those raving bloody feminist types are you? Oh no! There I go again. Can you do me a great big favour? Can you walk out the door and come back in again, please?' He came round from behind the counter and practically shooed me out of the door then closed it behind me. For some reason I did as he asked. Slowly, I reopened the door to be greeted with a great big smile.

'Good morning there, my name is Martin, I'm the owner of this shop. Is there anything in particular I can help you with today?'

I grinned broadly.

'Hi, Martin, nice to meet you. I'm Meredith and I'm the owner of the lighthouse. I'm looking for some bits and bobs. OK if I come in and look around?'

'It sure is, my lovely. And 15 per cent off anything you choose to buy today too. Special incentive for people new into the area. To welcome you an' all that.'

'Very kind of you. I'll bear that in mind.'

'And don't mind those busybodies at the mini-market. Their bark is worse than their bite.'

'Glad to hear it. But they were quite unkind to me. Not a nice welcome, I have to say.'

'Ah, they'll soon come round when they realise what a cracking sense of humour you have and how forgiving you are of ridiculously stupid oafs like me. Don't fret about it. Seriously though, is there anything in particular that you are after?'

'Not sure where to start to be honest. I think I'll only know what I need if I see it.'

'Well, take your time, m'dear, and just give me a shout if you need me. Me and my size twelve feet will be right behind this counter when you need us. I'm just repairing a clock for one of the villagers. Not sure how but I seem to be the local repair shop as well as the one flogging bric-a-brac.'

God, I loved a place like this. It was literally like Aladdin's cave, full of fabulous items that other people clearly didn't want any more. Out in the back yard, I spied a gorgeous white iron bedframe leaning against a wall and wrote it down in my notepad. I couldn't afford to forget anything, and I tended to be so easily distracted in such a shop I'd end up going home without the thing I needed the most. There were also two lovely armchairs that looked like they needed some love, but with a sand and varnish makeover, some new fabric and my trusty staple gun, they would look perfect up on the top floor, but I had no idea whether they'd fit up the stairs. I wished I'd brought a tape measure with me to work that part out. I'd ask Martin if he had one when I returned to the main shop.

Butterflies danced in my tummy as I started to feel something that I hadn't felt for a while. Excitement. And hope. Maybe I could do this after all. Footsteps interrupted my train of thought.

'If there's anything you would like to buy, then I could get my son to give me a hand to bring them down on the trailer. I think with that old place, it's going to be a case of try it and see. If there's something you like, we can drop it down to you and if it fits you can pay me, if it doesn't then we can bring it back. I can't say fairer than that now, can I?'

'That's really very kind of you, Martin, thank you. I love these armchairs, but I have no idea whether they'd fit up the staircase which I stupidly never thought about measuring before I came out. Wow!' My eye was drawn to the other side of the room. 'Look at that coffee table and bookcase. They'd be perfect too if they'd fit. Oh, and that old butcher's block. I'm desperate for some workspace in the kitchen and that's quite narrow so it might work. Not sure though. I'm not going to build my hopes up just in case.'

'Well, we can only try. Shall I get my lad to pop along with them later today? And then if they fit great, and if not, we can bring them back. Is that too soon?'

'That would honestly be amazing. Are you really sure?'

'The least I can do, m'dear. And hopefully it'll show you that we are actually quite nice around here.' He winked.

'Thank you. It really is very nice of you. Are you sure your son won't mind?' I had visions of a surly teenager being made to help his dad out. 'You don't have any paintings at all, or things to go on the walls do you?'

'There's some at the back, along with a few plaques and things with quotes on them. Would that type of thing be suitable for you? They're over here, look.' He moved to the back of the room and pointed out a big chest full of pictures and the most fabulous quotes on canvases and on wooden backgrounds. I pulled out a couple that seemed to be calling to me.

I moved two that I liked over to the counter. Gabby once said to me that I should only buy things that brought me joy and made me smile and this was the approach I was taking with my new home. While still browsing through the chest, I also found a wicker heart which was really calling out to me, and I thought would look amazing on the front door, make it feel more welcoming. It would also make me smile each time I saw it.

By the time I'd finished, unbelievably an hour had gone by, and I'd gathered quite a lot of stuff. Martin gave me a card with his number on, saying I should measure the stairway as soon as I got back and give him a call, so we could eliminate some of the stuff straight away.

There was still a lot of work to do when I got back, but first, a quick nip into the mini-market to pick up something for lunch and to get 'Operation Like Meredith' underway.

'Good morning.' I grinned at the same lady behind the counter.

The shop appeared to be empty, thank goodness. One at a time I could deal with confidently. 'Another beautiful day.'

'Is it?'

'It sure is. Makes you feel so much better when the sun is shining. Don't you think? I'm Meredith, but obviously you already know that because I told you yesterday.' I was gabbling now. 'I've just been having a chat with Martin next door, and he said that you'd been discussing the lighthouse and wondering what I'm planning to do with it. If you fancy having a break from the shop and a cuppa one day, I'd love to show you round the old place so you can see what I will have done to it. Give me time to get some major jobs done but you'd be most welcome.'

'Oh! Right!' Clearly, she hadn't been expecting that. 'And then what? You'll sell it on, I suppose, to the highest bidder and there'll be someone else new in the village?'

'Who knows what the future holds? It's a project for me right now, do it up and then see what happens. I might decide to stay. The locals are all so welcoming.' I decided to quit while I was ahead and smiled sweetly. Then I grabbed some fresh bread, a packet of ham and a bag of cheese and onion crisps and put the basket down on the counter.

'I see that the card machine is working again which is great. Do you prefer card or cash?'

'Either is fine.'

I grabbed an apple too and asked her to add it to the bill, grinning broadly, but my hands were shaking as I swiped my card. My nana had always taught me to hold my head up and smile, not letting people see what was going on on the inside.

'Thank you.' I supposed a muttered begrudging 'thank you' was better than none at all.

And with that I left. At least I was armed with knowledge today. And the expectancy that she might be hostile. I'd decided last night that I was going to dazzle her with niceness and see how that fared. I came away feeling so much calmer and more in control. Progress. Just a little but it all counts.

When I got back to the lighthouse, I quickly threw a sandwich together and sat on a tartan picnic rug on the top floor with the doors open. I wasn't brave enough to sit on the camping chair. It looked a bit too delicate for my backside, especially after all the food I was eating here.

The smell of the salty air and the sound of the gulls felt so familiar now that it already felt homely even if I did have to sit on the floor. Martin had told me that they would be round at about six o'clock with the furniture so I could do a massive blitz before then. I wasn't sure whether Gemma would appear again today but I was rather hoping she would. I had got quite used to the cakes she was plying me with, and yesterday she had seemed about to tell me something important, before she got the phone call, so hopefully, I'd find out what that was too. I loved a bit of juicy gossip.

## 10

The radio kept me company as I scrubbed and scrubbed. The section of wooden floors I'd attacked with vigour were coming up a treat, but it was incredibly slow progress and I realised that I would need to concentrate on one room at a time. I seemed to flit from one room to another doing a bit here and a bit there and therefore not really making a big impression. I'd sit down tonight with my notebook and get listing again. Perhaps I needed to prioritise the bedroom and the kitchen. And hopefully when I got an actual bed, I could get the mattress up off the floor and out of its protective wrapping and have somewhere to sleep. My time in the B & B would be up soon so I needed to get that sorted. Otherwise I'd be sleeping on the floorboards.

Sadly, there had been no interruption from Gemma today, so when I heard a vehicle approach, I didn't realise the time. I headed down the stairs to see a truck loaded with furniture reversing towards the building. I thought that maybe I'd seen it somewhere before – it looked quite familiar – but that puzzled me as I'd not been here long enough to recognise what cars people drove. Also, there were not that many vehicles around in this part of the village.

When the driver unfolded himself from the front seat, all became clear. We looked at each other in alarm.

'Oh God, not you!'

'Seriously, not you! Hogged any parking spaces lately?'

He tried not to smirk.

'When Dad told me to come down with some furniture for the "lady" who'd bought the lighthouse, you were the last person I was expecting.'

He mimicked speech marks when he said the word 'lady'. Twat!

'So, you bought this old place, did you? I can't believe it. I do hope your mood has improved since I saw you the other day.'

'There is and was nothing wrong with my mood, thank you very much. If you hadn't been so rude to me, I wouldn't have had to be rude back.'

Martin got out of the passenger seat where he'd been watching this exchange. 'What's going on here? Have you two met before?'

'Yes when—'

'Sadly yes.'

'Stop speaking at the same time. Do you think you two need to start all over again? Your old mum always used to say that there was nothing that communication couldn't fix. Isn't that right, son?'

'Suppose so.' His face turned into that of the surly teenager I'd been expecting.

I took a leaf out of Martin's book and made the first move.

'Hi there.' I held out my hand. 'I'm Meredith and I've bought the lighthouse. Nice to meet you.'

He shook my hand begrudgingly. 'I'm Martin's son, as you now know. Shall we get on with this then? Do you mind if I go ahead and see how the land lies?'

'Please do!' I smiled sweetly and then when he turned away pulled a face at him behind his back, though I didn't realise Martin had seen. He laughed and rolled his eyes at me. 'Kids, eh?'

Despite Martin's son being a grumpy so-and-so, and even though I thought we were having a 'fresh start', he was an absolute wizard when it came to manoeuvring furniture up the spiral staircase. Mr Rude managed to get both armchairs, the bookcase, and the coffee table onto the top floor. He grinned as he looked at all of his handiwork. When he smiled it took years off him. I tried to work out his age, which was quite hard to do as he kept scowling. Probably around the mid-thirties. He nodded towards the stripey dishevelled deckchair by the window, the one I'd found on arrival.

'Is that all you had to sit on?'

'It was already here when I moved in.'

'Looks like someone has been camping out, admiring the view.'

'Doesn't it?'

'Maybe it's the ghost of the lighthouse keeper. You're not scared of ghosts, are you? The estate agent I presume did tell you about the resident ghost?'

'Stop winding her up, son.' Martin grinned at him and then turned to me. 'Ignore him.' He winked. 'Time we got you into bed then, Meredith.'

'Best offer I've had all week, Martin. Lead the way.'

There was a little glint in Mr Rude's eye, but he was trying hard not to laugh. He was a right misery guts. I wondered whether he was related to the woman at the mini-market. The thought made me laugh out loud and he turned and glared at me.

'Something to say?'

'Nothing! At! All!' I mimed zipping my lips shut.

He picked up the bedframe and followed me as I moved down to the next floor, holding it as if it was as light as a feather.

'Want some help putting this together?'

'No, I'm good, thanks. I'll do it tomorrow.'

'I can help while I'm here, got my toolbox in the truck. Will only take me a couple of minutes.'

'Thanks, but I'll be fine. I'm used to doing stuff like this. Appreciate the offer though.' I didn't want him to think I was a helpless female, even if I was. I'd figure it out tomorrow. I'd have to. I needed to sleep somewhere.

'OK, if you're sure. Last couple of things on the way now. I reckon that old butcher's block might be too big for the stairs, but we'll have a go. Can you give us a hand with it please, Dad?'

They tried various ways to get it up the stairs, but it was solid and wouldn't shift. And even though I thought I could see a way round it, Mr Rude refused to listen to me. God, he was stubborn as well as grumpy. What a combination, although as I'd followed him up the stairs a few times already, I couldn't help but notice he'd got a really nice bum and I bet those lovely long legs looked good in shorts. *Meredith, stop. What are you doing?*

'Can you just try it my way? One last time and if it doesn't work then I'll admit defeat.' I really wanted this piece for the kitchen. It would be so helpful until the rest of the units were fitted, whenever that may be. Which also reminded me to get that blooming number for that Clement guy from Lucy. Must must must remember.

Lo and behold, it went up the way I had suggested. As I followed them up the stairs, and the two actually admitted they were wrong and I was right, I had a smug grin on my face.

'What are you doing about getting the rest of the kitchen fitted?'

'Not sure yet. I need to go through all of the boxes and work out what is here and what isn't. Then I guess I'll go from there.'

'I know someone who might be able to help.'

'Thanks, but I've already got someone in mind.'

'Please yourself.'

'Oh, I will.'

Martin looked from one of us to the other and shook his head. 'Right, that's everything then, my lovely!'

'Let me grab my bag and settle up with you.'

'No need. Just pop by the shop in the morning. We can sort it all out then. It's not like I don't know where you live, is it? We can have a cuppa and you can tell me all your plans for this place.'

'I'll wait in the truck.'

'OK, son, I'll be down in a minute.'

'Thanks,' I said. 'I appreciate your hard work.'

'S'OK,' he muttered and ran down the stairs, seemingly not able to wait to get away, but clearly forgetting to duck before he headed out through the front door as I heard him shout 'Shit!' and when I glanced out of the window, he was rubbing his head. That door wasn't made for big strapping lads, but it served him right for being an arse.

'Don't mind him. He's a funny bugger at times. I'll tell you more in the morning, but I'm gonna go and pop into the pub for a pint after all that hard work. I need me a rest.'

'Thank you, Martin. I really do appreciate all you've done for me. I've had mixed reactions to my arrival, and you've been so kind.' I reached up and kissed his grey beardy face. And despite the beard, I could tell he was blushing.

'You are most welcome, me darlin'. It's nice to get a bit of life into the village. I wish you luck here, I really do. Oh, and take no notice of him.' He inclined his head towards the waiting car. 'There's no ghost here. He was having you on.'

And with that, he raised his fingers to his head in a mock salute, just like his son had done the first time I'd met him – although that time it wasn't meant so kindly.

Great, I'd forgotten about that till now. A shiver ran down my spine and I decided that it was time to call it a day. My tummy rumbled. A stroll back to the B & B via the beach and a little sit-down on what I was now calling 'my rock' would be a perfect finish to the day.

\* \* \*

'Hi, is this Clement Penrose?'

'It is. How can I help?'

'I've moved into the village recently and I've been given your number. I was told that you might be able to help me to get some jobs done. Kitchen fitting mainly to start with but there might be some other stuff too.'

'I'm sorry, I can't hear you very well. I'm in the pub and it's quite busy. Can you text the details through to me? I'll message you back.'

'Sure.'

The call had gone dead before I'd finished the short word. This Clem didn't seem that bothered about the work. But I gritted my teeth. I would be nice. I'm sure I needed him more than he needed me. I texted him some brief details and he replied back immediately.

I live on a boat in the harbour. Any chance you could pop by in the morning and we can discuss details?

Oh, what a shame. Fancy not being able to afford a house and having to live on a boat. Perhaps he needed the work as much as I needed a handyman after all.

Sure! How will I know which one is your boat?

It's called *Penelope Plump*. Is 8 a.m. too early for you? I can provide coffee.

That's perfect. Thank you and see you then.

At least after I'd spoken to him I might have a good idea of what needed doing and hopefully the cost too. Maybe after tomorrow, I could put even more of a plan together and finally start making a bigger impact.

This was starting to feel exciting! But then I remembered the impending visit from my mother and my mood plummeted.

## 11

Miraculously, the person who was going to be moving into my room had asked if they could postpone their trip again, so Lucy offered me the room for a few more days, which was absolutely perfect. It would give me a little longer to get some order into the lighthouse before I moved in.

The next morning, Lucy packed a cool bag with some freshly cooked pastries and suggested I take these to Clement to 'butter him up'. Lucy had told me what a nice man he was, and had also mentioned that he was the local heartthrob, even though he had absolutely no idea.

I wandered round the harbour and found *Penelope Plump* parked, (is that what you call it?) next to the harbour wall. The name made me smile. This Clem clearly had a sense of humour.

Reaching the steps, I wondered what I should do. What was boat etiquette? Did you knock? What did you knock? Was there a bell? Did you have to ask for permission to go on board? Did you yell hello and hope that someone comes out? I had no idea. I past a few times, peering in, but there didn't seem to be any life on board.

It was just coming up to eight o'clock. Maybe I should text him,

I thought. Tell him I'm here. Yes, that's what I'd do. There was a bench just further down the wall. I'd sit and watch the world go by as I waited.

Footsteps got louder and a body appeared from the deck below. I walked towards the boat and heard a muffled hello from under a navy-blue towel that the person was roughly drying their hair with.

You had to be kidding me. There stood in front of me, looking dashingly handsome, although it killed me to admit it, with damp hair and clearly fresh from the shower was Martin's son. Dressed in shorts and a vest top, which I just happened to notice was showing off one hell of a muscly body, he stared at me with a half-crooked smile on his face.

'What? Why? Who?...' Words literally failed me as I walked towards the boat.

'I'm sorry, I couldn't resist not telling you. I knew it would be so much fun.' He grinned and his face lit up. The smile that he seemed to be holding onto yesterday burst from him. He was incredibly good-looking when he wasn't being surly. 'Now can we really start all over again?' He held his hand out to help me on board. 'I'm Clement Penrose. You can call me Clem if you like. It's a bit of a mouthful otherwise. Now, how can I help?'

If there was one thing I hated more than anything else, it was someone making fun of me. I'd had a complex about it all my life and Gabby always used to say that my going to therapy should have helped. But while there was part of me that was really annoyed with Clement Penrose for not admitting who he was, I clearly needed someone like him to help me and he was the only person whose details I'd got. That, and he was standing in front of me right now. I stood with my hands on my hips, wondering just exactly how to handle this. But somehow I felt the anger and tension melt away as quickly as it had appeared.

'Thank you! I'm glad you got a laugh at my expense.' He had the decency to look ashamed and while I was still annoyed at him, I reckoned that smile he was giving me was something that I could probably forgive.

'I'm not normally so annoying I promise. You must have caught me on a bad day.'

'Bad days you mean. You sure know how to wind a girl up.'

'Ok, well, truce? Coffee?'

'Truce.' I held up the bag. 'And pastries. Lucy sent them.'

'Now that is a good way to start a day. What that family doesn't know about baking isn't worth thinking about. Would you like to come aboard? Here let me help.'

Taking the hand he offered, I climbed onto the deck. I'd never been on a boat like this before and as I followed Clem, noticing his broad shoulders as I followed him down the narrow staircase into the main downstairs area, I was completely taken aback. There was way more space than I thought there would be and it was actually rather nice.

'Take a seat, Meredith. Make yourself at home.'

I looked around and took in the surroundings, hoping he might not notice me being too nosy. There was a doorway off the lounge-come-dining area and I could see a bed that hadn't been made. I flushed thinking about him in it and forced my attention back to him and his big blue eyes. I gulped.

'So how come you have to live on a boat then?'

'I don't have to. I choose to. Huge difference. Why would you not want to wake up looking one way to the harbour and the other to the beach? Just like your lighthouse, but in my case knowing that you could take off at a moment's notice and explore the world. Sailing is peaceful and wonderful. When the weather is in your favour that is. Have you ever sailed? Can't imagine it's your cup of tea, thinking about it.'

'Oh right. No, I haven't. But why do you say that? You don't know anything about me.'

I couldn't put my finger on why, but it felt like we were constantly offending each other.

'Just a feeling. You seem a little... well... uptight?' His voice lilted upwards at the end which made it more of a question than a statement.

'Well, I'm not so...' I didn't know what else to say because to be honest he wasn't the first person to have said this. I put it down to grief after Nana's death along with the other changes that had been going on in my life. I must make more effort not to do this and not to be so defensive. Not everyone has an agenda.

'Anyhow, I'm here to ask you about doing some work at the lighthouse. Would it be something you might consider? Do you even have time?' I got out my notebook and started to list the jobs that needed doing most urgently. 'The kitchen and bathroom mainly though.' I snapped the notebook shut and looked at him pleadingly.

'As it happens, I'm between jobs at the moment. I've just had a big one cancel on me, so I'm sure we could work something out. I can't do it today but how about if I come over tomorrow morning and have a look at the kitchen. It sounds like a good place to start would be working out what's in the boxes and whether we can make some cupboards up. Maybe get some more work surfaces fitted. What do you think?'

I could literally have jumped up and kissed his gorgeous beardy face. But obviously I didn't. Then I flushed again at the thought of kissing him. My eyes drifted to his lips which looked remarkably soft and full. Get a grip, Meredith. What is wrong with you? He's way too young for you.

'I think that would be fabulous. Thank you.'

'Don't worry. I'm sure between us, we can soon get things sorted out for you. Dad mentioned that you were a bit down, not realising what hard work it was going to be. Did the estate agent not mention the state of the place? Was his name Russell? He should know better if it was.'

'Yes, that's the one. You know him?' I asked. 'To be honest, I haven't actually met him apart from a couple of short phone calls. I've tried calling a few times since I arrived but he's not returning my calls. I think he knows what I'm going to say to him. But I'm here now and I just need to get the lighthouse liveable. Thank goodness for Lucy's B & B. It's been keeping me sane.'

He smiled at me, and I got a little flutter in my tummy as I looked into his lovely eyes. What was wrong with me?

'Let me give you the spare key.' I passed it over to him and as our hands touched a static shock surprised us both and we both jumped back.

'So sorry!'

'So sorry!'

We both laughed nervously.

'You should be careful giving your key out to any old stranger, you know. I could come in and rob all your stuff.'

'If you're desperate enough to want the stuff I have right now, you'd be welcome to it. There's nothing of value in there. Which reminds me: I must get a TV at some point.'

'With a view like the lighthouse has, why would you ever need a TV?'

I looked around his boat and noticed a lack of a TV.

'I don't have one if that's what you're looking for. I have books, my laptop and a radio. That's plenty for me.'

I didn't think I'd ever known anyone who hadn't got a TV and this really surprised me. He also didn't look like the type to be a reader. This was a man who was full of surprises.

'Oh well, I will need to get one at some point. Is there somewhere local that I could buy one from?'

He laughed. 'Local no. The nearest retail park is about an hour away. The beauty of living in a remote village like this one is that you don't get crowds on the roads because we don't really have much here. People who want that type of stuff on their doorstep don't end up living in Driftwood Bay.'

'I suppose so.' I put my empty coffee mug down on the table and added FIND TV SHOP to my notebook. I turned back to Clem. 'I'll be at the lighthouse just after breakfast so don't rush over. Thanks so much for the coffee.'

'And thank you for the breakfast.'

I stood nervously. 'I'd best be off then. See you in the morning.'

He followed me up the stairs and I couldn't help but wonder if he was thinking how fat my backside was – his face was so close to it. How mortifying. He was grinning as I turned at the top. I was pretty sure he knew exactly what I was thinking. I could feel the heat creep up my neck and into my face.

'It's beautiful here, isn't it?' He held his arm out and indicated the surroundings. 'You've picked a good place to come and live.'

'Thank you. Although I'm not sure whether I'll be here permanently or not yet. I'm just going to do the lighthouse up and see how I feel about it all. Even see how I fit into the neighbourhood.' I turned and we locked eyes. Those beautiful blue eyes. Time seemed to stand still although it had probably only been a couple of seconds. I swallowed a lump that had formed in my throat, and he seemed to be frowning at me but held my gaze. I was the first to look away.

'See you tomorrow, Clem.'

'Bye, Meredith,' he whispered.

# 12

I'd only been in Driftwood Bay a few days but I really felt like I was getting my own little morning routine. Each morning, James made me a drink, leaving it in a thermal cup at the bottom of the stairs and I headed to the beach where I'd watch the sun rise. What an amazing way to start the day.

After an hour or so on the beach, I made my way back to the B & B for a shower and then I headed over to the lighthouse. The front door had been propped open and I could hear a radio blaring and an appalling rendition of 'Uptown Funk' coming from the kitchen drowning out poor old Bruno Mars. Clem had obviously arrived before me. I headed up the stairs towards the noise and stood watching him as he danced around the kitchen, that expression 'dance like no one is watching' clearly extending to 'sing like no one is listening' too. He pivoted on his heel and realised that I was standing there. Mortified, he reached over to turn the radio down.

'Don't mind me.' I folded my arms and leaned against the stairway.

'Sorry. Didn't realise I had company.'

'Don't let me stop you. Are you auditioning for *Britain's Got Talent*? I think you might need to work on your pitch a little...'

'Cheeky.' His smile back at me made not only his eyes crinkle around the edges, but also made little butterflies dance around in my stomach. His whole face lit up and I literally had to drag my eyes away. He really was quite mesmerising and so different to how he was when I initially met him.

'So, I hope it's OK with you, but I made a start and have been through the boxes. I reckon that you need the carcasses of two more base cupboards and a matching work surface too. However, if you want them on the outside walls, I'm going to need to build some kind of unit for them to fit into because of the curved walls and the fact that they won't fit flush. Have you had any thoughts at all about how you wanted the kitchen laid out?'

I actually had no idea and his question flummoxed me. I had not realised that, with round walls like lighthouses have, it was going to be a total nightmare to furnish. I looked at him blankly and with no words coming out of my mouth.

He suggested I put the kettle on, if I could find it under all the cardboard from the boxes he'd opened, and said he'd draw me a rough sketch to show his thoughts.

I made the tea and sat on the floor next to him, not realising how close I was until I noticed that our arms were touching. However, it was one of those situations where I if had moved, it would have been really embarrassing so I tried to ignore it and concentrated on what he'd drawn. It was not easy. My mind was not on the kitchen but on the golden blond hairs on his forearms.

I shook my head and straightened myself up, and as he described it, the beauty of his vision, making the most of the amazing view at every opportunity, drew me back to the task at hand.

His plan was incredible and I could envisage what it would look like completely. He'd clearly put so much thought into it.

'You hate it, don't you? Instead, maybe I could do—'

I grabbed his arm, his sun-kissed rock-hard arm, and my eyes widened when I realised that it was a lot firmer than I thought it was going to be. I'd had a crush on Chris Martin from Coldplay for years after I'd noticed what amazingly strong arms he had. It was something I'd always admired in a man since. That, and I was also a sucker for a utility trouser.

'I love it.' Tears threatened to appear and I blinked them away. 'I'm nearly fifty years old and I've never had a brand-new kitchen before. Honestly, Clem, I just love it. You can really do all of that? In here?'

'Yep, I reckon I can. If you want me to.'

'That would be amazing. So what do we need to do to make this happen?'

'I reckon a trip to the DIY yard today is in order and I can make a start. You happy with that?'

'We haven't even discussed money. How much would you charge to do all of this?'

'Well, how would you feel if I said that you can pay me a daily rate of £160? And I'll do as much work as I can fit in, in a day. Does that sound fair?'

'That sounds more than fair but are you sure?'

'As I said before, I've had a job cancelled so I'd have just been bumming around on the boat for the next couple of weeks anyway, so this is more than I was expecting. If you pay for the materials and that daily rate, I'm very happy with that. Deal?'

I shook his hand before he could change his mind.

The alarm went off on my phone. It was nine thirty. Time to go and see Martin so I could settle my bill. I didn't want him to think I was taking advantage.

Clem laughed. 'You'll be lucky if Dad opens the shop before ten. Then he normally closes at twelve to go to the pub for a nice long lunch before he does a couple of hours in the shop in the afternoon. And he never works past four. He always says at his age there's no point having a shop if he can't keep his own hours.'

'Does he not lose customers that way?' I asked, intrigued. If shops back in Staffordshire weren't open, customers wouldn't come back in the hope that it might be open, they'd just find somewhere else. There didn't seem to be any loyalty around but there clearly was down here. How lovely.

'Nah. He's the only person for miles around who sells that type of old shite. Oops, sorry for swearing.' He grinned. 'Right, get yourself ready then and we'll head off to the yard and we can swing by Dad's on the way back. He'll be fine with that. I promise. And if the shop is closed, we can pop into the pub because I guarantee you, he'll be there.'

'Perfect. Let's go!'

'Oh, and by the way. Are you sure you're nearly fifty?' He looked me up and down and I couldn't quite discern what he was thinking. 'I thought you were around my age.'

'Well, thank you. You know how to flatter a woman. And what, may I ask, is your age?'

I'd been dying to know how old he was but didn't quite know how to bring it up.

'Forty last month.'

'A mere spring chicken in comparison.'

I smiled but felt a little deflated. My heart was telling me that it wasn't right for me to be fancying someone nearly ten years my junior. I should start acting my age.

## 13

It felt strange being in the car so close to Clem. When I thought he wasn't looking, I glanced at him a couple of times. He really was very easy on the eye, as Lucy had mentioned, and now his personality was thawing out a little, he was almost pleasant, but more than that he was clearly very good at his job and could make a massive difference in my life. His vision for the kitchen project was amazing, and it sounded like it was something he could get cracking on straight away. As we drove through the village and around the outskirts towards the builders' yard, he pointed out various sights: where he went to school, the doctor's surgery, the village church, the garage and the Chinese takeaway, and he had a little story about them all.

'Sorry, am I talking too much? I get a little over chatty when I'm nervous.'

'Nervous, why are you nervous?'

'Well, we don't really meet new people down here in Driftwood Bay, so when we do, it can feel a bit awkward.'

I sighed loudly. 'Driftwood Bay is a strange old place. Most of the people are nice – there's you, now that we're best friends obvs.'

He looked across and winked at me and I felt a little flutter in my tummy which I tried to ignore. Maybe I was just hungry. 'Your dad is lovely, Gemma, Lucy and James are great. And then there's the man I see walking a Labrador every day who never speaks even though I say hello to him and the woman in the mini-market who seems for some reason to really hate me.'

'Ah well, the man walking the Lab will be Dennis. He's staying with his grandmother, who lives in the village, for a couple of weeks. And the dog is Gladys. She's a proper sweetheart, not his dog. She belongs to Violet, but she's had a fall recently, really can't cope and is heartbroken at the thought of maybe needing to rehome her. Since the fall, she's really lost her confidence in walking the dog and she can't go chasing after her if she runs off. A dog like that needs a good run and the beach is perfect. If I didn't live on a boat, I'd consider having her myself.'

'Oh, that's so sad. I've always fancied having a dog but working in an office most of my life has meant that it would be left on its own all day long and it's not really fair on it. What a shame. How long is Dennis staying for?'

'I think he goes home tomorrow. Not sure what they're going to do. I must ask Dad if he knows.'

I thought back to our family dog from when I was a child and how heartbroken I was when my mother arranged for him to be rehomed. I was distraught for weeks.

Wandering around the builders' yard was probably an interesting thing to do if you're in the trade but to me it was a little dull. There was only so much wood you could look at. The best bit was choosing the materials for some more work surfaces. We couldn't get the exact same that was already in the lighthouse, but we went for a similar wood in a contrasting colour which we thought would look pretty cool. Tiles in various shades of blues and greens would bring the colour of the sea into the room so we took some samples so we could look at them in place. We stood at the counter waiting for my card payment to go through when Clem suddenly shouted at me.

'Knobs!'

'Sorry?'

'How do you feel about knobs?'

'Erm... well, erm... I suppose they're OK as long as they're not too hairy and being waved around in your face.' What a strange question. I frowned at Clem in disbelief not realising that we'd skipped ahead to the stage of our friendship where we discussed such things.

Bent double in hysterics, the sales assistant banged the counter, unable to speak. When I looked at Clem, he was proper laughing too and holding his belly.

'What?' I held both of my palms upwards.

He held up a packet.

'Cupboard doorknobs, you nutter.'

I put my head in my hands, mortified at my faux pas, my face glowing as red as a beetroot.

'I'll wait outside by the truck,' I said.

Oh my God. The best I could hope for was that Clem never mentioned this again. That would obviously be the gentlemanly thing to do. However, he was still chuckling when he got back to the truck with the trolley full of materials. I glared at him as I walked round to help. Sadly, that just made him laugh even more. My face then started to twitch, and I coughed to cover up a laugh which tried to escape. As he looked towards the noise, I saw that his eyes were full of tears, and he was trying so hard to keep a straight face. But then a laugh exploded from me, and he couldn't help himself either and we both fell about laughing.

'Don't suppose there's any chance of you ever forgetting that?'

'Not a cat in hell's chance. Sorry, but that's too good to keep to myself. You think that sales assistant isn't telling them all about it in there right now?'

'Oh lord! Get me out of here and remind me never to come back.'

'Come on, let's get this lot into the truck. I'm not sure about going out for lunch. I don't think you're safe to be let out anywhere else.'

We grinned at each other as we loaded the final piece of timber in the truck's huge boot, which was now brimming, and then jumped in the cab. It struck me that I couldn't remember the last time I'd laughed like that. Laughter is good for the soul. Once I'd calmed down again, I asked Clem to tell me more about his life growing up in Driftwood Bay. I thought it might take my mind off his knobs.

# 14

When we arrived back in Driftwood Bay it was time for lunch. Clem parked up in the pub car park, at the bottom of the steep hill, and while he went to get some drinks I joined Martin in the huge window seat which looked across the harbour. It was picture perfect, overlooking the ramp down to the jetty leading to boats bobbing on the sea. The thing that struck me about the image was it all looked so calm and tranquil. The sea had restorative properties. I had never felt so at peace in a place in my life.

'Hi, Dennis, how are you doing? How's Vi?' Clem shook hands with a guy who was sat at the bar nursing a pint and when he turned, I noticed he was the dog walker.

'Oh, I'm OK,' he drawled.

'You don't sound so sure about that, mate.'

'I have to go back home tomorrow and leave Nan. I don't mind admitting that I'm worried about her. The neighbours are great and said they'd pop in but she's not their responsibility. And I can't see any way around getting the dog temporarily rehomed right now. Nan is so worried and so sad that she's going to have to give her up for good.'

'Such a shame. I'm really sorry, mate. Maybe something will come up.'

My brain started to tick as I drank my coffee. I didn't even know this lady, but I was in a position where I could help, and she was clearly so desperately in need. Should I offer to help? Having a dog was too big a commitment for me right now but maybe I could pop in and walk Gladys once a day. It might do us both good. I walked on the beach anyway. I'd do some digging and find out where she lived. It could just work.

Lunch arrived. A cheese and pickle sandwich for me on doorstep-thick fresh crusty bread and a bowl of chunky chips smothered with salt and vinegar. Something so simple was so delicious. They sure knew how to feed people round here. I'm surprised the village didn't have a problem with obesity.

When Dennis muttered a gloomy goodbye, my opportunity came to do some digging with Martin and Clem.

'Where does Vi live?'

'In the pink cottage in the harbour. Been there as long as I can remember, on her own since her husband died years ago.'

'Do you think she'd let me walk her dog? It would give me the opportunity to see whether a dog would fit into my life and help her out at the same time. What do you think? I know I've only been here five minutes and none of you really know me, but I'd really like to help.'

Martin jumped up. 'I think she'd be over the moon. We could pop along and see her right now. Come on, come on.' Clem grabbed his glass and glugged down the last of his orange juice.

'Bloody great idea, Meredith. Let's go.'

\* \* \*

We knocked on the cottage's front door and Dennis appeared, still looking understandably gloomy.

'Can we come in and see your nan, mate?' Clem asked.

The three of us followed Dennis down the hallway to the front room where Violet sat, the dog curled up at her feet.

'Hello, Clem, Martin. What are you doing here? Not that it's not nice to see you, of course.'

'Hello, Vi, this is our friend Meredith. She's bought the lighthouse.'

'Oh, that one! The one everyone is talking about you mean. The lighthouse stealer?'

And there was me thinking Vi was a sweet little old lady. Was I going to regret what I was about to offer?

'Yes, I'm that one. I know you don't know me, but I've heard that you might have to rehome your dog?'

'Oh don't. I'm so devastated.' Tears began to well in her eyes. 'I love her so much. She's my best friend. I was just trying to work out how to say goodbye. Dennis has arranged to take her to the—' she sniffed and whispered the rest of the sentence '—dogs' home tomorrow.' Her eyes flicked to a box that had some dog toys and a couple of leads on the top, which it looked as if she'd put together for Gladys's departure.

'Well, I may have a solution.'

She sat up straight and wiped away her tears. 'Go on.'

'I've always loved the thought of having a dog but at the moment I don't know how or if one would fit in with my lifestyle. As you know I've bought the lighthouse and am not sure whether it's a short-term fix-up job or whether I'll stay. But I do walk on the beach every day and plan to do lots of that while I am here and it's going to take some time to get the lighthouse done up, thanks to Clem here who is helping me.'

'Ah, he's a good boy and I'm happy for you, dear.' She looked at me expectantly, clearly not knowing what this had to do with her.

'I thought that I could come and pick Gladys up and take her out for you. I could keep her at the lighthouse sometimes if you needed a break from her, or I could bring her back here to you. But it would give me some company and get her out for a good walk each day. Then maybe, when you are feeling up to it, you could come too, and build your strength up, and you'd have someone with you who can help if you need it.'

'Oh my!' She slumped in her seat. She must have hated the idea.

'Oh, I'm sorry, I didn't want to upset you.'

'Upset me? Meredith, did you say your name was?'

'I did and I'm sorry, I never meant any offence.'

'None taken. I'm just a little stunned. You'd do that for me? Someone you don't even know?'

'I would if you thought it was a good idea. But only if you are happy with the arrangement. If you think Gladys would be happy.'

Hearing her name, Gladys pricked her ears up and I smiled at her. She stood and came over to me, licked my hand and settled at my feet.

Vi held her hand to her heart. 'I think she knows already. I am truly flabbergasted. How can I ever repay you for your kindness?'

'There's no need. I'll be getting as much out of this as you will. Does that mean yes then? Maybe we could give it a try and see how we get on?'

Vi raised herself slowly from the chair and wobbled over to me. I stood up too and she flung her arms around me. 'Thank you, thank you, thank you. You've properly made my day.'

When she returned to her seat, she looked like a new woman, as if she'd been on the TV show *Ten Years Younger*. She looked visibly different and couldn't stop smiling. Gladys had settled back at her feet, and as we said our goodbyes, I promised that I'd be back around ten in the morning so we could work out what would be best for us all. I felt so happy. I'd been able to do what was a small thing for me but would be life-changing for her. Why should we not help others if we could? If we all did that, it would make the world a much nicer place to live in.

As we got back to the truck Clem looked at me wistfully.

'What?'

'You intrigue me.'

'Not sure if that's a good thing.'

'It is.' He winked. The heat I felt rising through my neck and face was somewhat overwhelming and I prayed for once that it was a menopausal hot flush.

## 15

'Right, let's crack on then getting this lot upstairs!'

Spiral steps were not the easiest thing when carrying timber and some of it had to be lifted through the straight part with Clem one end and me the other, but we worked well together and got everything up. It was around three by the time we'd finished. I presumed Clem would come back and start the next day, but he insisted on starting there and then.

'No time like the present. No reason not to start today.'

'Only if you're sure. Do you need me? If not, I've got some stuff to do in the bedroom.'

He raised an eyebrow briefly and smirked. Gosh, this man made me permanently blush.

'A bed to build,' I confirmed.

'Need some help?'

'No, I'm good thanks.'

'OK, but just holler if you need an extra pair of hands.'

I laid the bedframe out on the floor and got the screws out of the packet which had been fastened to the slats. There was an Allen key too and it looked pretty straightforward. What did give me a problem though was the fact that I had to hold one part with my leg and then stretch my arm to full length for the other, and the connection kept dropping out of the joint. I was determined to do it, though. Once I put my mind to something, it really annoyed me if I had to give in.

'Bugger!' It dropped apart again. Once more, I attempted to do it, this time resting one end on the top of a suitcase. And once more, it fell apart. It was also bloody heavy so the weight of it wasn't helping matters either. I was muttering expletives under my breath when I felt a presence behind me. Clem was standing in the doorway. I hadn't even heard him come down the stairway.

'It's not a crime to ask for help you know.' He knelt beside me and nudged my shoulder. 'Shove over. You grab that bit over there and I'll get the other side.'

Within minutes the whole frame was together and then all I needed to do was fit the slats in place, which I knew that I could do myself. After that, I just needed to decide where it would go. It made sense to face the window to make the most of the view.

'Thank you.'

'Teamwork!' He left the room and I sighed.

I really wanted to be able to do stuff myself. Asking for help made me feel weak and useless. I'd felt like that many times in my life, normally down to things that my mother had said to me and the memory brought those feelings back. Because she'd had to cope as a single parent, she assumed everyone should do everything alone and that help from a man made you a lesser person. Then when I was married, my husband wouldn't let me do anything, which at first I found endearing but I eventually worked out that it was patronising, especially when he told me that I was useless and couldn't do anything right.

Gabby had always tried to tell me differently but these feelings were so deeply embedded in my brain that I really struggled to balance them. I was trying. But then, aren't we all a work in progress?

The floor in the bedroom was wooden and needed a good sweeping and polish. I popped up to the kitchen to get some cleaning bits.

'What are you after?' Clem asked as I stood there, dithering about what to use.

'Something to clean the wooden floor with.' I chewed my lip as I looked through the cleaning box.

'Did you know that hardwood floors aren't as delicate as you think? Because they're finished with polyurethane, they're actually one of the most durable floors you can have.' I turned to stare at him as he gave me this nugget of information. 'I reckon if you give it a good sweep, then go over it with your Hetty hoover, who, by the way, looks like she has her beady eye constantly on me, and then use some specialised hardwood floor cleaning spray, it'll come up a treat. I've got some on the boat if you want to try it. Sorry, but I'm a bit of a geek where wood is concerned. And I've worked on the boat a lot since I've had her, so I've learned lessons along the way. Don't want to come across as a know-it-all.'

'That would be fab. I've still got another couple of nights at the B & B before they kick me out so if you could bring it tomorrow that would be fabulous. I could do with doing an online shop too. Which supermarket comes out this way?'

Clem laughed. 'You're in the depths of Cornwall now, my girl. None of the supermarkets deliver this far. I head up to the super-store once a month and stock up on all the big stuff. I try to bulk buy but it's hard because on the boat I don't really have much space to store it. You could always come with me when I go, and we could load up the truck.' He paused and looked at me with a smirk. 'And it's much easier to get a great parking space when you have a big truck.' He winked again. He really wasn't helping matters. 'Can't imagine you can get much shopping in your Mini.'

'You're right there. Six carrier bags of shopping and the boot is full and that's if the roof is not down. There's even less room when most of the roof goes in it,' I said. 'But that would be great if you don't mind. Let me know when you go, and we can share the petrol cost.'

'You're on. Maybe at the weekend. Unless you have other plans.'

'The only plans I have for the foreseeable future are this place, mealtimes and now a daily hot date with a golden Lab.' That actually made me sound really sad, but it was true for the time being. Moving your life to a new village wasn't easy. You needed to make friends and that is hard to do as it is as you get older. You must make the effort yourself, find and join clubs, which I hadn't got as far as doing yet, so I had an empty diary. Maybe when I started working again things would look different but as I would be doing that mainly from home too, I wasn't sure what that would look like.

'What a loser!' Clem winked at me. 'We'll definitely have to do something about that. It's quiz night in the pub tonight. Highlight of the week. You should come down. Bring Lucy, James and Gemma.'

Did I really want to go to a quiz night in the local pub? It wasn't really my thing.

'Unless you're thinking you'll lose.'

He clearly didn't know about my competitive side.

'You're on.'

# 16

I was determined to head back to the mini-market again although, being later in the day, it would be just my luck for the owner to not be there. I didn't even really need much if I was going to the supermarket at the weekend but I'm sure there would be something I'd need before heading back to the B & B.

I loved the pretty little high street with its quaint shop windows. Walking towards the door of the shop, I could see that one of the ladies who was in there the other day was just leaving. As I said good evening to her, she just looked straight through me and let the door close behind her rather than holding it for me. Miserable mare.

As I suspected, there was a young girl behind the counter. She was singing along to Take That which was playing on the radio and seemed quite nice, which made a pleasant change.

'Hi, I'm Meredith. Big Take That fan are you? I am too. Probably their biggest fan ever actually.'

'Oh, so you're Meredith, are you? I'd heard that you'd arrived in the village.'

'Is that from the frosty woman who owns the shop?'

'My mum, yes.'

I covered my face with my free hand. 'Gosh, I'm so sorry!'

'Don't worry. She is a frosty old cow. And I'm sure especially towards you.'

'Why towards me? Have I done something to offend her? I've only met her twice.'

The girl looked at the door behind her and pulled the handle to make sure it was shut.

'The whole lighthouse thing. You outbid one of the villagers for it. Surely you know that?'

'No wonder I've been getting some funny looks. Although that didn't seem to bother your mum when I offered to show her around when I've done it up.'

'Ah, don't mind her. Her bark is worse than her bite. She's just very protective of the folks round here. She's lived here all her life and doesn't have much else to think about apart from me, my big sister, Da and the village.'

I must remember to ask Clem later who it was that I'd outbid. He knew everything and was bound to spill the beans.

I walked back via the beach to the B & B and stopped at my rock. It was a place where I always managed to get four bars of signal on the phone so I dropped Gabby a message, hoping she'd checked her diary to see when she might be able to come down.

I saw Dennis walking down by the sea, throwing the ball for Gladys. He was laughing and chatting away to her. This time, he acknowledged me with a wave and came over.

'Mind if I sit?'

'Be my guest.' I shuffled over and Gladys sniffed at my hand, sitting down with her backside leaning up against me.

'I've just come from the lighthouse actually. I was hoping to see you.' Dennis had kind eyes and was actually quite good-looking close-up. I hadn't noticed earlier as I was so concerned with Violet and the dog.

'Have you changed your minds?'

'No, not at all. I just wanted to say thank you. I never even considered doing a kind of dog-share arrangement and it really is the perfect solution. Thank you for being so kind and offering. I honestly can't believe the change in Nan today. She's like a different person.'

'I'm really glad to help. It will give me a purpose too, as well as doing up that old place.' I nodded my head towards the lighthouse.

'Yes, I'm sure that will keep you busy. I thought maybe, erm... Well, I wondered if I might be able to give you my number. Maybe you might erm... well... feel like giving me a call sometime.'

I looked into his eyes. He was blushing profusely, and I didn't want to make him feel worse.

'You could let me know how things are going with Nan and Gladys,' he continued. 'Or if you just... you know... fancied a chat.'

'I'd love to keep you posted about your nan and Gladys. Maybe I could send you some pics from time to time too.' I wanted to choose my next words very carefully, not wanting to offend but wanting to make sure I didn't mislead him in any way. 'I'm going to be really busy doing up the lighthouse and what with walking Gladys and popping in to see your nan too, and keeping up with friends, I'll be keeping quite busy. It's nice to have new friends though.'

He nodded. 'Yes, I can imagine. Well, it would be lovely to know how things are going. I have pushed my number through your front door, so you'll have it and if you need anything for Nan, do let me know. And thanks again, Meredith. It really is very kind of you. Goodbye.'

He bent across and lightly kissed my cheek. He seemed like a nice man – for someone, but that someone wasn't me. There was just no spark between us. When I was ready to fall for someone next time round, I wanted the whole shebang that I'd never really had before. The fireworks and fizziness that you read about in epic love stories and see in romcom films. At that point, Clem's face flashed into my head. He wasn't what I needed either, despite him being the most handsome man I'd seen for a long time. Way too young for me. I really hadn't got the time or inclination for romance in my life right now. I had a lighthouse to renovate. A business to get back on its feet and friends to make. I already felt like Clem and I were becoming friends now that we'd both put our stubbornness behind us. Gemma, Lucy and James were fab, of course, and Gladys would be the perfect companion for me too.

When I got to the B & B I suggested to Lucy about the pub quiz. She was over the moon. 'God, I never normally get a night off from this place, and luckily for us again, there's no-one in tonight so I don't need to be around. Let me ring Gemma now. How exciting. Another night out.'

James laughed. 'You'd think I never take you anywhere.'

'That's because, one, you don't, and two, we own a bloody B & B and rarely get a night off work. Thank goodness everyone is at an event in the next town tonight to give us a break.'

'Well, it wasn't me that wanted a B & B. I did tell you this when we bought it.'

'I know, my love! But it doesn't stop me having a moan about it every now and then does it?'

She bopped him on the nose with her finger and headed down the hall to their private quarters. 'I'm off to doll myself up. You can clear up.'

'Anything you say, darling wife.' He grinned and asked if I wanted any pudding, which I declined. I was sure that I was putting on weight just by looking at food. I'd already opted for a salmon salad for tea because I'd already been to the pub for lunch and something lighter suited me.

I headed up to my room and showered, feeling so much cleaner without all that dirt and grime in my hair, and when I emerged half an hour later, I felt like a new woman. I'd dressed in clean jeans, a pink sparkly top, and a navy cashmere cardigan. It felt nice to dress up. It also reminded me that I needed to get a washing machine as it wouldn't be that long before I ran out of clean clothes. I'd had a massive sort out before I left Gabby's home and had donated bags and bags to charity – a plan so I'd only bring things that I really needed and not things that had sat in my wardrobe for years and years untouched.

The Harbourside Hotel was packed when we arrived, and we squeezed through throngs of people to get to the far side of the room where Clem was. Clearly not wanting to be thrashed by me, he'd decided that the five of us could be in a team together. We weren't a bad team, with Clem and James doing well with the sports and music rounds and Lucy, Gemma and I coming up trumps with general knowledge.

We cheered loudly once all the rounds were complete, and it was announced that we were joint leaders and that it was all down to a tiebreaker. When I looked to see who we were tied with, I saw it was Dyllis from the mini-market with her daughter and the friends I'd seen in the shop. They were all glaring across the room at me.

'So, the tiebreaker question is... Who was the second member of Take That to leave the group? That's the second member to leave. Answers to be written down and handed to me, please.'

A hum went around the pub as discussion took place. I knew this. No one was a bigger Take That fan than me and I knew 100 per cent that it was Jason Orange because he was my favourite, and I was blooming devastated when he left. So much so that Gabby thought it funny to send me a sympathy card in the post. Robbie was definitely the first. He went it alone and had his strange thing going on with Liam Gallagher, but it was definitely Jason who was second.

The rest of my team hadn't got a clue. They must have been living under a rock. I looked across at Dyllis's table where they were all huddled together. She looked up and caught my eye. Now was my moment to shine. There was silence. I wrote a name down and passed the piece of paper to Geoff the landlord, who was wearing a quiz master hat tonight. Maybe this was my chance to be in Dyllis's good books.

'Congratulations to Dyllis's team. It was indeed Jason Orange. Bad luck to Clem's team who thought it was Robbie.' I muttered apologies to the table and did actually feel quite bad for getting it wrong on purpose.

'Robbie Williams was actually the first member to leave. And that didn't work out so badly for him now did it, folks, as he went on to have a mighty successful solo career.' Dyllis's daughter looked at me, smiled and whispered something to her mum.

'Ah, I'm so sorry. I thought I'd got it right. Drinks are on me for getting it wrong.' I wrestled my way to the bar and was gutted to see that the person who had come and stood next to me was Dyllis. Great. She nodded her head in acknowledgement.

'Evening.'

'Congratulations.'

'I heard what you've done for Vi and Gladys.'

'Ah, yes. It will do me a favour as well as them. Hopefully it'll work out well for us both.'

'Well, it's a nice thing to do. But just because you've done that, doesn't mean that we're going to welcome you with open arms. And our Leanne told me that you would have known that answer.'

'I guess you can't know everything about your favourite pop group now, can you?'

Someone pushed in between us to get to the bar, and I turned away to get back to our table, trying to balance a tray full of drinks and dodge those standing in the way. I smiled, realising that some things are bigger than being right. Sometimes it's about making a gesture with the right sentiment.

'You see that tall guy with his back to us in the black T-shirt?' I craned my neck to see who Clem was talking about. 'That's Russell. You know, the estate agent that you've been trying to get in touch with.'

So that was the infamous Russell.

I caught his eye as I headed towards the ladies', and thought I'd grab him on my way back. There were definitely a few choice words that I'd be having with him – but when I reached the bar, he'd vanished into thin air. At least I knew who to look out for now though. I'd grab him the next time I saw him. Although I'd stopped calling him over the last couple of days as I just wanted to get on with the work.

This was easily the best night out I'd had in a long time, the three large glasses of red wine clearly helping the evening along and I stumbled back to the B & B with my arm linked in Lucy's one side and James's the other. It wasn't until I fell into bed and started drifting off to sleep that I remembered that I still hadn't asked who it was who had also put in a bid for the lighthouse.

## 17

Much as I needed a full English to soak up the red wine from the night before, I couldn't bring myself to have anything but coffee. I had three more nights left at the B & B so had to really knuckle down and at least get a decent bedroom space organised at the lighthouse.

Clem had very kindly brought along the floor cleaner he'd mentioned, so I made a start with that, and it was amazing what a difference it made. After admitting to myself that I couldn't physically do a lot of the stuff that needed doing, he also helped me to put the bed in place and we lifted the mattress onto the frame so that I could make the bed up. It was starting to look quite cosy. I'd put the two bedside tables that I'd brought with me either side of the bed with a table lamp on each.

'Where are you going to hang your clothes?'

'I was thinking of getting some rails off the internet. I presume Amazon know where this village is?'

He grinned.

'There's a matching chest of drawers and wardrobe in that building in the garden, but the removal men couldn't get them in, so I guess I'll have to sell them and maybe do an Ikea trip at some point and get some flat pack stuff to build.'

'You know the nearest Ikea is in Exeter, don't you?'

'Seriously? That's probably a couple of hours away. I remember passing it on the way here.'

'Yeah, you can probably do it under that if there's no traffic and you go early, but it doesn't open till ten each day. Although there are some other shops around there too. You could go and look round while you were there.'

'Yeah, I could. I love the furniture I've got so I want to try and match it up if I can. Such a shame but never mind. It's not the end of the world. I'm going to pop round and take Gladys for a little walk and see how we get on if you're OK here for a bit.'

'Sure, say hi from me to them both.'

\* \* \*

When I knocked on the door I could hear Violet shout that it was open.

'Violet? It's Meredith. Can I come through?' I bent down to greet Gladys who had come running through to see who was here. She clearly liked a tickle behind the ear; she pulled a funny face and curled her lip up.

'Violet, are you sure you should be leaving the front door unlocked?'

'Ah, it's fine. I've got nothing worth taking and we all know each other round here. I can't keep getting up and down to the door each time it goes. Come and sit down and I'll tell you all about my Gladys.' At her name, the dog licked Violet's hand and curled herself up at her feet.

'First things first, call me Vi. Can't bloody stand Violet. Makes me feel like I'm being told off by my mother. God rest her soul.

Secondly, there's a box by the front door with some toys in for Gladys for when you go for a W. A. L. K. Sorry but you have to spell it because she gets herself into a bit of a tizzy when she knows she's going out.' I laughed. 'Her lead is hanging up on the coat hooks by the front door along with her winger wanger.' I lifted my eyebrows at this phrase. 'You'll see. She'll be fine off lead once you get to the beach. She might chase squirrels if you see any, she will definitely chase ducks and she'll try and chase seagulls till they turn round and fly towards her. She likes to paddle in the sea, but I wouldn't want her to go too far in. And she'll do anything for a treat, like most Labradors. I think that's all you need to know for now. Are you going to take her out today?'

'Well, yes if that's OK. I thought I'd take her out around this time every morning. I'm normally up bright and early and on the beach but that would be way too early for you.'

'Oh, I'm up every morning at five, dear. Not sure why as I sleep well, but I suppose I go to bed early, so if you wanted to do first thing, if that fits in with you better, I wouldn't mind at all.'

'Shall we just see how it goes? I'll take her out for a bit now and then maybe do an early one tomorrow. How does that sound? I'll grab her lead.'

'That sounds perfect.' I started to walk down the hallway, when Vi shouted out. 'And Meredith...' I turned to see her with her hand on her chest. 'Thank you again. The thought of giving her up broke my heart. I'm truly grateful to you.'

'It's you who's doing me the favour. I need something to fill my time while I'm here and Gladys will be a very welcome distraction for me.'

\* \* \*

We had a lovely walk on the beach. I was a bit wary of letting Gladys off, in case she didn't come back, but I made sure that she knew I had a pocket full of treats and gave her one every time she came back, telling her that she was a good girl, so she didn't stray far from my side. She was a lovely dog and was having fun running around. And the same for me: all this fresh sea air was doing me so much good. I'd gone from constantly waking three or four times in the night at home, and feeling quite crabby and tired in the days, to sleeping through every single night, which meant that I felt completely different in the mornings with loads of energy and totally invigorated. I think it suited me here. I hadn't used my car for days, there was nowhere locally that you couldn't walk to, and everything was on the doorstep anyway.

'Only me, Vi.' I knocked on the door and walked straight in, as she'd told me to, Gladys running off into the lounge as I hung up her lead in the hallway and took off my boots. 'Have I woken you? I'm so sorry.'

'Oh, don't mind me, dear. I was just having a little power nap. I try and have a few throughout the day. That's the trouble with getting up so bloody early.'

'Shall I make you a cup of tea before I go?'

'That would be lovely. Would you stay and have one with me? Or do you have to get back to your lovely Clem straight away?'

I blushed.

'I'd love to stay and he's not my lovely Clem. He's just helping me do up the lighthouse.'

'Mmmm. OK. But I've seen the way you look at each other.'

'I think I annoy him quite a bit to be honest. We didn't hit it off straight away and we're just starting to get to know each other. For work purposes of course. And I'm very happy on my own. I'm not looking to find love. And if I was, I'd have to find someone more my own age.'

'Pah! My husband was nine years younger than me and it caused a right old palaver in our time. Age doesn't matter these days though. But sometimes you don't have to look to find love. Love finds you when you're least expecting it.' She studied me and I fumbled to unbutton my cardigan. She must have the heating on full blast.

'I'll go and make the tea.'

We sat chatting for a good while about her family and how she'd always lived in this house. Vi talked about her husband and how she'd been on her own for thirty years since he'd died from a heart attack. I asked if she'd ever found anyone else since he'd gone, and she said that she didn't bother because she knew that no one would be able to replace him. She talked about Albert with such love and affection that I wondered what it must feel like to have that in your life. My marriage was more a marriage of convenience. We bumbled along together but more through habit than anything else. Existing rather than living. He had his life, a social job, played golf, but he didn't like it if I did anything apart from go to work.

I think I constantly annoyed David, and after we split up, while I was sad for the end of our marriage, there was a little part of me that felt relieved. I could do things without someone constantly watching over my shoulder telling me I wasn't doing things right. It was all I'd ever known though and I didn't even realise this until Gabby told me how she hated the way that he'd changed me. When she first met me, my dream was to have a big family. It wasn't till well after we were married that David said that he'd changed his mind and didn't want children, shattering my vision for our future. He wouldn't budge, so my dream never happened and it wasn't till years later, now, at this age, that I realised what Gabby had meant.

Now was my time to live for me. I might not have the family I wanted, but I had a new chance to make a new life in a new place. And if I didn't have a love like Violet and her husband, then I'd be better off on my own. That was the sort of love I wanted. Someone who loved me so fiercely that nothing would ever come between us. And that was why I was unsuccessful with dating back home. Gabby had pushed me to go on an app, and I went on a couple of dates but there was no one that I got that feeling about when I met them. I know it's not all about love at first sight, but I wanted some sort of bells and whistles and they never appeared. So, I gave up. I would be happy alone.

When I glanced at my watch and noticed the time, I made a hasty exit.

'I'd better get back before Clem sends out a search party and accuses me of leaving all the work to him.'

Vi looked at me knowingly and I grinned.

'He's fit as. That's what you young ones say these days, isn't it? If I was your age, I would definitely be up for a fling with someone who looked like that. If he's that talented with his hands at woodwork, imagine what he'd be like in the sack.'

I nearly choked. I wasn't expecting that at all and proper laughed out loud.

'Well, obviously it hasn't gone unnoticed that he's a good-looking guy, but even if he was my age, he's not really my type,' I said, rubbing the back of my neck. It was getting a little warm. 'Anyway, I must go. OK if I call in about seven in the morning then? Are you sure that's not too early?'

'It will be perfect.'

I quickly swilled the mugs and dried them before shouting goodbye, still laughing about what Vi had said about Clem and feeling happy that I'd made another friend. Through something I'd done, I had changed her life, and that made me feel all warm inside. My own nana had brought me up saying that we should always help people if we could, said we were all put on earth, not just for ourselves, but for others too.

As I strolled back to the lighthouse, I was still thinking about Nana and how much Violet reminded me of her. She'd been more of a mother to me than my own mother and I was totally devastated when she'd lost her very short battle with cancer, but glad that I got to hold her hand through it all and that she knew how dearly I loved her. For the first time in a long time, instead of feeling sad about the memories, I felt happy – that she'd been in my life and that I had some wonderful memories of her. Really, once people are gone, that is all you have left. Photos and memories that are embedded deep in your heart. I wondered what Nana would think of my hare-brained idea to buy a property I'd never even seen in a village I'd never visited. Would she think I was brave and bold, or would she think like my mother did, that it was a 'foolish and irrational' thing to do? I hoped very much that it would be the former.

When I got back to the lighthouse, I couldn't find Clem in the kitchen but knew he must be around somewhere as the front door was open. I heard a noise from the garden building and headed there to find him scratching his head looking at the wardrobe and chest of drawers.

'OK there?'

'Oh, hiya. I'm glad you're back. I've been thinking.'

'That sounds ominous.'

'You know I'm a carpenter, right?'

'Of course.'

'Well, I reckon that if you let me butcher these pieces of furniture, I could make something that you would really love for your bedroom. All I can say is that you have to trust me and not make any judgements until I've finished. What do you think?'

'So, you want to take the furniture apart? Do you really think you could do something with the parts? It would be really great to get something that matches what's there already, but surely it would be too much trouble and even more hard work for you to do.'

'Working with wood is one of my most favourite things to do. I know that makes me sound like a complete and utter nerd but it's my passion. Remind me to show you all the before and after pictures of my boat one of these days. I worked so hard on it for so long to get it to where it is today, and I love it. Wardrobes and a chest of drawers are a doddle compared to that. The boat still has a long way to go, sure, and the furnishings need some attention but all the groundwork has been done now, just some minor tweaks to make.'

'You did it all yourself? That's incredible.'

'I did. It nearly killed me, but I did it. And I know I could easily sort out this furniture for you. But I'll only do it if you want me to. You might want to sell them and buy that flat-pack stuff from Ikea. But looking at the quality, I reckon you're not really a flat-pack type of girl. I've got some ideas already but I'm only doing it if you are sure. You would have to trust me, Meredith.'

I looked into his eyes. I hadn't known him long and we hadn't got off to the best of starts but I felt that we were becoming good friends and he seemed like a good man. A kind man. And in my experience, there weren't all that many of those around, so you had to appreciate the ones who were. Our eyes locked and something strange and fluttery was going on in my stomach. I was the first to look away.

I couldn't speak. I nodded.

'OK, let's do this.' As he peeled off his T-shirt and powered up a chainsaw, I began to walk away. Mainly because I was scared to death of what he was going to do next but also because he looked really fit. I laughed again, remembering what Vi had said earlier. She was so right but I think it was best that Clem and I were just friends. But it didn't hurt to look, did it? I wasn't blind.

\* \* \*

When I walked back into the lighthouse later that day, I could see that he'd made real progress in the kitchen and a part of me regretted that I'd stopped him from doing that to move onto the furniture, but I couldn't be a control freak and knew I'd have to ease back and let him do his thing.

I heard his footsteps clatter on the metal stairs. You definitely couldn't creep around in this place. Thank goodness he'd put his T-shirt back on.

'I've made a list of a few things I need. Is there any chance you could find your way to the builders' yard again?'

'Oh, to the place where I never wanted to show my face again, you mean?'

'Yep, that's the one. I'm sure they'll have forgotten all about you now.'

'Hope so, and yes, I'm sure I could. I've got satnav so as long as I have the address that should be fine.'

More approaching footsteps alerted me that we were no longer alone.

'Helloooo! Anyone here?'

Gemma appeared. 'Wow this is coming along. Are you working hard, Meredith? It's my day off and I wondered if I could persuade you to come for a Cornish afternoon tea with me? Let me show you the proper way to do it.'

'Go, Mere,' Clem piped up from inside a cupboard. 'There's nothing really that you can do here until I've got these cupboards sorted and you could pick those bits up while you're out. I won't need them till tomorrow. Go and enjoy yourself. You don't need to babysit me.'

\* \* \*

Gemma and I had the loveliest afternoon. We went to a posh hotel and sat outside on the terrace eating dainty sandwiches with the crusts cut off, and fruit scones with clotted cream and raspberry jam, which were delicious. We then popped along to the builders' yard, arriving just in time before they closed and was mortified when the sales assistant winked and said, 'There's your change, Knob Lady.' I was glad Gemma had waited in the car, so I didn't have to explain. But I must remember to tell Clem, I thought to myself; he'd find it amusing.

Back in the car I was still smiling at the thought and Gemma asked me what I was grinning at. She laughed as I decided to explain after all.

It had been so lovely to sit and chat with her and get to know her better. I knew that we'd never be as close as Gabby and me, but it gave me hope that I did have people down here who I could call friends. I was starting to feel part of a real community. Maybe I had been bold and brave after all and buying Driftwood Bay Lighthouse had been one of the best decisions of my life.

## 18

Clem had already told me that I wasn't allowed back in the lighthouse the next day until after I'd taken the dog out. He wanted me to have a surprise when I next went in and said he'd still got a couple of hours' work to do. He really was a hard worker, and I knew I should have a think about something thoughtful to buy him to say thank you. For the daily rate I was paying him, I was getting way above what a tradesman should do. He was putting effort in as if the lighthouse were his own and I was truly grateful for the love and attention he was pouring into it.

Around 7 a.m. I popped into Vi's to pick Gladys up as promised. An hour passed by so quickly on the beach, playing catch and chasing the gentle waves. It was fun for both of us and I hoped that the arrangement would work out. Although I couldn't see it not, as long as I was still here. There was no rush; I would just build my work around my life, instead of the other way round. That's how I always ended up getting burned out. There didn't seem to be any rush to make a decision about whether I would stay here long term. Maybe time would give me the answer.

I'd brought pastries along again today and thought I'd beat

Clem by getting to the lighthouse early, but it looked like he'd been there a while. He said he'd meet me 'up top', which was becoming our nickname for the lounge, the most impressive room of all. The view was incredibly special, and we sat on the two chairs I'd got from Martin's shop and watched the boats sailing in and out of the harbour. Clem talked about the fact that as a child, he, and some of his friends, used to get up in the middle of the night, unbeknown to his parents, and come into the empty lighthouse to have midnight feasts. He talked about the fact that as he grew up as an older teenager, he found it a place of solitude, somewhere he could come to grieve his mother's passing, and that it really was quite a special place for him. Clearly that was why he was pouring his heart and soul into it. I was glad that I'd asked him to do the work and not someone else because there was no way that they would have loved it the way he did. And I was glad because I liked spending time with him. Moving into a new home was hard when you didn't know anyone and along with Gemma, Lucy and James, Clem was another person I classed as a friend and it felt good that he felt able to open up to me.

After breakfast, he made me promise to stay out of the bedroom and kitchen for a couple more hours, so I stayed on the top floor and gave it another good clean. Those wooden floors sure did generate some dust, but they came up beautifully. I put the book-shelves in place and sat sorting through a couple of boxes of books I'd brought with me before placing them on the shelves.

'Mere! Can you come down please?'

I stretched my back as I stood – sitting hunched over the boxes had made it ache – and headed halfway down the stairs to the floor below.

'Stop. You need to close your eyes before you go any further.'

I laughed. 'I can't walk down the stairs if I close my eyes, you numpty.'

'You have to. Pretend it's the middle of the night and you're feeling your way down with your feet. Take your time.'

When I reached the bottom, Clem came and stood behind me. He produced a black silk scarf from his pocket, which he tied loosely around my head, before pulling it down over my eyes and then also covered my eyes with his hands. I couldn't concentrate on a thing apart from the fact that his warm, firm body was behind me, pressed into mine. With my sight covered, all my other senses were working overtime and I was literally tingling all over. He kept nudging me forward into the kitchen with his body. Gosh, it was hot in there!

'OK, you can look now.'

It wasn't very often that I was speechless, but he seemed to have taken all the thoughts I'd had in my mind as to how my dream kitchen would look and make them into reality and I literally couldn't speak. My eyes filled with tears.

'You hate it, don't you?' he asked quietly. 'You can tell me. I'm a big boy.'

That was something I didn't need to think about right now. I was still cooling down after being so close to him. I swallowed down the lump in my throat and whispered, 'I love it.'

'Really!'

'Oh really. Thank you, Clem. It's just perfect. Thank you.'

I looked around. Just like the plan he'd sketched up, the cooking area and breakfast bar were perfectly situated in the middle of the room looking outwards to make the most of the views of the harbour and bay and there was so much cupboard space at the back of the room, I couldn't believe that he'd managed to squeeze it in.

I turned and he was so close to me that I could smell a mixture of aftershave and sweat but I didn't care. I flung my arms around him and hugged him tightly.

'Wow, what a reaction. Are you sure? Is there anything you'd like me to change?'

'I wouldn't change a thing. I absolutely love it.'

'Fantastic. There are still a few things to do, figuring out where to put the appliances. I just really needed to see how you felt about it.'

'I honestly love it. Thank you.' Our eyes locked for what felt like minutes but was only seconds.

'Right then,' he said, looking away. 'In that case it's time we got that blindfold back on and I got you into the bedroom. Erm... I mean, erm... I'd like to show you what I've done downstairs too.' He was getting a little flushed in the face, making me break out into a huge grin.

'Best offer I've had all week,' I said casually. 'Do you always like to blindfold a woman before taking her to the bedroom?' I tilted my head to one side and he grinned back, his face turning even pinker. Adorable.

'I do feel that on this occasion it might be appropriate.' He took my hand and led me down the next flight of stairs. I hated not being able to see but I felt like I could trust this man with everything I had.

As we stood in the bedroom, he positioned himself behind me once more, pressing his body into mine as he gently untied the blindfold. My body started to sizzle all over and I'm sure he must have been able to hear my heart pounding. When his soft fingers brushed against my cheek, I thought I might explode.

'Ta-dah!'

I had no idea how he'd done it, but there were built-in wardrobes all the way on the side wall which matched the rest of the furniture and he'd managed somehow to get the dressing table in too.

'What? How? When? Wow!'

'Make me another cuppa and I'll tell you what I've done.'

* * *

It was quite incredible how this man had been able to get inside my head and make my ideas a reality. He had done exactly what I would have asked for if I'd had the room professionally designed. He deserved the big mug of tea that I had just handed over to him.

I stared at his handiwork.

'You're amazing, Clem. How have you managed to do all of this?'

'It's not perfect. I need to put some lattice work in where I've taken those doors out and fill in the space behind so that you can't see inside.'

'It's perfect to me. I was going to make some cushions for the bed and re-cover that bedroom chair when I can find a fabric shop. I wonder what it would look like if we were to put some matching material behind the lattice work.'

'You can re-cover furniture?' He looked at me in disbelief. 'I thought you were a graphic designer.'

'It's amazing what I can turn my hand to. You'd be surprised if you knew my hidden talents.'

'I bet I would.' He raised his eyebrows and tilted his head. 'I shall look forward to learning more about them one day.'

Blimey, this man sure knew how to make me get hot under the collar and I stuttered a little. 'I... I... I studied textile and interior design at college but fell more into the graphic design side when I needed a job. It's a long story, but I still did a bit of interior design work for friends and family. I used to be a dab hand with a sewing machine, although it's been a while.'

'Well, you are a dark horse, Meredith. Why "used to be"?'

'Oh, I suppose when I married, and we had enough money to

buy things, I didn't need to make do and mend. My husband liked us to have everything brand new.'

'But what about you? Is that what you wanted too?'

'I suppose at the time. I didn't even think about what I wanted. I felt like it was my job to keep him happy.'

'Not at your own expense though surely?'

'Yep, I can see that now.'

I became lost in my own thoughts. Why do people change to suit others? Why do we, when in a relationship, change how we look, what we feel, what we want, because we feel that we don't want to rock the boat? That what the other person wanted from us was so completely different to what we wanted for ourselves? If I could go back and teach my young self anything, it would be to keep my own identify. Not settle. For years, I tried to make my mother happy, and then when I met David, I found myself doing the same thing there too. For what? For me to end up on my own starting all over again and trying to work out who I actually was for myself?

Clem could see that I'd drifted off somewhere and brought me back into the room.

'I need all the seats re-covering in my boat,' he said. 'Maybe you could have a look at that and give me some advice. Or I could pay you to do them.'

'It's the absolute least I could do after you've done—' I gestured around the room '—all this.'

'What a team we make.' He grinned, his gaze lingering on my face.

I smiled back at him. I had smiled more since arriving in Driftwood Bay than I had in years. Living with Gabby, I had started to find myself again, but I think it suited me here even more. What's not to love about living by the sea?

Maybe I should consider staying in the long run after all, I thought, put down some proper roots. Although I might change my mind once I'd moved out of the cosy B & B and into the stone-cold lighthouse.

* * *

The harbour was looking particularly picturesque, the sun glinting off the windows of the pretty terraced properties painted in various pastel colours, and I walked towards the high street with a spring in my step. I was honestly so chuffed; so much progress was being made in such a short space of time, but I needed to take stock and work out what to tackle next. My list was never-ending. I'd ask Clem what other things he needed to finish the kitchen. I wanted to see what the sample tiles looked like behind the cooker and check out whether the floor would be OK for the time being. I could do with finding a couple of bar stools to sit alongside the breakfast bar. And I still needed to chase up when the internet was being installed; that was a priority really as I'd be moving out of the B & B soon and would need decent Wi-Fi sorted for when I was going to start work again.

There were two people waiting in the bakery, so I thought I'd pop into the mini-market first.

'Hello, Dyllis. How are you?'

'You're perky today,' she muttered through pursed lips.

'Today's a good day that's why.'

'Is it?'

'It is if you choose for it to be. And I do.' I smiled at her.

'I noticed you and Clem getting cosy in the pub the other night. What's that all about? Don't you go messing him about now. He's gone through quite enough in the last few years.'

Dyllis seemed to be the queen of hinting. She'd done it a few times now, as if she were loading a gun, readying me to fire the bullets. I needed to be careful with this trait of hers. I was sure she could lead me into trouble.

I grabbed a four-pack of bottled beers off the shelf, thinking it would be nice to keep them in the fridge for when we finished working at night. There were a couple of things that Vi had said she needed too so I popped them in my basket.

'Clem is doing a fantastic job for me and there's nothing more to it than that.'

'Well, like I said: make sure you don't be upsetting him, girl. No one round here will forgive you if you do.'

'Not sure why you think I would. You don't know me at all but seem determined that I'm a baddie. It's a shame really because I'm actually quite nice if you made the effort to get to know me.'

'Well, we'll see about that.'

'Yes, we will,' I said as I left the shop, again offering a cheery, and forced, goodbye.

Nothing like a bit of negativity to bring a girl down.

'You OK?' Gemma asked when I walked into the bakery.

'Oh, I suppose so.'

'Well, tell your face that.' She laughed. 'Come on, spill. What's up?'

'It's just her at the mini-market. She's just quite unpleasant every time I see her. I've never known anyone have such disdain towards someone they don't even know. She's now warning me off Clem. As if anything is going on between us anyway!' I noticed that Gemma very quickly raised her eyebrows and I wondered if I'd imagined it or not.

'What?'

'You and Clem do seem to be getting on well.'

'So what if we do? We're working together and it's better to get on with someone you are with all day long, isn't it?'

She looked at me a little longer than was absolutely necessary and very slightly raised an eyebrow.

'It is. Do you fancy doing something at the weekend? I do love having someone to do stuff with, you know. I've been starved of female friendship for so long, it's so lovely to have another single person here. Please say yes.'

'I can do Saturday night or Sunday.'

'What are you up to on Saturday day then?'

'Erm. I'm going to the supermarket with Clem.' There it was again. Split second eyebrow lifting seemed to be a Gemma-ism. 'Because I can't get much in my Mini. He offered to take me.'

'I bet he did!'

'Oi!'

'I'm sorry. I'll stop winding you up. I think it's nice that you and he are friends. He's a really nice bloke. But I just want you to be my friend.' She pulled a pouty face. She did make me laugh.

The grin that Dyllis had wiped off earlier reappeared back on my face. I loved it here. I really did.

## 19

At the end of that Friday afternoon, I stood at the top of the lighthouse and gazed out over the bay.

'Nice view!' I hadn't heard Clem come up the stairs. I must have been in a world of my own.

'Yeah, stunning, isn't it?'

'Yeah, the outside isn't too shabby either.'

Once again, the heat rose up my neck and I'm sure my face would be blotchy before long. I wasn't the most beautiful of blushers.

'Smoothie!'

'You should be so proud of everything you've achieved already, you know, Meredith. Not many people would have been as brave as you have taking on this project and just getting on with it.'

'Oh, Clem, thank you, but there is absolutely no way I could have done this without you. If it was me on my own, I'd still be trying to put my bed together, wishing I was an octopus to hold all the corners at the same time.'

'I'm glad I've been able to help and make a difference.'

'Honestly, Clem, I'm not sure how I will ever be able to repay you. Money and words just don't seem enough.'

He tilted his head. 'Oh, I'm sure we can think of something.'

I gulped. He appeared to constantly tease me and I didn't want to misconstrue anything. After all, why would someone of his age flirt with someone so much older than him? Perhaps it was just his way.

'Right, what time do you want to go tomorrow?' I was the master of changing the conversation. If he continued looking at me in that way, I might not be responsible for my actions. I was not looking for love in any way whatsoever. My new start down here was about finding myself, but leaning up against the staircase, with those bright blue eyes boring into mine, I was definitely wavering.

'How does eleven grab you? We can grab a late lunch while we're out and find your material shop too. Plenty of time to get everything in if that suits you.'

'It does, thanks so much, Clem. For everything. I really do appreciate you.'

'You are most welcome, Meredith. The pleasure has been all mine.'

## 20

It was my last night at the bed and breakfast, so I wanted to get up and over to the lighthouse bright and early to get some more unpacking done.

It felt good to have a kitchen that I could use so I unpacked all my crockery and pots and pans and found them a home. I hadn't got that much food to put away but I would decide where it was going to go when I got back from the shops later.

I couldn't believe that it would soon be my first night staying here. I was still feeling a little nervous but knew that Gemma, Lucy and James weren't far and Clem was only a stone's throw away in the harbour – although after being quite defiant when I met him that I did not need rescuing by a man, it would have to be a dire situation for me to call on him and admit defeat.

My bedroom was looking cosy and even though there were still some finishing touches to do on the wardrobes, I could hang my clothes up which was nice as I'd been living out of a bag for the past few days over at the B & B. I headed up to the top floor and put some of my belongings around. I also hung the wooden signs that

I'd bought from Martin's bric-a-brac shop. It was starting to feel quite homely and I could have pottered all morning but Vi would be expecting me around now.

\* \* \*

Gladys and I were enjoying our lovely walk on the beach, which I thought was deserted, but then a lovely chocolate Labrador bounded up to us gracing us with his presence. He began prancing around Gladys, who went running off with him, ignoring my shouts for her to come to heel. His owner apologised for Charles's behaviour.

'I'm so sorry, he's not normally like this at all.' The owner looked a little familiar. He must be one of the locals I hadn't got around to meeting yet. I also happened to notice he was quite good-looking as he strolled over, wearing a white T-shirt which clung to his body extremely well, a pair of knee-length linen navy shorts and flip-flops,

'Neither is she. Although I've not known her long in fairness.'

'Have you just got her then?'

'Ah no, I'm walking her for a friend. She's struggling to walk her.'

'That's incredibly kind of you.'

'It's lovely actually. I've always wanted a dog but never quite got round to getting one, so it's good practice for me, to see how I'd cope. And it gets me out here every day on this glorious beach. Gladys, come on, back over here please.'

Gladys turned and looked at me, stuck her backside in the air, then turned her back and went sauntering off with Charles.

'Charming.'

'There's no one else around so they're not bothering anyone.

Are you walking that way? Are you happy to walk together? Are you new to the area?'

'I am, I've recently moved into the lighthouse.'

'Oh, my goodness. You're Meredith then.'

'Er, yes. How do you know my name?'

'I'm Russell, the estate agent who sold it to you.' He ruffled his hair bashfully. 'I've been meaning to get in touch to ask how you were getting on and wanted to pop round to see you. I'm so sorry but I had a call from my family in the north and had to go back up there as my dad was in hospital. I know I left you in the lurch a little. I wanted to be here when you arrived, but I got the call that morning and had to leave right away. My assistant said that they were going to call you from the office to tell you why I wasn't around. I literally got back last night.'

So this was the elusive Russell then. This should be an interesting conversation.

'Not a word from anyone from the office. To be honest, I thought you'd done a runner. I couldn't get a response from your number. It would only let me leave a message and it even stopped letting me do that at one point.' I paused, looking him up and down, trying to see whether he seemed genuine. There was something about him I couldn't quite put my finger on. I also hadn't finished saying my piece. 'But let's be honest. It wasn't quite what you sold me was it? What was it you said – a part-renovated project? So come on then, do tell. Which part was actually renovated?'

'Ah well, maybe I was a little creative with the wording, but I knew, in my defence, that the person who bought her would fall in love immediately and want to bring her back to life.'

'I sure did that.' When I thought about all the work that we'd done and how well my vision for the property had come together with the hard, manual work that Clem's skills had brought to the table, I smiled. 'She's becoming a beauty. However...' My frown returned. 'I really do think you should have been more honest with me from the start. I could have ended up not having anywhere to stay if it wasn't for a cancellation at the B & B. That's not on, Russell. You told me it was habitable. I couldn't stay there for days. It's totally not acceptable.'

'I'm sorry that you couldn't get through to the office. I had to leave my work phone behind but clearly my voicemail was full of messages. I'm annoyed that they didn't get in touch with you though. You must have thought I was awful to leave you in the lurch like that.'

'Yes I did. I just thought that you'd done a deal and run to be honest. You wouldn't have been the first and I'm sure you wouldn't have been the last. But weren't you in the Harbourside Hotel a few nights ago?'

'Never. That's not the type of man I am. I'll have you know that I'm full of decency and integrity. Maybe when we know each other a little better, you'll let me show you that you might even quite like me.' That cheeky grin again and I couldn't help but thaw a little towards him. After all, it was all working out OK now.

'No, definitely not me in the pub earlier in the week. I only got back last night as I said.' He shook his head and scratched his neck. He didn't quite meet my eye.

'Oh OK, I must be mistaken then. It's just that Clem said...'

'Oh yes, I heard that you've had Clement Penrose doing some work for you. I bet he couldn't wait to get his grubby hands on it.'

'Yes, Clem has been working on it with me. He's been amazing actually.'

'I'm sure he has been.' He smiled sweetly.

I didn't want him to think he was completely forgiven, but all of the animosity had left me. So I excused myself.

* * *

Back at the lighthouse, I heard a beep and looked out of the window to see that Clem had pulled up. I quickly nipped into the bathroom, ignoring the mess as I knew that, after the spare room, this was the next room to be tackled. My next priority was to make sure Gabby had somewhere to stay when she eventually came. Although by the time she was able to get herself down here, all the work would be done. Typical. But good actually, because it meant that I could spend quality time with her showing her around my fabulous new abode and village. I didn't have time to change so I just applied some deodorant and sprayed some dry shampoo, fluffing up my hair a little. I also added a little tinted lip gloss and finally a squirt of perfume. That would have to do. Clem had seen me in far worse states during all this building work, and anyway, I was doing it for me, not him.

'Morning. You all set for our exciting day out shopping?' He grinned as I climbed up into the cab.

'You know how to treat a girl, don't you?' We grinned at each other, and time stood still as we held each other's gaze.

He spoke and it broke the spell. 'Oh, don't worry, if this was a real date, I know exactly what I'd be doing with you and it wouldn't be shopping.'

Good lord, it was getting hot in here. I broke away from his big blue eyes.

'Meredith, that came out way more pervy than it was meant to.' He smacked himself on the forehead. 'What is wrong with me?'

I felt like we were in quite dangerous territory. I wasn't used to someone flirting with me and didn't really know how to behave. And of course, I wasn't interested in Clem in that way, as I kept telling myself. We were just friends and I didn't want to cross any boundaries and lose that friendship. I thought back to something

Gabby had suggested when we last spoke but I'd assured her at the time that I did not have a crush on Clem. I assured myself now too. I just liked him, we were spending a lot of time together and I knew that wouldn't be forever. I was grateful to him as he was helping me achieve my dreams. It was definitely not a crush and the over-heating thing every time he said something a little flirty must have just been my age.

I did something that I'm very good at: I changed the subject.

'So, what's the plan for today then?'

'First stop builders' yard, which is on the way, just got a couple of small things I need to pick up as well as those lovely tiles that you chose so I can crack on with them next week. Then second stop the material shop. Third stop lunch and fourth stop supermarket so that all the cold stuff will still be cold when we get back. How's that for a plan?'

'Impressive, Mr Penrose. Let's get this show on the road.' I watched his hand closely as he grabbed hold of the gear stick and swallowed a lump in my throat. I really needed to pull myself together. I tried to focus my eyes on the road ahead.

The day was a beautiful one and the scenery stunning as we drove along the coast road with Clem, once again, pointing out interesting places along the way. We chatted about safe subjects such as how much he loved being out on the sea in his boat, and how I didn't think I'd ever be a sailor as I'd once been violently sick on a ferry to the Isle of Wight, which he found highly amusing. He told me about how he'd spent much time and poured much love into refurbishing the boat. He was good company and I was quite disappointed when we had to stop first at the builders' yard.

When we arrived at our next stop, Clem said he had a couple of calls to make, so told me to go in and have a wander around and he'd join me shortly.

When I got inside the material shop, my heart soared. I was in

my element in a place like this. As a very tactile person, I walked
around touching some of the fabrics to feel the quality. There was
so much choice, I was behaving like a child in a sweet shop.

Then I felt eyes on me and turned to see Clem leaning up
against the door, watching me. I was a little embarrassed though I
didn't know why.

'What?' I asked as he sauntered over to me.

'I wish you could see what I can see.'

'Which is?'

'The smile on your face as you are walking round. You are obviously loving being in here.'

'I am. Thank you for bringing me.'

'Found anything you like the look of?'

I raised my eyebrows. If only he knew. Stop it, Meredith. You're
not helping matters.

'Yep, plenty. What do you think of this?' My enthusiasm took
over as I explained what I was planning to do with the various
fabrics. He just stared at me. 'Sorry, am I boring you?'

'Not at all. I love the way your face lights up and you wave your
hands around when you express your plans. Your passion for this is
really shining through. I can't wait to see what you'll do with it all.'

'All that excitement has made me hungry.'

'You being hungry I can cope with, but you being hangry. Now
that's a whole different matter.'

I laughed.

'Come on, I'm starving too. And I have the perfect place for
lunch.'

After Clem loaded the truck with my purchases, he held the
door open for me.

'Your carriage awaits, madam.' He gave me a little smile that
somehow made me feel like a teenager with a crush. I had to

concentrate hard to compose myself and told myself that I was being a silly old fool with a bit of a crush on a man way too young for her, as his arm brushed against mine and made all the hairs on my forearm tingle.

## 21

'I'm absolutely stuffed.' My hands resting on my stomach, I wished I wasn't wearing my jeans because I could do with undoing the buttons and letting my belly hang out.

'Would you like to see the pudding menu?' the waitress asked.

Clem smiled at her. 'We could have a little look maybe?'

'Seriously, how can you possibly eat anything else after you've just polished off that mixed grill?'

'Does that mean you're not having a pudding then?'

I batted his arm with the menu. 'Doesn't hurt to have a look, does it? My nana used to say, there's always room for something you like.' It was lovely to think of her and smile instead of feeling sad.

'Do you miss her?'

'Every day.'

'What was her name?'

'Alice.' I smiled.

'Nice name. Pretty. Grief is shit, isn't it? Really tough.'

'It is. I presume you mean your mum. Your dad told me that you'd lost her? How long ago was it?'

'Four years now. Sometimes it seems like yesterday and some-times it seems like it's always been that way.' He rubbed his jaw.

'It's weird. It feels like a really heavy bag that you carry around with you. It never gets any lighter but if you swap it from one hand to another it temporarily feels lighter but then the weight just comes back. All you can do is just get used to the fact that it's really heavy.'

'You're so right. And there are so many people who just expect you to "get over it". I honestly don't think I'll ever get over it. It's not just that I lost my mum. It's that I lost a whole future that I thought I'd have with her: the fact that one day I might have kids and she would be a grandma, and that she'd look after them, and take them to school, and just be part of their lives really. She'd have been an amazing grandma too. It's all that.' He looked out the window into the distance and whispered, 'It's just hard.'

I covered his hand with mine. 'It is hard and I don't think that unless people have experienced it, they understand and that's not really their fault, I suppose. I know when Nana died, I apologised to a friend of mine who'd lost her nan. I should have been more helpful to her.' I turned to him. 'I know everyone's journey is different, but maybe we can be grief buddies together.'

He smiled at me but the sadness was still there.

'People say stupid things too, don't they?' he said. 'I had someone say, "Well, at least you've still got your dad." As if that makes things better. Dad's amazing actually and he's handling it much better now than he did at first. He was like a lost sheep back then. They'd been together since they met at school, so over forty years. Dad is young enough to find someone else. You can never replace your mum though.'

'But perhaps it's not about replacing that person. It's about finding something new with someone.'

'Yes, but that's what I mean. Partners can move on. Children can't. It's a different love.' His eyes were wet with tears that threatened to spill out.

'True, but maybe if your dad found someone, they could become a mother figure in your life. Not as a replacement but just someone in a different role.'

'I honestly never thought of it that way. Thank you.' He squeezed my hand and looked deeply into my eyes.

A voice boomed across the room from the bar. 'Clement Penrose, as I live and breathe!'

'Oh, my goodness. It must have been... ten years. How are you, Mike?'

This person strode across to our table and Clem stood. They shook hands. Mike turned towards me and reached his hand out. 'And this is...'

'This is my friend Meredith.'

'Meredith, nice to meet you. Do you live near here?'

'I've just bought the lighthouse in Driftwood Bay. Clem is helping me to renovate it.'

'The Driftwood Bay Lighthouse? Isn't that—'

Clem cut him off.

'Are you still going out with Kay?'

'I'm not no!'

'Oh, thank goodness. You know everyone knew that she was shagging about behind your back. She was a right old slapper.'

Mike's face turned puce. 'Thanks for that, mate. I actually married her.'

Clem looked like he wanted to crawl up into his own backside but then recovered quite quickly.

'You never could tell when I was joking, could you?' He laughed nervously.

'Oh, don't worry, mate. I found it out for myself when I caught her in bed with my best mate. One of the other lads told me she was up to no good a few weeks before, but I didn't believe them. I wouldn't have a word said against her. So, I'm young, free and on the pull now, so if you have any friends, Meredith—' he winked at me '—send them my way.'

'I'll do that although I don't know many people here myself. I've moved down from the Midlands.'

'Nice to see our Clem here showing you the ropes then. He took you out on the water yet?'

'Sorry?'

'You still sail don't you, mate?'

'I do, I live on a boat now. You'll have to come down one weekend and I'll take you out for a spin.'

''Bout time you settled down with a wife and some sprogs, isn't it?'

'Ha, not me. I'm good, thanks.'

'God, remember that frightful girl who used to moon around after you all the time?' Mike said to Clem. 'Is she still around?'

'Not sure who you mean.' Clem scratched his beard. I got the feeling that he knew exactly who Mike meant.

'You do. That Sophie bird.'

'She moved away.'

'Thank goodness. She was desperate to get you up the aisle.'

'Mikey... Are you ready?' A lady tottered across in high heels.

'This is the current girlfriend, Debbie.'

Debbie laughed and somehow managed to sound like a horse neighing. Clem and I stared at each other, trying not to giggle.

Mike took a card out of his pocket and handed it to Clem before making a phone shape with his fingers. 'Call me, dude. You can take me out on that boat of yours.'

'Look forward to it, mate.'

We watched them walk out of the pub and when they were out of sight, I let out a big breath.

'Crikey, he's quite a character, isn't he?'

'God, yes, I thought I'd dropped myself right in the shit when he said he'd married Kay. How embarrassing. Thank God they got divorced. Talk about putting your foot in it.'

Clem held my gaze as if studying me.

'So, what brings you to Cornwall, Meredith?'

Even though we'd spent time together over the last few days, this question hadn't been raised before.

'Not much to tell really.' I was trying to work out just how much to say. 'I needed to do something different in my life. My mum lives abroad, not that she's ever been around much. My nana, well you know how that ended. And my best friend, who I've been staying with since my marriage ended, is all loved up and moving her partner in. So it was time I started again. I thought maybe somewhere new where I can make my own new memories would be good.'

I wasn't quite sure whether to go ahead with the rest of the reasons, but then thought, oh what the hell.

'To please Gabby more than me, I've spent the last year on the dating scene, had some nice dates that didn't go anywhere and some pretty awful ones too, and, to be honest, I'm a bit disillusioned with the whole thing and feel like I'm better off on my own.'

'And why do you think none worked out? Were you on apps or something?'

'Yes, that's right. I think most people who are on them are just there for the crack. You find someone who you don't think looks too much like a serial killer and leave yourself open to chat with them and before they even introduce themselves properly you get a dick pic in your inbox.'

'I hope that's not a euphemism!' Clem grinned and I blushed as I realised that sentence had sounded much better in my head.

I laughed and carried on. 'You block those and then get people blocking you for no reason at all. It's the weirdest thing ever. A lot of people have loads of success on them, but like the lady who recommended the site to me said, "You might have to kiss a lot of toads before you find your prince." I just don't think I like toads to be honest and my self-esteem was taking a bit of a battering so I deleted all the apps, realised I needed a huge change of scenery so opened a property website instead and after one too many glasses of wine one evening, I woke up to discover that I'd bought a lighthouse. As you do.'

'Well, some do clearly!'

'Not sure if it was brave or stupid. Especially as I'd never even seen it. My friend couldn't believe it. I'm not the most spontaneous person in the world so I'm not sure why I did it, but it just felt like the right thing to do at that moment.'

'Any regrets?'

Now that was a question and a half to ponder. This decision of mine had been a bit of a roller coaster from the moment I clicked buy on the website and it had all happened so quickly I hadn't even had a chance to really think about whether it was a good thing or not.

'God knows what I'd have done if I hadn't met you and you hadn't been able to help me. I think I would have still been sat on the concrete floor in the kitchen crying into my hands.'

'Well, it's a good job I was able to help then. Perhaps the universe was giving you a helping hand.'

'Oh, you're not another one of those woo-woo people who leave everything up to the universe are you?'

'Ooh, I love me a bit of manifesting and affirmations.'

'You'd get on so well with my friend Gabby. She's into all that malarkey too.'

Gabby was forever trusting that a higher force would help her make the right decisions. It wasn't something that sat that well with me. Maybe I was too practical for my own good.

'You should try it; you might just surprise yourself.'

'Nah! I don't really think it's my thing. All a bit "out there" for me.'

'OK, but don't say I didn't offer to teach you my ways.'

'I think the villagers already think you are showing me quite enough of your ways, Clement Penrose. Especially that miserable old cow up at the supermarket.'

'Ah, ignore her. She means well but she gets everything wrong. She just doesn't know when to stop meddling in things that don't concern her.'

'That sounds like you've experienced her nonsense first hand?'

'Like I say, just ignore her.' He turned to grab his jacket. 'Are you ready to make a move and get some shopping done?'

Seems like I wasn't the only one who was good at diverting a conversation.

I let out a massive sigh, wishing I could undo the button on my jeans and let my very full and contented belly hang out. The waistband was digging into me, and I got up feeling like I was nine months pregnant. I mock waddled over to the door, with Clem laughing at me.

I was a tad disappointed when Clem mentioned us splitting up to do our shopping and meeting up in the coffee shop at the front of the store. I think I'd envisaged us wandering around like a married couple, which was ridiculous because we both had a trolley each and were shopping for our own stuff. I walked around the store checking against my list and filling up my trolley with a lot of store cupboard necessities. I was a little too excited than was necessary; it was like starting from scratch all over again. I had thrown away so much stuff before leaving and this was my chance to stock up.

The journey back was relaxed and we didn't stop chatting. Clem was such easy company and we found that we had plenty to talk about with the renovation plans for the lighthouse. I had one more week before his next job started, so it would be interesting to see how many tasks we'd be able to work through before his time was up. It would be strange not seeing him every day. He'd very quickly become a fixture in my life and it had made my integration into village life so much easier. Everyone knew him and liked him, and as we were out and about, he had introduced me to many new people too.

Where I had come from, everyone kept themselves pretty much to themselves but here it was like you only had to cough and someone would know about it. Some people would hate that, but I felt like this new little community was perfect for me and just what I needed right now. Who knew what the future would hold? Though at the moment I was just looking towards getting the lighthouse finished and then I would think about the next stage.

There was no pressure to go back to the Midlands. Gabby and Luke were starting their lives together, and apart from Gabby, there was nothing to go back for anyway. My divorce was finally through and all the money side of things settled, so that part of my life was well and truly over. At least here, being away from my old home, meant that I wouldn't have to keep bumping into David and his new partner.

Funny how we'd spent all our married life without children because that was what he wanted, yet now he'd met someone younger, his tune had well and truly changed. He was quite sheepish when he came round to tell me about her pregnancy and it hit me like a steamroller, but I suppose it made me realise that you should never change your dreams to fulfil someone else's. In hindsight, I only had myself to blame.

I'd always said I'd love to live by the sea and never thought that it would be possible, but now here I was and I was loving it. Would I stay or would I go? That was the big question, but not one for right now. Maybe it was actually OK not to have all the answers and see where life took you.

## 22

Clem had been so kind in helping me to get all my shopping in. It never occurred to me that having a third-floor kitchen and having to traipse all my shopping up the stairs and then going back down again for the next lot would be an issue but it was a real pain in the rear so I was very grateful to him for his help. We'd had a really good day and it had been nice to take some time out from the renovation project and just potter around a few shops, especially with pleasant company; someone who was fast becoming a good friend. He was long past being that mardy arse I'd met when I first arrived and now I felt like I could talk to him about anything. We were never stuck for words.

When it came time for him to go, we did an awkward little hug and I kissed his cheek, thanking him. His beard felt soft against my face and even though it only touched me for a split second, it made my tummy tingle. It had been a while since I'd been that close to a man so I was sure that was the only reason and I told myself to get a grip.

When I got back to the B & B I was shattered. A bath and bed would have been perfect but Gemma, Lucy and James had organised a special meal for me, in their private quarters too. I really was grateful that they'd gone to so much effort. Nipping upstairs to quickly get changed, I felt quite sad that this short period of my life had come to an end. This B & B was the cosiest, comfiest place I'd ever stayed, probably helped by the fact that I'd become firm friends with the owners. I'd recommend it to anyone who came to visit for sure. That thought reminded me that my mother would be visiting in the not-too-distant future. Maybe it would be better if she stayed here rather than at the lighthouse. The second bedroom was still just a shell right now and once Clem was back on his own work, I wouldn't have his constant help on hand. I'd be glad to avoid my mother as much as I could when she came. I couldn't stand having her constantly digging at me and criticising everything I did. I was a grown-up and she needed to treat me as such.

'I honestly don't think I've ever eaten as much in my life since I moved here,' I said later that evening after a large, sumptuous meal. The food was amazing and the Prosecco flowed freely. This family sure knew how to cook. Freshly and locally caught lobster salad to start, with thick crusty bread slathered in butter, home-made delicious Cornish pasties with the most divine shortcrust pastry and then we had to have a big rest before Lucy served up sticky toffee pudding and vanilla ice cream. Obviously, it would have been rude to have left any when she'd gone to so much trouble, and even though I'd had lunch out, I had eaten every bit. 'That was amazing, thank you. I'm sure I've eaten more in the last week than I have in the last year. It's a good job I'm moving out or you'd literally have to call the fire brigade to lift me out.'

'We've loved having you here, Meredith,' she replied. 'You've been a breath of fresh air. I hope you don't forget us after you move out. We thought that if we fed you up with proper Cornish food, you might want to come back.'

'You've got no chance of that. It's more likely that you'll never get rid of me. I'll miss your company so much. I've never been made to feel as welcome as you guys have made me feel here and it's really helped. I honestly can't thank you enough. Moving to a new place where you literally don't know a soul is harder than I thought it would be and you guys have made it such a great experience. I'm so grateful.'

'And Clem too. Having him around can't have been so bad. I told you he was easy on the eye, didn't I?' James batted his wife on the arm and she grinned at him. 'There's only one man for me, babe, and you know you're it. Why would I want a big burly builder type with suntanned muscly arms and long luscious legs when I could have someone who comes home stinking of fish every day? It's a no-brainer!' She reached across and kissed him. They were clearly very much in love.

The two of them had first met when James came to Driftwood Bay on holiday with his parents. They were both eighteen and they'd fallen in love immediately. When he returned home, they realised that they couldn't live without each other and he moved back down.

Such a romantic tale. It reminded me of that epic love that I had dreamed of. Maybe one day I'd have someone who looked at me the way that James looked at Lucy. But till then, I had plenty to be getting on with.

Heading off to bed that night, after way too much Prosecco, I lay with the window open listening to the sound of the waves lapping at the shore. I realised I'd laughed more tonight than I had in a long time and I was truly grateful to have these wonderful people who had come into my life.

## 23

So, this was my big day! I was both apprehensive and excited in equal measures. Leaving the B & B did feel strange. Back to the lighthouse, on a Sunday where there was no one to keep me company, no one working in there to make tea for or have a conversation with. It was just little old me. On my lonesome.

I slotted my key into the front door feeling like I was doing it for the first time. The ground floor had been cleared of some of the boxes and was reasonably tidy, though a bit of a nothing room, an entrance hall which definitely needed something to make it more welcoming. Perhaps Martin might have a piece of furniture at the bric-a-brac shop to have a big vase with some fresh flowers on. He might even have the perfect vase too. Or maybe I should see if Clem could build me something, maybe a bench seat which I could make a cushion for, with a coat rack above and some shelving and shoe storage space. I'd have a little ponder and see. The walls needed a lick of paint or two too. I was pretty sure that on those old stone walls one coat wouldn't go far. A light wall colour would give it the illusion of feeling bigger and maybe a huge mirror would also work.

Yes, I definitely needed a trip to Martin's and a good rummage through his stock.

I walked up to the next floor, to the second bedroom with a small en suite. A partition wall needed to be built so that the room had its own door. That would cut down on the room space, but as it would only be a spare room, it should be fine.

The next floor was my room, which was looking lovely and just needed painting. The furniture Clem had built looked amazing and went perfectly with the cast-iron bedframe. With the beautiful material I had bought yesterday, in peacock green, turquoise, pink and lime, made up into a bedspread and pillows, along with a gorgeous turquoise cashmere throw that I'd bought from – of all places – the supermarket, I knew it was going to look gorgeous. Contrasting but plainer material on the bedroom chair, along with another throw would blend well and would also go behind the latticework that Clem was going to fit to the wardrobe doors. I'd bought enough material to also make some roman blinds for the window in here as well as in the main bathroom next door. The bathroom needed quite a bit more work and we needed to book an electrician to fit some spotlights, but the free-standing bath was a gorgeous feature and I was happy with where we were going with it.

Up another flight took me into the open-plan dining kitchen, the main work surface and breakfast bar overlooking the large picture window and making the most of the amazing views. There was a huge space for a dining table and chairs, which would have been great if I had one. But plenty of time for that.

And finally, my favourite place in the building and possibly the world. The top floor. Again, open plan so the staircase went straight into the room. The stunning views literally took my breath away every time I walked in, the huge windows and French doors which opened onto the narrow balcony capturing the essence of this amazing building. I wanted to get some big pots with plants out on the balcony and make it pretty. I'd never been particularly green fingered but you never knew. Gemma said last night that Driftwood Bay had its own microclimate so it was always possible. There was just enough room for a small bistro table and a chair which would make it pretty darn perfect.

I walked out onto the balcony which Clem had checked out and assured me was safe, and breathed in the fresh salty air. Seagulls swooped around me, wondering if I'd brought them a treat.

'Not today, birdies.' Gosh, I really did need a head check if I was talking to the birds. I laughed at myself. You have to sometimes, don't you?

As I took in everything around me, my heart filled with joy and it brought a lump to my throat. I felt incredibly lucky and grateful for what I had. There was a therapeutic quality to the brightly coloured boats bobbing around in the harbour and the rhythmical chimes of the metal clinking away. I might feel differently if they were still at it in the middle of the night and I couldn't sleep, but right now it was soothing to my soul.

I watched a woman playing and laughing with what I presumed was her young daughter and couldn't remember a time when I ever did that with my mother. You'd have thought I'd have hardened to Mum's nature over the years. She constantly told me how she would have done things instead. I went through one stage of my life where I really clashed with her, but Nana taught me to ignore her because she'd only do it more if she knew that it wound me up. Very strange behaviour from someone who didn't really have a maternal bone in her body. And either not bothered or totally oblivious to the fact that a child might carry that kind of damage with them through their life.

I did ignore it as much as I could but the number of nights I'd gone to bed in tears, feeling that I would never be good enough for her, were too many to count. When she moved to America, it was like a weight was lifted from my shoulders. Nana tried to explain that it was because she was pregnant so young in life, but that was no excuse. She was hurtful and spiteful, and many times, it was intentional. She used to say that it built strength and character. If I'd ever had kids, I would have chosen my words so carefully – once spoken you could never take them back. And as a parent, surely you should want to nurture your child and inspire them to be the person that they could be? I went through my childhood with my head and shoulders down, the knowledge that I should always have done better constantly haunting me. It was only when Mum moved out of the country that I realised what a bearing it had had on me and I felt finally free – only for the old wounds to open whenever she called me. But at least it was so much easier over the phone with the tools that my therapist taught me to manage those conversations.

Pushing those childhood feelings to the back of my mind, I locked up and headed over to Vi's. At least she and Gladys were always pleased to see me.

## 24

After a lovely walk around the harbour, it was time to get back to Vi's for the Spanish Inquisition about my day out with Clem, and I grinned as I opened the door. I could hear her pottering around in the kitchen and the clanking of teacups. I hung up Gladys's lead, although I wasn't sure why as she always managed to get it down again to tell me it was time to go out.

'Let me take the tray through for you, Vi. You should have just waited for me to come back. I could have done that.'

'Oh, I know you could have, dear, but I have to do something. I'll go insane just sitting here fannying around all day long otherwise. It takes me a while but I can shuffle my way into the kitchen and just take it slowly. Honestly, don't get old, Meredith. I know I should be grateful to still be here but I do wish my poor old body could keep up with my mind. I'm still only twenty-three in my head.'

She grinned and made her way back into the lounge. I followed her through with the tray on which she'd gone to town with china cups and saucers, a teapot and even a plate of chocolate biscuits. She shuffled into her wing-backed armchair and let out a big sigh.

'Everything is such a buggering effort these days.'

I thought back to how Nana used to spend her time and it sparked an idea.

'Do you knit or crochet at all, Vi?'

'Do you know I don't. I wish I did; it's always been something I'd like to do. The doctor suggested it as a way of keeping my hands mobile to stop this blithering arthritis but I have no idea.'

'I saw the other day on the window of the mini-market that there was a crocheting club up at the church hall.'

'Is there? I never knew that. I suppose I've not been out the house for a while though.'

'Is it something that you'd go along to?'

'Well, I probably would have gone years ago, but since my fall, I've lost all my confidence. That's why I'm so grateful to you for walking Gladys for me. I'd never be able to do that steep walk to the church at the top of the hill on my own these days. I'm sure if I was there, I'd enjoy it but... It's a nice idea though, dear.'

'What if I helped you to get your confidence back?'

'What do you mean?'

'What if I walked with you?'

Vi's face was a picture of horror. 'Oh no. I couldn't ask you to do that.'

'But you're not asking me, I'm offering. Totally different thing, as my old nana used to say.'

'You're doing enough to help me with the dog. And I'm ever so grateful for that. It would be too much.'

I could see her brain ticking away so I just sipped my tea and left her to ponder on it for a minute or two.

'Well, it's entirely up to you. The offer is there.' I smiled sweetly. 'I'd just hate you to be missing out on all the fun that I've heard goes on, just because you're a little apprehensive about getting there and won't accept some help.'

She lifted her cup to her mouth and then put it back down, splashing tea on the saucer.

'Oh, feck it!' she muttered under her breath and I giggled as Gladys, previously fast asleep, was there like a shot, only too happy to lick it up.

'It wouldn't be fair to Gladys either to leave her on her own. She's so used to me being around every second of the day that I think she'd get that – what is it they call it nowadays? I saw it on that programme with Phil and Holly...' She clicked her fingers and huffed. 'Ah, that's it, separation anxiety?'

'Well, if you really wanted to go, Gladys and I could walk you to the church hall, leave you there for a couple of hours and then we could come and fetch you back. The company would be good for me and save me chatting to myself. When Clem finishes working for me next week, I'll be all alone so it'll be nice to have her with me at the lighthouse while I'm working. No pressure though. I'd hate to force you into enjoying yourself.'

'Oh, I know your type, lady.' She laughed. 'Make me think it's my idea, won't you?'

'Oh, Vi, how could you possibly suggest such a thing.' I grinned. 'You are very kind; do you know that?'

'Thank you. You remind me so much of my nana, Alice her name was, and I'd hate to think of her sitting alone at home when she could be enjoying herself learning a new skill or hobby or even just chatting with friends. If she'd been well enough to do it, she would have, but sadly, towards the end, she was just too poorly.'

'I'm sorry, but I'm sure having you around made her very happy.'

'I hope so. I really do. Although what she'd think of me buying a lighthouse without even seeing it, I have no idea.'

Vi waited until I'd stuffed nearly a whole chocolate biscuit in my mouth before speaking – probably so I couldn't answer immediately. I reckoned she was a right crafty old bird. 'Do you know what I think? Well, I'm going to tell you anyway. I think Alice would be incredibly proud of the woman you are today. You clearly have a huge heart and even by just taking Gladys out you've changed my life. You'll never know how much that means to me and now you are offering to help me again. How will I ever be able to repay you?'

I moved across to the footstool next to her chair and perched myself on the edge of it, hoping it didn't collapse under my weight. I took her hand in mine.

'There is nothing to repay me for. Kindness goes a long way and Nana always used to say that you should do things for people, not because of who or what they are, or what they can do in return, but because of who you are. Kindness costs nothing and means everything. It's something that's stuck with me and I've always tried to live by that.' I smiled as I thought about the wonderful woman who'd brought me up.

'She sounds like a very wise woman. Meredith, you talk about your nana a lot, but not about your parents. Are they still around?'

'Ah, Mum.'

'Now that sounds like there's a story there, the way you said that. Here, check and see if there's some more tea in that pot would you please and you can tell me about her.'

I poured her another cup and told her my story, a single mum who struggled with having a young child and that she moved to Florida when I was eleven to be with a rich man she hardly knew, leaving me with my nana to bring me up. What I didn't share with her is that I'd never felt good enough for my mother and that my self-esteem had suffered all my life because of it. It was also probably why I agreed to marry the first man who showed me some attention and why I was now divorced.

'So, she's rich now then?'

'She's certainly comfortably off. He died at a young age and she's had three husbands since. Her second husband Bill was lovely, but she drove him round the bend and he said he couldn't cope with her any more. And of the three, I do think he had a positive influence on her. When she was with Bill, she didn't seem to be such a...' I paused, not being able to find the word.

'Bully?'

'Well, that's a bit harsh. I'm not sure I'd say that.'

However, it was a word that Nana used in reference to her all the time. And I was her daughter. 'Cow maybe? I think she just felt hard done by, bringing me up alone, and she always seemed to be bad-tempered and unhappy. She blamed me for a lot of it.'

'You should never mix bad words with a bad mood. You can change your mood but you will never get the chance to replace words that have already been spoken. Words are so very powerful. That's why you should always choose them very carefully. They have the ability to create a beautiful moment, but they also can destroy many others. What did my husband used to say now? "Taste your words before you spit them out." He always used to tell me that when I was young. I had to think before I spoke. "The mouth is such a small thing but can do enormous damage" is what he'd say.'

'He sounds like a wise old owl, Vi.'

'He was indeed. You'd have got on with him like a house on fire. You're just his type of person. So, tell me more about Alice.'

We spent over an hour chatting about Nana and it felt so good, remembering what a wonderful person she was but also what an influence she had been on my life. She came to all my parent's evenings at school, ferried me around from one activity to another, and to and from my friends' houses. She was everything that I thought a mother should be and she hardly ever badmouthed my mum in my company. I had heard her a few times talking to her friends but it was only through me overhearing; she never intentionally did it in front of me.

'I think Alice and I would have been good pals you know, Meredith.'

'I think you are right there, Vi. I really do.'

Before I left, we made a bit of a plan that I would check the times and day of the crochet club and let Vi know, and we'd start to build up her confidence by just walking around the garden for a few days and then maybe stretch a little further afield.

She hugged me tightly as I left.

'Maybe Alice and Albert are looking down on us and have thrown us together for some reason. You're a good girl, Meredith. And one day I'll find a way to do something nice for you.'

'You already have done plenty, Vi. Not only are you lending me Gladys but you've also welcomed me into your home and I feel like you're my new best friend. Just don't tell Gemma or Lucy I said that because they're both vying for that position too, not realising it's already been filled.'

It's really cool to have a multi-generational friendship, and as I walked back to the lighthouse, I thought about how much I'd missed having an older person in my life. If we limit our pool of friends to those in the same age range, we're missing out on tons. We can learn so much from older people, who share their worldly experience and wisdom with us. And hopefully they can learn from us too; we can ease their trepidation of the modern world by helping them understand its ways. I was so glad that I'd made a new friend in Vi. She really was a shining star in my life.

## 25

I straightened the wicker heart on the front door and made a mental note to add another nail in the bottom to stop it from going wonky every time I opened and closed the door. I loved the front door now I'd given it a lick of paint. The hibiscus plant was blooming beautifully, its vivid pink flowers contrasting against the cream render of the building. It needed something on the opposite side. Maybe another matching plant. I was also thinking of maybe making an area downstairs with some nice rattan lounging furniture. I stopped to make a note to have a look and see if I could find a garden centre somewhere.

Every time I walked into the lighthouse, I saw it with new eyes and noticed things that I'd never seen before. On the floor where the second bedroom would be, there were a couple of small arched shapes cut into the walls. This room would probably be the last room I tackled but I reckoned that Clem could put a wooden shelf at the bottom and they would make fabulous shelves. I had to make the most of him being around this week so it was another thing on his list. I wanted to get over to the builders' yard again or find out where the nearest B&Q was so I could choose some paint. Every room needed at least a coat of paint and I was actually pretty good with a roller. Having a brass bed meant that I couldn't have a fancy headboard so my thoughts were veering towards a feature wallpaper behind it. If my phone's internet would pick up a connection, I'd try to have a look online, although it would be nice to go and see the choices in person. And finally, my en suite should become a little less basic, with a towel rail being fitted by the electrician tomorrow. It was going to be a busy day with the electrician, Clem and the internet provider. Hopefully there was room for everyone and they wouldn't get in each other's way.

After spending a good couple of hours sorting through some more boxes and hanging even more clothes, I was just trying to decide what to have for tea when my phone rang. My heart gave a little skip when I saw Clem's name on the screen. Get a grip, Mere. It's just Clem.

'Hi there.'

*Hi there?* I never said *Hi there!*

'I was just wondering whether you'd eaten.'

'Oh, I haven't. In fact, I was just thinking about what I was going to have.'

'Good. Fancy an adventure?'

'Er, what sort of an adventure?'

'Grab a blanket and a bottle of wine and come on over to the harbour. You said you'd never been out on a boat before, didn't you?'

'I did say that yes, but...'

'But nothing. You told me at the pub yesterday that you should be more spontaneous. Get yourself over here. We're going out sailing.' The call disconnected.

Shit the bed. I'd literally not been on the sea since that trip to the Isle of Wight. Throwing up when you were a visitor on a boat was not really the look I was hoping for, so I just hoped that being on a smaller boat rather than a bloody great ferry would feel differently. It was also a different time of year and the sea was much calmer than that choppy crossing.

Oh, bugger it. What did I have to lose? Gabby always mocked me for being a planner and told me to be more impulsive – although I don't think she'd really meant me to take her literally when I'd bought the lighthouse.

I slid my feet into some white pumps, grabbed my handbag from the breakfast bar, and a bottle of Pinot Grigio blush from the fridge and nipped upstairs to pick up one of the throws. My heart was hammering in my chest as I ran down the stairs and I'd got proper butterflies in my tummy but the one thing I noticed more than anything was that I was beaming broadly, and it was a feeling that I liked. Very much.

I felt myself practically skipping along to the harbour. For a sleepy little fishing village, there sure was a lot going on down here, and I don't think I'd ever felt like I'd fitted in more.

'Ahoy there.' Clem beamed at me when I arrived at his mooring. He placed a bright orange life jacket over my head. It needed fastening by my breasts and he blushed a little. 'I'll let you do that then.'

I fumbled at the clasp and finally snapped it into place.

'Don't look so nervous, Mere. I'd never make you do something that I didn't think you were going to enjoy. It's going to be fun, trust me.'

And in that moment, I realised that I did trust him. I know I'd not known him long but I trusted him with everything I had. Instinct I suppose and friends like that were worth hanging on to.

## 26

I had no preconceptions about sailing as I had never done it before so I asked Clem to tell me what I could do to help but he told me to just sit back and enjoy the scenery. As we left the harbour and headed out into the open water, I noticed how tranquil and peaceful it was.

'OK?' he asked.

'Yep, I'm good thanks.' Strangely I did feel very OK. It was a warm, still evening so the water was more like a millpond than the sea. Not sure if I'd have felt the same if it had been choppier, but for my first time, it was perfect. It was nice of him to check on me, knowing that I'd been a little apprehensive at first.

As we passed the lighthouse, I felt a little burst of pride from within. I'd left a couple of lights on inside so it wasn't in pitch darkness when I got back, but looking at it from the sea, instead of from the land, it looked pretty and the light glinted off the French doors at the top.

'She's a mighty old girl, isn't she? And she's coming on a treat you know, Mere. You're doing a wonderful job of renovating her.'

'Well, it's you doing all the grafting so you should be congratulating yourself not me really.'

'I've just done the work, but it's been mostly your ideas and they've worked really well. I love how the colours you've chosen work so well and I can't wait to see all the reupholstery that you're doing.'

'There's still a long way to go but we're getting there.'

'I bet when I finish at the end of the week, it'll be completely different again.'

I felt sad at the fact that he wouldn't be there after next week. I'd only ever really known it when Clem had been there and it almost felt as if we were an old married couple, working in silence alongside each other, but happy in each other's company. It had felt quite strange being there this morning on my own and I think he'd purposely invited me out tonight knowing that. It was my first night alone and he was trying to take my mind off it.

'So, I thought we'd sail around the coastline a bit and show you some of the scenery from the sea. You miss so much from land. Then I thought we could drop anchor and I could cook us some tea. Nothing too fancy, just some new potatoes, pan-fried steak and some seasonal veg. Does that sound OK?'

'OK? It sounds amazing. It feels like I haven't cooked for so long I shan't know what to do with myself when I have to start making my own tea at night. And steak will make a lovely change from fish too. I'm a bit fished out.'

'Ah, well, you live in Cornwall now, me lovely.' His over-exaggerated Cornish accent made me giggle. 'You'll soon be sprouting your mermaid fins and diving for pearls.' I noticed that we were getting further and further away from the rugged shoreline and I was trying not to get stressed. I'd swum in the sea before, and I was a reasonable swimmer, but I do like to be able to touch the bottom.

Clem drew attention to some of the landmarks along the way,

telling me who lived in some of the clifftop mansions and pointing out the white sandy stretches of beach and which ones were good for surfing and which were good for paddle-boarding. I couldn't imagine either of those things would be useful for me to know – I wasn't one for water sports; being on this boat was about the most adventurous around sea that I thought I would ever be.

'Look left. Quick!' He suddenly stood and yelled and his face lit up. 'Yes! You're so jammy on your first trip out!'

At first, I couldn't see what he was looking at, but then I gasped as I noticed three dolphins leap out of the water, all in formation, and then dive deep underwater to appear a little further ahead. They were so incredibly graceful considering how big they were and how fast they swam, and I felt so incredibly lucky to be experiencing this very special moment. They came really close to the boat at one point and Clem explained that they were just being inquisitive. They certainly seemed to be having fun doing their glorious display of acrobatics to their audience of two. After a minute or so, they swam away out into the deeper waters.

I could not stop grinning.

'You're so jammy, honestly, Mere. Some people come to Cornwall just for this experience and never see them.'

'Well, clearly they know I'm considering becoming a local and they've come to say hello. I do feel very honoured I have to say.'

'And let's hope they can persuade you to stay!'

I blushed. Was this Clem saying that he'd like me to stay too? I thought it might be a possibility. I wondered how I felt about that.

'Right, I don't know about you, but I'm getting hungry so shall we find somewhere to drop anchor and get some food cooked?'

'Perfect. I'm starving.'

Clem went down to cook, leaving me on the deck to just relax and look out to sea. As I gazed at the different shades of gold, copper and bronze in the sky, I realised again how nature is so clever. The beauty of the sky literally took my breath away. It was starting to get a little darker on one side of the boat but not the other and it made me wonder where we would end up if we kept on sailing out to sea. It seemed bonkers to think that we were still in England and that France was just there somewhere ahead of us.

I was in a little world of my own when Clem appeared again to set the table. He asked me if I was OK again – he was so kind, making sure I was comfortable with the surroundings.

'I'm actually having a lovely time. Thanks for asking me. If you'd have given me more warning, I might have been able to find an excuse but I'm honestly so glad to be here. Just look at what I would have missed out on if I'd said no. Gabby would be so proud of me.'

'Here, pass me your phone and you can send her a pic of you.' He snapped a couple of pictures, getting me to pout and pose which made us laugh. He then surprised me by suggesting we have a selfie and proceeded to take quite a few of us both together. I sneaked a peek at the photos after he'd gone back down below deck and I didn't think I'd ever seen myself look so happy. My face and shoulders had a golden glow from being in and out of the sun each day, my cheeks were naturally sun-kissed, and my hair was blonder than it had ever been, and even though I say it myself, it suited me. I liked being happy. It wasn't as if I had been miserable before I came here, but I had felt like I was just existing – something was missing but I couldn't work out what. Since I'd been here, I was helping people, mainly Vi, and I'd made good friends too.

In one of the pictures, I was staring at Clem in what could have been misinterpreted as sheer adoration. I'd better not send that one to Gabby, I thought. I was sure she'd have something to say about it. I sent my favourite one of me and one of us both and just said:

Living my best Cornish life!

Dinner was gorgeous – simple but delicious. The Pinot Grigio blush was ice-cold and light and went down perfectly with the meal.

'What is it with you Cornish people and food? I'll have to start jogging again just to keep my weight at a steady level. I haven't done it for a couple of years but I think it'll become a necessity soon if I keep eating like this.'

'Ah, well, if you're ever up early enough, you'll see me out every morning jogging. If you fancy coming along, let me know.' He paused and gave me a wink. 'Unless, of course, you don't think you could keep up with me.'

I batted his arm. 'Cheeky! I'll take you on, Clement Penrose, but only after I've done some training to get back into shape. Maybe Gladys would like a jog every so often instead of a walk.'

'I don't think Labradors are made for jogging. She'd be stopping every time she found a bit of food that had been dropped.'

'You're not wrong there. She's a right greedy one!'

I suddenly got this feeling in my tummy and I started to worry. Oh lord. Wind. It was going to come out one way or the other and I hoped more than anything else in the world that it came out the right way. The feeling built in my chest and up inside my throat and I let out a massive burp.

I looked at Clem in horror and apologised.

He laughed. 'Don't mind me. Better out than in. Sign of a good meal. And at least it was up and not down. I always say that you can't really be held responsible for bodily functions. A few years ago, I went to an osteopath with a bad back. I was in agony. She was such a pretty little thing and I was trying to be all smooth and cool and chat her up, so I was totally mortified when she cracked my back and I farted really loudly.'

I proper laughed out loud.

'I honestly couldn't leave quick enough. Can you imagine my

alarm when I saw her in the pub a few weeks later with all her mates? I could hardly bring myself to speak to her when she asked me how my back was. So, burping, really, it's nothing. We all do it.'

I was still giggling as he cleared the plates away to the kitchen, insisting that I stayed where I was. When he came back up, he was holding a couple of hoodies. 'I brought these. You might want to put one on. It'll start to go quite chilly soon – it's amazing how much the temperature drops out at sea – and you'll want your blanket over your legs too. You'll be nice and toasty then.'

He threw a navy-blue hoody in my direction, and as I pulled it over my head, I closed my eyes and breathed in deeply. It smelled of Clem's aftershave and a little shiver ran up my spine.

I must be feeling that chill already.

Up above, shades of indigo and aubergine merged with the remaining amber and big bright stars were popping up everywhere dazzling against the colourful evening sky. It was like someone had thrown a net of sparkly fairy lights far above us. So very pretty.

As Clem poured us both another glass of wine, emptying the bottle, he pointed out the constellations above us and explained that the stars showed up more in Cornwall because of the amount of natural light. He seemed at one with nature and here, sitting side by side chatting away to each other like friends who'd known each for years, it felt so natural. And I felt incredibly privileged to be experiencing this beauty right now, wrapped up warm under a blanket in Clem's oversized hoody which swamped me. What a wonderful idea it had been to do this tonight. Right there, in that moment, there was no place that I would have rather been.

\* \* \*

By the time I laid my head on my pillow that night, shattered, thoughts of the lovely evening swirled around my mind. Clem had very chivalrously walked me home even though I'd said there was no need, but he insisted, and we parted with a bit of an awkward hug-cum-kiss on the cheek under the light of the lantern by the front door.

I'd had a thoroughly lovely evening, an enjoyable new experience which I hoped would happen again, and when I arrived back the lighthouse felt welcoming and warm. The table lamps that I'd left on cast a lovely cosy glow in the rooms and instead of feeling uneasy at being here alone, I felt extremely comfortable in my surroundings. Before I headed down to my bedroom I sat for a while in one of the armchairs on the top floor, just staring out to sea, wanting to commit this feeling and image to my memory banks never to be forgotten.

And as I drifted off into a deep sleep, to the rhythmic hypnotic ticking of my bedside clock, I wondered what Clem was doing at that moment and if maybe there was a remote chance that he might be thinking of me.

## 27

A door slammed and the noise woke me. I wasn't sure if it was part of my dream but when I heard footsteps on the metal stairs, I realised they were for real. I glanced at the clock. It was eight. As I leaped out of bed, I realised that it must be Clem and grabbed my dressing gown. Glancing in the mirror, I wiped the black smudges from under my eyes and smoothed my hair down, trying to make myself look at least a tiny bit respectable.

'Won't be a minute,' I yelled as I heard steps go past my bedroom door. I felt a little discombobulated and pulled my dressing gown tighter around me.

'No need to ask if you slept well then?' Clem was filling the kettle.

'I can't believe it. I literally just woke up. I think I had one of the best night's sleep I've ever had. I'm so sorry that I wasn't up though.'

'Well, lighthouse life and a sail on the open sea obviously suits you and I'm glad I didn't go with my original plan of coming round at seven. Coffee?' He held up the tin of posh instant coffee I insisted on using.

I nodded. It felt perfectly natural for Clem to be offering me coffee in my house. This strapping big man who was taking up a whole lot of room felt as much part of the furniture as I did. Sitting at the breakfast table while he was pottering about made me smile and wonder what he'd be like to live with.

My phone started ringing. Gabby on a FaceTime call. I answered it without thinking but then when her voice boomed across the kitchen realised that it wasn't such a great idea.

'So, did you get lucky last night with the fit builder then? Nice work, Mere.'

'Er... actually, Gabby—'

'You are a dark horse, aren't you? You definitely looked like you were getting all kinds of cosy in those pics you sent me. I bet that boat was doing some bobbing about! I'll have to get you one of those signs. "Don't come a knocking, when the boat is a rocking!"'

'Gabby!' My voice was getting louder and deeper and with the faces I was pulling at her too, I had rather hoped she realised that I was trying to tell her something.

'Mind you, I don't blame you. He is hot as f—'

'Gabby! Say good morning to Clem, who's just arrived for work.' I turned the camera around and he grinned broadly at her.

'Good morning, Gabby.' How he managed to make those three words sound sexy was a real skill.

'Morning, Clem. So, hang on a mo, Mere. You're in your dressing gown and Clem is making you your morning coffee. Are you sure that's all that he's been making you? Are you sure he's just turned up for work and hasn't been there all night? Looking a bit suspect I should tell you.'

'Gabby, if you don't behave yourself, I will disconnect this call.'

'Oh no. Clem, have you met Stroppy Meredith before? She's a proper scary bird.'

Clem continued to laugh, finding the whole situation hilarious.

'Sorry to disappoint you, Gabby, but I really have just turned up for work and sleepy head over there really has just woken up. But yes, I have met Stroppy Meredith before. Don't ever piss her off in a supermarket car park when she's hangry, will you?'

'Ha, you've met that Meredith too. Poor you.'

'Excuse me, I am here you know.'

'Yes, I do know. Anyhow, I'm going to go now and leave you two lovebirds to it. I'll call you a bit later. Love you.' The screen went blank.

She really was incorrigible.

'Sorry about that.'

'No problem to me. Flattered that she thinks I'd be capable of pulling you to be honest.'

I blushed and slid off the stool.

'I'll go and get dressed.'

I leaned up against my bedroom door. How bloody embarrassing was that? I'd kill Gabby when I saw her. Then I realised that I wouldn't kill her at all. I would hug her tight and tell her how much I missed her.

It had been nearly two weeks and it felt like a lifetime. More than that I wanted her down here. I wanted to show her around my new home and see how well I'd fitted in. I would pin her down to sorting out a date when I called her back later.

I quickly swilled my face with water and cleanser, slapped on a bit of moisturiser and threw on the nearest clothes, which just happened to be some denim shorts, a strappy vest top and a cardigan I grabbed from the chest of drawers. Make-up today would have to wait till later if at all.

'Right, lazy-bum. There's your coffee. That's my list for today and that's yours. Shall we have this coffee and crack on?'

'God, you're a slave driver. I wanted to pop into your dad's shop today too.'

'Not on a Monday you won't. Cornwall closes on a Monday. Surely you know that by now.'

'Oh, bum. That can be tomorrow then. I'll take Gladys out at lunchtime today.'

'Fab, drink up then. Let's get cracking.'

## 28

Next morning when Clem arrived, I was much more prepared. I'd slept like a log and while I'd woken early, it felt like great restorative sleep, something I'd been sadly lacking back at Gabby's, as I frequently woke early thinking about all the things I had to do to get through each day. This change of pace really did suit me.

I'd jumped out of the shower and dressed in shorts and a T-shirt, leaving my hair to dry in its natural waves. I'd just flicked the kettle on when Clem arrived, bright and breezy. My marriage to David was like a roller coaster: one minute he was lovely to me, and the next, he wasn't speaking.

I shook the memories away. They had no place with me in my new home.

'You look like a proper surfer babe this morning.' He grinned.

'Now that's something that I'll never be.' I laughed. 'My balance is appalling.'

'You know me well enough by now to know that I like a challenge, don't you?'

'Seriously, surfing is not for me. I tried it once years ago and fell off more times than I cared to count. I think I swallowed most of the sea too. My husband said there couldn't be a person in the world with less co-ordination than me.'

'Oh, now there's love for you. I thought your spouse was supposed to be supportive and want the best for you.'

'Ha. Perhaps some are, but mine certainly wasn't.'

'Maybe you just didn't have the right teacher.' His eyes lingered on mine.

I gulped.

'In that case tell me when you have a few hours free and I might just have another idea.'

'Most of my time is free, but I'm taking up enough of your time with work.'

'I'm enjoying having a project.'

'Oh, so that's what you call me is it? A project? Charming.' I pretended to huff as I moved over to the other side of the kitchen to make some coffee.

'You know what I mean. Sorry, I didn't mean to insult you.'

'I was only joking. You'll have to try far harder than that to insult me.'

He walked closer and then turned to look out of the window. I flicked him with the tea towel on the backside but then wondered if I'd been too familiar.

He turned round and glared at me. 'Right, lady! You think you're gonna win that competition, do you?'

He picked up another tea towel from the side and we ran around the kitchen whipping each other with them like children.

'Ouch, that hurt.'

'Good. Does that mean you're going to give up?'

'Not on your nelly, mate. I won an award at Scouts for being a champion flicker.'

I stopped. 'Scouts? You were in the Scouts? You?'

'Dib dib.' He raised two fingers to his head in a mock salute and I burst out laughing.

'What's so funny?'

I seriously didn't know why I had found this so funny but every time I tried to stop laughing, and looked at his serious face, it set me off again. Suddenly, in a big hiccupy type of burp, I very unattractively and uncontrollably snorted snot out of my nose.

Mortified at what had happened, I ran down the stairs followed by the sound of Clem roaring with laughter. I slammed the bedroom door behind me and wiped my mascara-streaked face but my eyes were still glossy and bright. There was nothing for it. I could never face him again.

After a minute, there was a tap at my door. 'Mere, are you coming out?'

'No. Never.'

'You might have to come out at some point.' I could still hear laughter in his voice and it made me smile.

'I can't. I can never leave my bedroom again. Call the estate agent. I must sell the lighthouse and move on. I'll move out tonight when you've gone and it's dark and I'll never have to see you again.'

Sliding down the door, I sat with my right side against it. I heard him do the same the other side. My whole body tingled as I realised that it felt incredibly intimate that we were so close with nothing but a door between us.

'What if I promise to never tell a soul? Would that help?'

'It might, but what if you renege on your promise? I've not known you long and I don't know how good you are at keeping secrets.'

'Oh, trust me. I'm the master at that.' Suddenly, his voice changed and he sounded sad. It felt like there was a definite shift in the mood. 'I've had to keep quite a few over the last few years.

Maybe I'll share some of my own darkest secrets over a pint one night.'

'You can't do that if I do a moonlight flit.'

'Ha. You don't want to do that though. Gladys would miss you. Vi would miss you. And... Well... I might miss you a little bit too.'

My breath caught in my throat. I would miss him too. Very much. He made me feel more alive than I had for years. Two minutes ago, we'd been larking around like kids. Now it felt like it had got very serious all of a sudden.

'Mere. Come out.'

I sighed. I loved the way he said my name. What was going on here? I wasn't meant to be feeling this way. I was meant to be finding myself, not trying to find someone else. I heard him stand and I mirrored his movements from my side of the door.

'I'm going to come in now.' The door handle started to turn and within seconds he was standing before me.

'You can't just walk into a girl's bedroom, you know. What will people think?'

'They can think what they like. I gave up worrying what this village thought about me a long time ago. And you are not a girl. You are very much a woman.'

He moved a step closer to me and his hand grazed my cheek as he tucked a stray strand of hair behind my ear. My body shivered at his touch. He ran his index finger gently down the side of my cheek as I looked deep into his eyes. He held my gaze. My eyes flickered to his lips. Nothing else mattered at the moment when he dipped his head towards mine. I caught my breath as I closed my eyes, hoping that I hadn't got this wrong and that I hadn't made a mistake. That he really was going to kiss me and I really, really wanted him to. More than anything. I could sense how close he was to me now. I could feel his breath on my face and sensed that his lips were just millimetres away from mine.

'Cooee! Anyone home.'

We sprang apart and our eyes locked.

'Shit!' I whispered.

'Fuck!' he muttered and took another step back.

'Up here, Gemma.' For some reason, I smoothed my clothes down.

Clem turned and fled down the stairs to the second bedroom calling hello as he passed Gemma on the landing.

'Hope I haven't called at a bad time.'

I heard him cough and I bit the inside of my mouth, stifling a smile.

'No, it was probably just the right time. Are you stopping for a cuppa?'

'Can't stop, sorry. Just dropping these cakes off.'

'I'd love you and Lucy and James to come to dinner on Friday night. Are you free?'

'Damn right I'm free. You know I never go out, Mere.'

We heard footsteps behind us.

'Sorry, I just need to get...' Clem and I did an awkward dance around each other. Once more, I blushed and Gemma looked at me and raised her eyebrows.

'All right Clem? Are you coming to dinner on Friday night too? You've already invited Clem, right Meredith?'

'Oh well... erm.' I rubbed at the back of my neck and the heat in my face intensified. 'I hadn't, but yes of course, if you're free, do come along Clem.' I felt like I had no option but to ask him.

'Thank you, Mere.' He grinned that great big daft grin and ran his fingers through his hair before heading back to work and those pesky butterflies in my tummy did a little jig. I avoided Gemma's eyes for a moment or two as he went back downstairs and she raised her eyebrows. 'I have to go but this conversation is far from over.'

\* \* \*

I could hear Clem whistling away through the open windows. The sound made me smile. I headed for the garden room and dragged the corner table in front of the window. If I was going to work in here, I may as well have a nice view while I was at it. The rolls of material I'd bought were leaning against one of the walls and I heaved them over and onto the tabletop, waiting for inspiration to hit me. Maybe if I brought one of the chairs down, it would help. As I headed up the stairs and reached the landing outside the second bedroom where he was working, I heard him answer a call.

'Hey, Soph. How are you?'

Ah, a woman. Interesting. I couldn't really help overhearing and curiosity got the better of me so I stayed to listen. His voice seemed to soften and I had this strange feeling come over me. Jealousy maybe?

'I know. Try not to worry. Whatever happens we can work things out. We've never had a problem before that we can't sort out, have we? We can talk to your mum together if it makes it easier.' He seemed to be calming 'Soph' down and ended with 'OK then. See you at the weekend. We can discuss it more then.'

I tiptoed as lightly and as quickly as I could back up the stairs wondering what the conversation was about. Clem appeared a minute later.

'Sorry, Meredith but I need to finish early today. I'll make up my time but something's come up. Bye.'

'Oh, OK. Is everything all right, Cl—?'

He was already heading down the stairs and out of the door. I heard his truck rev up and his tyres spun on the gravel as he scooted away.

What on earth had this Soph said to him to put him in this sombre mood? He'd been so mellow until now.

I looked at my watch; it was only 2.30 p.m. and it felt like I'd got a long afternoon ahead of me, alone. I'd got used to Clem's company but it was time I got used to my own. Not right now though. I headed out for a walk.

\* \* \*

'Hello young lady, and how are you?'

I'd come to see Martin as it had been a while since I'd been into the shop because I'd been focusing on the hard work going on at the lighthouse. I also thought it might be an opportunity to do some discreet digging about Clem.

'Working hard, but it's all coming along nicely,' I replied. 'You'll have to come and have a look round when you get chance. Your son is a wonder with his hands.'

I blushed at the memory of Clem delicately touching my face and thought about the other places that it might be quite nice for him to touch too.

'That's what all the girls say.' He laughed. 'And what can I do for you on this fine afternoon?'

'Just came for a mooch. Need some bits and pieces but not sure of what until I see them if that makes sense.'

'Makes perfect sense to me. Make yourself at home and mooch away. Fancy a cuppa while you're looking?'

I didn't fancy to going back into the lighthouse right then and I was parched so took him up on his kind offer. I spent the time at Martin's shop moseying around. I picked up some trinkets, a couple of large ornate vases, a small wrought iron table which would be perfect for the entrance hall and a particularly stunning table lamp.

One of the things I loved about a shop like this was the feeling that it gave me, wondering who had owned these items before and thinking about the stories that they could tell. When I'd finished browsing, I sat chatting to Martin and grabbed my chance.

'Is everything OK with Clem do you know? He's been a bit quiet and I'm not sure if there's something going on.'

'Ah, I'm not always sure what goes on in that head of his, but I'm sure he's fine.'

He didn't seem to want to elaborate and changed the topic, instead telling me lots of the history of the village and in particular the lighthouse. Apparently it had been in his family once upon a time. He said he'd have a look through some of his old photos and pass them on to me if I wanted to keep them.

The more work I did on the lighthouse the more I was beginning to imagine what a life here would be like. It even made me think about what it would be like to live here full time and how nice it would be to be part of the community forever. Maybe Driftwood Bay Lighthouse wasn't just a project, maybe it should become a home. It was certainly starting to feel that way.

I decided to call in on Vi after leaving the shop. Anything really to stop me thinking about Clem. I still heated up in the face every time I thought about our near-kiss.

Gladys was very excited to see me, almost programmed now that every time she saw me, she knew she got to go out. I decided to take her down to the beach and then come back and walk with Vi for a bit. My talk with Martin about the village had been so fascinating but it just made me think of even more questions and I knew Vi would be perfect as she'd lived here all her life.

'I've taken Gladys out, it's your turn now,' I said when Gladys and I had returned from the beach. 'Then when we've done some walking with you, I'll make you a nice cup of tea.'

'Are you sure?'

'I most certainly am. I have all the time in the world so I think we may as well get you started. I've bought you a pedometer so you can count how many steps you've done. Here, clip this onto your waistband.'

Vi gripped my arm tightly as we made our way down to the garden, and as we meandered around, I could see her confidence growing with every step. Vi's garden was beautiful, with a path all the way around the outside so we could walk steadily and admire the plants along the way. She was concentrating hard and finding it difficult to talk at the same time, so I just wittered on about the plants and the birds.

She stumbled a little.

'I think it's time to go in now.' She looked worried.

'Just a little bit longer,' I insisted, and she looked at me sheepishly. 'When a baby stumbles do they give up? No, they just get back to it and keep on until they can do it confidently. And that's going to be you too. I'm right here to help you.'

'But what if I fall?'

A saying that Nana used to say flashed into my head.

'But what if you fly...'

She smiled sweetly and patted my hand before tucking her arm back in mine. 'You're such a good girl, Meredith. Thank you for helping Gladys and me. And for no reward too. I wish there were more people like you in the world.'

'The reward I'll get is seeing you walking up that hill to crochet club and telling me that you wish you'd done it years ago.'

She laughed. 'I think you know me too well already, young lady.' She stopped and checked her pedometer. 'Oooh, I've clocked up a thousand steps. That's not too shabby, is it?'

'Not too bad at all. Let's go for the same tomorrow and then another five hundred. If we add on five hundred a day, we'll soon have you running up the hill to the church hall in no time. But for now, let's get you back in the lounge and I'll go and put that kettle on.'

We chatted about the area and she filled me in on her life in Driftwood Bay as a child but I could see that she was struggling to keep her eyes open. Just that little walk had tired her out so I made sure she was comfy and had everything she needed around her and left her to doze. I'd have to ask her the burning questions that were swirling around in my head another day. I bent down to say goodbye to Gladys and she rolled over for a belly rub. When she rolled back she farted really loudly. Vi's eyes sprung open.

'Oh lord. Was that me?'

I laughed. 'Don't worry, it was just your flatulent Labrador.'

'Oh, thank goodness for that. Thought I might have shit myself for a minute then.' And she closed her eyes and went back to sleep. I only just made it through the front door before I let out a hoot.

On my way out, as I was undoing the latch of the garden gate, I heard a voice and turned to find Dyllis standing with her hands on her hips and a sneer on her face.

'Christ, everyone's gone mad round here since you've moved in. You're clearly contagious.'

'Hello there, Dyllis, and how are you today?' I said, trying to be amenable.

'Fine, if it's anything to do with you. Still hanging around mooning over Clement Penrose, are you?' She was a proper charmer...

'Clement is helping me to renovate the lighthouse. I'm not mooning over him; I'm paying him for a service.' I crossed my arms.

'Mmm. I bet you are.' She pursed her lips and glared at me.

'I beg your pardon? Are you implying something else here?'

'We don't need outsiders coming into our village, taking our properties from those that it rightfully should belong to and also taking our men for that fact. At your age too. You should be ashamed of yourself.'

I couldn't believe the cheek of her. I had done absolutely nothing wrong.

'Would you rather I paid someone from outside the area to come in then? Would that make you happier?'

'It would make me happier if you'd never arrived in Driftwood Bay, Meredith Robinson. That's what.' And with, that she stuck her nose in the air and stomped off.

Honestly, that woman. Just as I thought she was thawing, this is what I got.

I looked around to see if anyone else had seen our exchange but there wasn't a soul around. I could feel the fury in my body and had to give myself a minute to calm down. After a lovely walk with Gladys, and a productive morning at the lighthouse I wasn't going to let her spoil my day. But I was also determined to get to the bottom of why she had this vendetta against me.

## 29

Thursday afternoon soon rolled round. Mine and Clem's near-kiss had happened a couple of days before and neither of us had referred to it since, keeping a distance where we could. I hadn't a clue whether he felt like it was a mistake or whether the mysterious phone call was the trigger but there was clearly something wrong. He'd not tried to get anywhere near close to me, being more of a professional carrying out a job, waving as he left on time every day and not stopping during the day at all, saying that he wanted to get on and get finished. He seemed to just want to get the job done and get away from me, so it was a surprise when he made me close my eyes and led me up the stairs. He grabbed my hand to steady me, and I couldn't help but notice how utterly perfectly my hand fitted into his. But I tried to remind myself that we were just friends.

'Ta-dah!'

'Oh my God!'

'Do you hate it?'

'I bloody love it. You've literally left me nothing to do. I didn't realise you were painting the walls too. When did you get the paint?'

'I just wanted to make it perfect for you. I know you have guests coming next week, so thought I'd try and get as much done as possible to save you the work. Got to make sure you're getting your money's worth out of me.' He raised his eyebrows and I pulled my eyes away from his and looked around. He'd built shelves into the walls and a small wardrobe along with a wooden frame for the headboard which I was going to pad out with upholstered material. And he'd somehow made a small dressing table shelf and stool. A very small en suite with shower, washbasin and toilet was just behind another door. I couldn't believe that he'd been able to create what he had from a blank canvas.

'Clem, you've been absolutely amazing. I can't thank you enough for what you've done. You've turned this place around and it's more than I could have ever imagined.'

A tear ran down my cheek, and he reached across and wiped it away tenderly. Then he tucked his hand back into his jeans pocket.

'It's your dream, Meredith. Basically, you told me what you wanted, and I just built it.'

'But you haven't just built something here, Clem. You've built something absolutely fabulous. Your work is beautiful. You really are incredibly gifted. You've turned my dreams into reality.'

He smiled and leaned against the door frame.

'Did you finish the headboard?'

I nodded.

'Shall we go and grab that and the mattress then?'

I nodded again. I looked around the room again and was just so stunned by what he had done, I could hardly speak. All I could do was grin.

We grabbed an end each of the headboard and carried it across the garden, manoeuvring it through the front door and carefully up the stairs. We fixed it into place on the wooden frame and it finished the room off perfectly. Then we did the same with the mattress.

'Tell you what,' I said, 'why don't you go and grab us a beer each out of the fridge and I'll give you a shout? I just want to get the bedclothes on so we can see it finished.'

He went up to the kitchen and I went back out to the workshop and grabbed the bedclothes and ran back over to the main building, quickly popping a sheet, pillowcases and duvet cover on and then finally a runner which sat across the bottom of the bed.

'I'm ready for you, Clem.'

'Not every day a girl calls you into her bedroom and says that, you know. A different man might take that the wrong way.'

'Well, it's a good job you're not that type of man then, isn't it?' I batted his arm, his solid, muscly arm, and I noticed how sun-kissed the little blond hairs on it were. I dragged my eyes away. 'What do you think?'

'Very nice. I like what I see.' I turned back to him and he wasn't even looking at the bed, he was just looking at me.

'Er hello! Are you sure you're not that type of man? I meant the bed. What do you think?'

He laughed.

'I think it looks amazing. The whole lighthouse looks amazing, Mere.' That lilt again when he said my name... 'You've got such a fabulous eye for this you know. Why on earth are you not doing this for a living?'

Now that was a question I couldn't answer.

'What are you doing now?' he asked sharply.

'Er, no idea. Why?'

He looked at his watch. 'I have an idea.'

To be honest, I could have done with just sitting and chilling for the evening. My back was aching from bending over the workshop table and sewing machine. I could do with an early night.

'I know that face. And I'm not taking no for an answer. I promise that you are going to love it.' I couldn't help but grin back when he smiled at me in that way. He was like a little boy with a new toy. How could I refuse? And in fairness, I did say that I wanted to be more spontaneous and have more fun.

'I'm gonna go and grab some stuff, put your cossie on and meet me at the beach and I'll be at our rock in fifteen minutes.'

I laughed as he leaped up into the Jeep. I then clocked that he'd said 'our' rock and that gave me a warm fuzzy feeling inside.

\* \* \*

I sat on 'our' rock gazing out at the sea. I could have been there for ten minutes; I could have been there for ten hours. Time just drifted by. The water was mesmerising and the late afternoon sun a delightful sight as it cast shimmery shadows on the water.

'Ahoy there!'

'Oh shit. You have got to be kidding me!'

'I kid you not. I take these things very seriously, you know. Now, I know you said I'd never get you on a surfboard, but these aren't surfboards. These are paddle-boards. Much easier as you can just relax once you've found your balance and it's so much easier than surfing. Come on. This one is yours.'

I shook my head at him as he grinned that ridiculous grin and laughed out loud.

'Don't look so scared. You know I'll look after you.'

I did. I knew I was in a safe pair of hands.

'So you're going to wade out and carry the board until you are knee deep, then set it down, OK?'

I nodded nervously.

'Then I'll hold your board while you work your way onto the board. Don't worry, I'll hold it firm, so it should be easy.'

'Easy. Hah!'

'Do you trust me?'

I looked into his deep blue eyes. 'I do.'

'So, climb on then, and just lie on the board – to start with.'

Mounting the board was not the most graceful thing I've ever done in my life, and I was sure I could feel my arse hanging out the back of my swimming costume. Great, the last thing I needed right now was a wedgie, but I was on and holding on for dear life. I couldn't exactly reach around to sort it out.

'That's it. And relax. The worst that can happen is that you fall off and get wet.'

'I guess that's not the worst thing in the world.' I let my shoulders relax a little and stopped worrying about my backside.

'Use your hands to push yourself out a little bit. I've got your paddle, don't worry. Just get your balance to start with. I've got your board too. We can work up to your knees when you feel confident enough. Paddle out a bit with your hands, just like you are swimming.'

'I'm doing it, I'm doing it.' I whooped and he laughed and when I turned towards his voice, I realised that he wasn't even holding on any more. 'Clem, hold me.'

'You don't need me to. You're doing great. You're a quick learner.'

I let go with one of my hands and punched the air and the board wobbled. I cried out.

Within seconds, he was beside me kneeling on his board. 'I've got you. You have nothing to worry about. OK?'

I nodded.

'Ready to go a bit further?'

I nodded again, still quite nervous.

'And when you're ready you can smile and at least pretend you are enjoying it. Relax those shoulders. I'm right beside you. You're doing so well.'

I grinned at him. 'I'm really paddle-boarding!'

He laughed back at me. 'If I'd told you this is what we were going to do, would you have agreed?'

'Hell no!'

He laughed. 'And that's exactly why I didn't tell you. Wanna try to get on your knees?'

'No! I like it down here. Can I stay here? Please?'

'OK, but next time we do this, you are going on your knees!'

'I bet you say that to all the girls.' I paddled away from him and bravely went further out into the open water, leaving him grinning innately at me from behind.

'Look at you. Getting brave, aren't you?' He drifted back over to my side and we paddled contentedly side by side for a while before he could see that my arms were starting to get tired. 'Come on, let's head back into shore. There's a beer in that freezer box with my name on it.'

We dragged the boards out of the water and laid them on the sand by the side of our rock. He threw a towel at me and I draped it around my shoulders. He'd brought a couple of oversized fleece hoodies with him too and I put one on after I had wriggled into my denim shorts. He handed me a beer, which tasted delicious. He really did think of everything.

I noticed Russell walking Charles on the beach and raised my hand in acknowledgement.

Clem's phone buzzed and he reached across to check a text, which made his brow furrow. He glanced at his watch.

'Right, sorry, Meredith, but I didn't realise the time. I need to go.'

He started to pack up, leaving me sitting there feeling quite bewildered by his change of mood, again.

'Is everything OK?'

'Yeah, all good. See you tomorrow.'

And just like that he walked away.

I wandered back to the lighthouse wondering what the hell had just happened. We seemed to be having such a lovely time yet all of a sudden, everything changed.

When I arrived back, I saw a shadow emerge from the side of the building.

Clem.

What was he doing here?

Before I could blink, he leaned in towards me and gently kissed my cheek.

'You should be happy being you,' he said. 'You're perfectly lovely. And if we're nothing else to each other, I'm very lucky to have you as my friend.'

And as quickly as he had appeared, he had gone.

Inside, I held my hand up to the place where his soft warm lips had met my cheek, wondering what the hell that was all about.

But it at least confirmed one thing, as devastating as it was to admit. I wished more than anything that he felt differently about me. That he didn't just think of me as a friend.

But he clearly didn't feel that way about me, so then yes, I was glad he was my friend too. Perhaps some people were just not meant to be 'the one'.

# 30

I woke to the sun streaming in through my window and the sound of seagulls squawking.

Back in the Midlands, I'd wallow in bed each morning, hitting the snooze button at least twice before I dragged my backside out of bed. Here, I couldn't wait to get out of bed and start my day. I had more energy than I could ever remember. I grabbed my dressing gown which was draped over the back of my bedroom chair and slid my feet into my furry slipper boots. Those cast-iron steps were as cold as ice first thing in the morning. I headed upstairs into the kitchen area, filled the kettle and while waiting for it to boil, I just stood admiring the view. With the birds swooping down onto the sea and the sun rising, creating its glorious myriad of gold and orange glowing in the distance, seemingly lighting up the whole harbour and the beach, what could be better than this to start the day?

Coffee hit the spot that morning and I went to collect Gladys who was eager for a walk. When I reached the top end of the beach, Charles appeared from nowhere, closely followed by Russell who had, by the look of his sports attire, and beads of sweat, been for a run.

'Hey there, do I need to be waving a white flag?' he called out as he approached.

'Not sure yet, I haven't quite decided if I'm speaking to you or not.'

His face broke out into a grin that could have melted an ice queen and I couldn't help but smile back.

'How's it going? Is it starting to take shape yet?'

Proud of the work that Clem and I had done, I started to explain the changes that we'd already made and found myself gabbling about the plans.

'I'd love to see it some time.' He looked into my eyes as he swept his hair back and grinned, openly flirting with me. Gosh, I hadn't noticed last time because I was so furious with him but his green eyes were stunning and – wow – that smile. We stood staring at each other, grinning aimlessly, when an idea struck me.

'I know it's short notice but I don't suppose you are free tonight, are you?'

'I might just be free actually. Especially if it's you that's asking.'

I giggled like a schoolgirl and flicked my hair. What on earth was going on? Just because someone was flirting with me, didn't mean to say I had to do the same back.

'I'm having a few friends round for dinner and to show them the work that we've done. I suppose it's a bit of a housewarming. Why don't you come along? I'd really love you to see the changes. I'm not sure you'll believe what we've achieved in such a short time.'

'I'd love to.'

We broke eye contact and turned back to the dogs to see that Charles had mounted Gladys from behind and was happily humping away to his heart's content. Gladys, the little hussy, seemed to be enjoying every moment. We both ran over to them, shouting at them to stop. Vi would kill me if Gladys ended up having puppies. She'd never be able to cope with that.

Russell grabbed Charles's harness and pulled him away, apologising for his dog's behaviour while I went off in the other direction scolding Gladys for being such a little strumpet.

'Dinner is at seven thirty,' I shouted over my shoulder. 'You know where to come.'

'It's a date,' he shouted back. 'Can't wait'

I was grinning all the way back to Vi's house and, I think, for other reasons, so was Gladys!

'What are you looking so happy about? Shagged the payroll, have you?'

'Vi! You're incorrigible.'

'And you're too slow. Bloody hell, if I was your age, I'd have done it in every room in that lighthouse.' She winked at me.

'Vi, seriously! You are so naughty.'

'Oh, life's too short, Meredith. You have to have a laugh, don't you?'

'You do indeed. Come on,' I said. 'Fancy a spin round the garden?'

'Well, you'll be surprised at me, because yesterday, I did two thousand steps.'

'Blimey, I bet you needed a lie down after that.'

'I bloody did but now I've got a spring in my step for the first time in months. You walking me round the garden seems to have given me the little lift that I needed. I feel ready to take on the world. When does the crochet group start up again?'

'Next Tuesday, but that's only four days from now.'

'I'm nothing if not determined. I shall do this, Meredith. Are you still OK to help me?'

'Just you try and stop me. Come on, show me what you've got!'

Vi put her arm in mine and when we reached the gate her eyebrows lifted.

'Are you coming, Gladys?'

Gladys, who was lying down on the patio by the front door, lifted her head, gave me the filthiest of looks and put her head back down to the tune of a great big sigh. I think Charles had worn her out. I considered telling Vi about Gladys's antics but then thought better of it. I didn't want to worry her unnecessarily.

So, while the sun shone down on our bare shoulders, Vi and I strolled – slowly – arm in arm around the harbour.

'I'll have you in the top room at the lighthouse in no time, Vi.'

'I'm not sure if I'll ever be up for that, much as I would love to see it. Me and my Albert used to sneak up there and sit in front of the fire with a blanket around us and watch the stars at night when we were courting. In fact, that's the very first place where we—'

'Stop! Too much information.' I stuck my fingers in my ears. 'La, la, la! I can't hear you!'

'Helloooo!' A voice carried down from along the harbour walk. 'I thought it was you two. I spotted you both from the shop window. Here you go.' It was Gemma, and she was holding a thermal bag. 'I've brought you both a Belgian bun and a cuppa. Thought you might need some carbs to get your energy back. And I could do with a break too. Budge up, Mere.'

'If I'd known I'd get given food all the time, I'd have made friends with a baker years ago. Thanks so much. You are kind.'

Gemma wedged her bum next to me on the bench.

'And look at you, Violet. You're looking spritely today.'

'Well, I'm not sure about that but I'm definitely getting back on my feet again thanks to this one.' She patted my knee. 'Such a superstar.'

'We've got four days to get her up to the top of the hill to the church hall. That's our goal. The crochet club is starting up again after a bit of a break and even though I'd offered to drive her, Vi's insistent that she's going to walk.'

'It'll take me those four days if we set off today.' Vi laughed.

'Four days of intense training is what I meant and you well know it.'

We sat in companiable silence for a few minutes, eating, drinking and watching the world go by, mesmerised by the sound of the clanking metal of the boats which was like wind chimes in the breeze. And then when it was time for Gemma to get back to the shop, we said our goodbyes and headed round the harbour wall back to Vi's house.

'Thank you again, Meredith. Do you really think we'll make it on Tuesday afternoon?'

'I think you can do anything you set your mind to!'

'Only because you have given me the confidence to do this. I honestly would not have even mustered up the courage if it weren't for you. I think I was giving up before you came along. Dennis, even though he was wonderful by coming down for a couple of weeks, was talking about me going into a home and rehoming Gladys. I didn't want either of those things but didn't know how to tell him. I want to end my days in my lovely little cottage here on the harbour front, but I don't want to be a burden to anyone. Which is why I want to get out walking again. But you've honestly turned my life around.' Vi had a tear in her eye.

I really did know what it meant to her. Driftwood Bay had turned my life around too.

Selfishly, it also gave me a boost, being able to help someone else, and I was honestly over the moon.

I could see that Vi was tired so I made sure she was settled in her armchair, and kissed her papery soft cheek before I left, closing the front door behind me. As I meandered back home, I thought it was about time that Clem and I addressed the elephant in the room. I was going to be brave and mention our near-kiss. Up until that point I felt like we were getting on so well and this awkwardness had spoiled all of that.

However, when I got back to the lighthouse, there was a note from Clem pinned to the front door saying that he'd finished up and headed off and would see me later. I'd missed my chance for that day. Now I'd be fretting all night trying to work out when I could raise it again.

# 32

Rat-a-tat-tat went the front door. I skipped down the stairs and was greeted by Lucy and James. James was holding a bottle of pink Freixenet Prosecco in one hand and a box of Corona beers under his arm.

'Apparently, so my darling wife tells me, when it's empty the bottle will look pretty with some lights in, which if you put your hand in my front pocket, we have also brought along.'

'Oh, thanks for the offer but the last time I ferreted around in someone's front pocket, I was nearly arrested so I'll leave that job for Lucy if you don't mind.'

Lucy laughed, appearing from behind him, holding a long wooden planter, brimming over the sides with the most vibrant purple flowers, and giving out a smell which was both floral, herbal and woody at the same time.

'Ah, lavender – my favourite. And that planter is beautiful. Look at the craft work. I love it, thank you.'

'Well, you can thank Clem for that, he's been finishing it off this afternoon. He measured a spot on the balcony and apparently, it should fit perfectly. Bloody heavy though. Not sure why I ended up with this and you ended up with the drinks, dearest husband.'

'Here, let me give you a hand.' Clem appeared behind them and smiled. He took the planter from Lucy, sweeping it out of her hands as if it were weightless. 'Do you like it, Mere?'

Why did my heart skip a beat every time he said my name that way?

'It's stunning.' I leaned forward and gave him a brief hug, not trusting myself to make it longer. 'How can I ever thank you?'

Gemma sprang up in the hallway next, as if from nowhere. 'Oh, I'm sure you'll think of a way.' She winked most obviously as she thrust a huge arrangement of pale pink hydrangea and eucalyptus at me, which again smelled divine. I didn't realise how much I'd missed having fresh flowers around the place and made a little promise to myself to always have them in my home.

Home. That was the first time I'd called the lighthouse that. Just the thought of it warmed my heart.

'Sorry, let's all get out of the hallway and head upstairs. We'll put these things in the kitchen and then I'll give you the guided tour. I hope you love it as much as we do.' I looked over at Clem and smiled.

'Gosh, you sound like an old married couple.'

'Well, maybe not that, but we've made a great team haven't we, Mere?'

'I reckon we have.' I noticed that Clem's eyes were bluer than ever tonight. He was looking mighty fine in a pair of navy linen trousers and a white shirt. He looked casual but smart. And if I thought he wore a pair of utility shorts and a T-shirt well, then this combo was definitely making my temperature rise.

'Meredith? Did you hear me?' James raised his voice. 'Shall I crack open the Prosecco? Maybe we should make a toast.'

I dragged my eyes away from Clem. 'Sorry, I'm not with it tonight. Not used to having so many guests.'

'What a great idea. James,' Lucy said, 'perhaps you could say something nice?'

'Meredith, you've laid the table for six people, you nutter. Though it does look gorgeous.' Gemma ran her hands along the edge. 'I love this wood and you've made it look so pretty.'

'Ah, well...'

There was a knock at the door.

I skipped down the stairs again and opened the front door to greet Russell, who thrust a bottle of Dom Pérignon at me and sprang forward to kiss both of my cheeks.

'Oh, er, thank you.'

'I love it already !' he said effusively. 'You've worked wonders. I can't wait to see the rest.'

'Go on up. The kitchen is on the third floor. You may remember but it might look a little different to the last time you saw it. The others are in there.'

I walked up the stairs behind him and couldn't help but stare at his pert little bum in a pair of tight-fitting black jeans. I mean, honestly, I couldn't help it, it was right there in front of my face.

We reached the kitchen and Russell began to make his greetings.

'Hey, guys, nice to see you. You too, Clement.'

'I never thought to ask if you all knew each other,' I said, watching as the group welcomed him in. 'How great is that?'

Russell kissed Gemma and Lucy on the cheek and then moved to shake hands with James and Clem. Clem's face didn't move a muscle, I noticed. Surely he wasn't still annoyed about the lies he'd told me about this place?

James handed Russell a glass of Prosecco, who took the bottle of champagne from me. 'OK if I pop this in here?' He gestured to the fridge. 'Prosecco is always lovely, but we can have the proper stuff later, eh?' He wedged the bottle into the shelf in the door and returned to my side slinging an arm around my shoulder. 'Well, Meredith, I have to say, you know how to make a silk purse out of a sow's ear. What an amazing job you've done.'

'It was just my ideas really. Clem is the one who did all the hard work and turned it into reality.'

'Yes, but that's the easy part surely. It's the ideas that take all the creativity and you seem to have them by the bucketload. Who'd have thought that this rickety old place, would end up like this. This kitchen is to die for.'

A glance from Lucy to Gemma across the table made me feel a little uneasy. I wasn't sure what was going on here but every time I mentioned how amazing Clem had been there seemed to be a snidey comment from Russell. Was there something that I was missing? Did they have a history that I wasn't aware of?

'Like I say, I have Clem to thank for everything. That's why I wanted to invite you all here tonight. To thank you for being so amazing. To Gemma for knocking on my door on that very first day when I was about to burst into tears when I saw the state of the place.' Russell did have the good grace to look down at the floor at that point. 'To Lucy and James for giving me bed and board at the B & B when I couldn't even get my bed in here to sleep on. To you all for making me feel so welcome into your wonderful community, and for making me feel like I've been here forever already. But, most of all, to you, Clem, for making my dreams come true.'

I held up my glass to Clem and his face softened from his previous frown. His eyes crinkled and he raised his glass back to me and replied, 'Teamwork makes the dream work. The pleasure has been all mine.'

The world felt as if it was standing still as his eyes bore into mine. There could have been a hundred people in the room, or there could have been just him and me. A special moment held in time that I knew I'd never forget.

'And don't forget thanks to me for selling you the lighthouse in the first place, of course.'

And there it was. The moment was broken by Russell's words. There was definitely something in the air tonight that felt a little 'off'.

'Something smells good.' Lucy grinned, changing the subject. 'Thank the lord that dinner doesn't smell of fish for a change!'

'Some people would kill for a fisherman for a husband you know.' James pouted pretending to be hurt.

'Really? Perhaps a week of washing your stinky boiler suits would make them change their mind.'

'Oh, my cod. I do have feelings you know.' He grinned and she went to his side.

'Oh, shut up, or I'll batter you.' She kissed his cheek.

'I'm so lucky. You're the gill of my dreams.'

She laughed and her eyes shone. The love between the two of them was so apparent it was almost overwhelming to be an outsider watching.

'Don't be so shellfish and share that Prosecco around, James.' Lucy turned to the rest of us. 'The secret of a happy marriage is to still laugh at each other's crappy puns, even though you've heard them a hundred times before.' She laughed. 'Now snapper out of it, husband, and let's find out what's for dinner. I'm bloody starving. Can we eat and then do the guided tour? I think I may have to chop off my own arm and eat it if I don't get fed soon, and I need something to soak up the Prosecco.'

I began to get the food out. We could definitely do the tour after dinner.

'Here, let me give you a hand,' Russell said and reached out to take a plate from me.

I looked over at Clem to see he was still staring at Russell and frowning.

'I'm fine thanks,' I said, waving Russell away with the tea towel in my hand. Despite me refusing his help, he still came over to my side and rested his hand on my arm for a little longer than I was comfortable. Behaviour that I thought earlier was flirty, fun and friendly, was now feeling a little overfamiliar.

'But I insist. You tell me what to do and I'll do it. Another secret of a happy marriage, hey, Lucy?'

'Very true.' She smiled at James.

It felt awkward having someone else moving around my kitchen space. Clem and I just fitted together naturally, but with Russell, we seemed to be banging into each other and getting in each other's way. Perhaps I was just being oversensitive. And it wasn't as if Russell would be a permanent fixture. He was just here for the meal. There was a little bit of me that wished I hadn't been so spontaneous and invited him. I never even thought to ask him if he knew the others, and even whether they got on. Trust me to speak before I thought. Something my mother had always pulled me up on in my younger days before she headed off to the States.

I took the lid off the slow cooker and gave it a stir, which led to a chorus of oohs and aahs from the table, the aromas of the food that had been marinating all day diffusing into the air. I put the lid back on and hoped it would stay warm while we had our starters.

I'd made a rosemary and garlic focaccia, which was still warm, and so succulent and light that it literally fell apart when I tried to cut it into pieces. Slices of red and yellow peppers lay alongside celery and spring onions with various dips that I'd picked up and put together that afternoon along with some sundried tomatoes that had been marinating in basil-infused olive oil.

'So how do you guys all know each other then?' I asked as I cleared away the dishes from the first course and carried over more crockery to start the next. Clem seemed particularly quiet tonight, although with Russell around, it was quite hard to get a word in. He was quite the larger-than-life character and seemed to have plenty to say for himself and liked the sound of his own voice.

Clem and Russell spoke at the same time.

'Now that's quite a story!'

'We used to go to school together.'

'They used to be best mates but fell out over a girl,' Gemma added.

The room fell silent. My eyes were drawn to Clem as he and Russell looked daggers at each other across the table. This was about to get interesting!

The timer suddenly rang out and the room was deathly quiet.

Then I heard Russell mutter, 'Phew. Saved by the bell!' under his breath.

'Oh, we've all grown up since those days,' James said, either saving the day or spoiling all the fun; I wasn't quite sure which. 'It's all water under the bridge now, isn't that right?'

Clem and Russell were still looking like they were about to challenge each other to a duel.

'Let's not spoil Meredith's special night by dragging up the past, eh?' The last sentence was more of an order to be obeyed rather than a suggestion.

'So how did you do your pulled pork, Meredith?' Lucy asked, diverting the attention away again. What a tag team she and her husband made. 'I'd love you to share your recipe with me.'

Coming from one of the best cooks I've ever met, I knew that she was just trying to make conversation, so I shared with her my nana's recipe as I placed the casserole dish in the middle of the table and lifted the lid, letting the aromas permeate the air, which – I did have to admit – smelled delightful.

Comfortable chatter resumed around the table while we ate, although Clem was quieter than usual and not his normal self at all.

I started to collect the empty dinner plates. 'Anyone for pudding yet, or do you want a nosey around and have a bit of a break?'

Lucy leaped up from the table. 'Look round please. I've been dying to see what you pair have been up to.'

My eyes shot across to Clem and there was that eyebrow raising again, this time accompanied by a twitch of his lips – something that no one else would probably have noticed. Once again, my heart rate started to rise.

'You OK there, Meredith? Got a bit of a flush going on?' I glared at Gemma; she knew exactly how to wind me up.

'All good thanks, just a bit hot and bothered with all the hot food.'

'And the hot men too,' I heard her mutter as she moved away to the top of the stairs. She winked at me. 'So where shall we start? The bedroom?'

I laughed as I headed over. 'You're so funny.'

'I am, aren't I? Don't let me have any more wine. God knows what might come out of my mouth. Or go in it for that matter.'

I batted her on the arm. 'You're terrible, Gemma.'

'I am, but I'm one of your only friends round here, so you need me.' She grinned and I couldn't help but grin back. I loved her sense of humour and hoped that she and Gabby would get on when Gabby arrived.

As everyone wandered around from one room to another, taking it all in, there were lots of positive sounds coming from Lucy, James and Gemma. Russell was very quiet though. When we arrived back upstairs, he offered to get the champagne from the fridge.

I didn't have any champagne flutes so I had to wash up the glasses we were already using. Russell stood very close by me at the sink. Clem glanced across at me but I couldn't read his expression.

'You know, you'd make a fortune if you sold this place now.

You've worked so hard on it. I could pop round and do a proper valuation, take some pictures, see what interest you'd get. I know you said you were looking to stay here for a while before you decided, but I think you should strike while the iron is hot. I reckon I might already know a buyer who'd snap your hand off.'

I would have felt more comfortable with his advice if he'd have been open in front of my friends, but the way he was speaking in a low whisper was making me feel uneasy. It also felt rude to be having a private conversation when we were all supposed to be together for the evening so I smiled and moved away.

As the cork hit the ceiling, Russell proposed a toast.

'To Driftwood Bay Lighthouse, and all who live in her. And to Meredith and all the hard work she's done to get it to this standard in such a short amount of time.'

'Ah, well, it's Clem I'll be thanking for that. It's him who has done all the hard work, I just threw some ideas at him and he transformed it into what it is. I couldn't have done any of it without him. Thank you, Clem.' We all raised our glasses in his direction and he offered a smile in return but it didn't reach his eyes.

'Good old Clem, eh?' Russell knocked his drink back and I realised that he'd drunk more than any of us so far tonight. 'Anyone would think he had an ulterior motive. But then he always did like to be the hero, didn't you, Clem?'

'That's enough, Russell, don't spoil the evening.' James felt the need to step in.

Why on earth did I invite him tonight? He seemed to be taking a dig at Clem at every opportunity.

Clem's phone dinged and he picked it up. It looked as if he was reading a message.

'Don't worry, mate.' He stood and rested his hand on James's shoulder. 'I need to get off now anyway. Thank you for a lovely meal, Mere. I'll see you soon.' He reached across and pressed his soft lips to my cheek. It felt as if he'd burned an imprint on my skin.

'Are you leaving already?' I could feel my brow furrowing.

'Yes, I'm shattered and could do with an early night. Thanks again. You stay up here with your guests and I'll see myself out.' He raised a hand in a high wave. 'Night guys.'

'Is everything OK, Clem?' I put my hand on his arm as he started to move away from the group.

'Yes, fine thanks. Just a few things on my mind. Goodnight, Mere.'

As Clem descended the stairs, Russell turned to the group and said, 'Poor old Clem.'

'What's that?' I asked of him.

'No money, no prospects and has to live on a boat because he can't afford anything better.'

'I think you'll find that Clem chooses to live on his boat,' I defended.

'You've only just moved here so you don't really know him like we do. I think you'll find that Clem isn't the person you think he is.' He grabbed the nearest bottle, filled his glass, this time with red wine, and knocked it back. 'Bloody superhero Clem.' His words were starting to slur and he slumped back in his chair.

'I think you've had enough, mate. Shall I take you back home?' James walked round the table and started to pull him up. Russell was so tipsy he nearly fell over. I honestly hadn't noticed how much he'd been drinking, which was surprising. My ex-husband was a big drinker and wasn't the nicest drunk, becoming insulting and quite nasty after a few too many. I was reminded of this now. We were all just having a nice relaxing time.

Although I'm not sure Clem enjoyed it as much as the rest of us. Maybe I'd drop him a text later. I know he said everything was OK but it didn't feel like him being tired was the issue, but more the things that were on his mind.

'I'll come back as soon as I've got him home,' James said to Lucy and Gemma, nodding at Russell, who was limping towards us.

'See you, gorgeous.' An arm flung around my shoulders and his lips seemed to be heading for my mouth, but luckily, I turned my face and he left a big slobbery wet kiss on my cheek. 'Thanks for everything and remember what I said.' He waved his arm around the room. 'We would make a packet on this place.'

James led him down the stairs and we heard a yell and a bumping noise.

'Oh, sorry, mate, mind your head,' we could hear James saying, and then he raised his voice as he called out to us. 'We're fine. Back soon.' Then the front door slammed shut. The one thing about living in a lighthouse was that it echoed, a lot.

'Jeez. Thank God for James. Your husband is a saint, sis.'

'I know. Russell was totally off his face. Don't know how it happened so quickly? No one else was.'

'So strange,' said Gemma. 'And I thought that he and Clem had buried their differences years ago. But clearly not. Don't suppose there's any chance of a coffee is there, Meredith? And let's get some of these plates and dishes off the table and we can tidy up.'

The food had gone down well. There was nothing left, which was always good to see, and between the three of us, it took a couple of minutes to clear the table and load the dishwasher.

We headed upstairs with a tray of drinks.

I flung the French doors open, letting the balmy late-evening air in, and then lit some more scented candles making the room glow a beautiful colour. I looked out to the harbour, and even though I couldn't see where Clem's boat was moored, I wondered what he was doing right now. Did I feature as just a tiny part of the things that were on his mind? I turned to Gemma and she smiled gently at me as if she knew what was going on in my head.

'What?'

'Clem's a good guy. Don't let Russell tell you anything different. They have history, but it's Clem's story to tell not mine. But I promise you he's a good un. Don't you be thinking any different.' Gemma tapped the side of her nose and took a sip from her cup.

## 34

The next morning, I couldn't stop checking my phone beside me on the coffee table, but there had been no message back from Clem. I'd texted him before I went to bed just saying that I hoped he was OK. When he'd suddenly left after receiving some mysterious text, it had given me a funny feeling in my tummy. Feminine intuition, I think it's called. Something was awry, I just knew it.

Feeling restless, I decided to take Gladys for an early walk.

The good thing about Vi was that she was an early bird like me, so getting a knock on the door early morning wouldn't come as a surprise. However, that morning, it was me that got the surprise because she was already out doing laps around the garden.

'Morning, my lovely! How are you?'

'Not as bright and breezy as you. You're making an early start today.'

'I am, and I thought when you and Gladys get back we could take a little walk together. I'd love to go on the beach again. It's been such a long time but I didn't want to tackle it on my own. Would you take me?'

'I will and I think it's a good idea to do it when Gladys has already been out; she's always so excitable that I wonder if she's going to knock me off my feet, so I'd really worry that she'd do the same for you.'

'Yes, I was thinking the same. Silly old me, getting myself into a state about the things I used to take for granted. Shall I see you in around an hour then?'

'Perfect. Come on, Glad, let's go walkies.' She went and found her own lead and brought it back to me. I rubbed her head. 'Clever girl.'

The beach was quite deserted. Maybe because it was the weekend and people came out a bit later as they were having a more relaxing time. I kicked off my trainers and left them on my rock and we skipped down to the water's edge. Gladys went in up to her undercarriage, but there was no way I was going in quite that far.

All of a sudden, she darted away and started to run across the beach. Shocked, I looked up only to see that she was running towards Charles, who was running towards her too. It was like a scene from a movie. They greeted each other like kids playing kiss chase. Behind them, Russell was approaching.

I turned back towards the sea, where the sun was twinkling away.

'Morning, Meredith.'

'Morning.' I knew I was being frosty but he had nearly spoiled the evening with his behaviour.

'Before you say anything, I owe you an apology.'

'Go ahead.' I turned to face him and stood with my hands on my hips, suddenly deciding that I wasn't going to make this easy. In fact, I was quite pleased with myself that I wasn't being the pushover that I normally am.

He took his Ray-Bans off and perched them on the top of his head.

'I don't know what came over me last night. All I can think is
that I'm on some tablets from the doctor, and when I checked the
packet this morning, it said to avoid drinking alcohol with them.'

'That'll probably do it.' I folded my hands in front of my chest. I
was glaring at him, but he couldn't really tell because I'd left my
sunglasses on.

'I'm sorry. Honestly. James called me earlier, waking me up, and
told me that I was a total tosser. I don't remember a lot after we did
the tour of the lighthouse. And may I just say what a spectacular
job you've done of it.'

'Clem and I have done a spectacular job, you mean?'

The old Meredith would have accepted what he'd said and
moved on, not saying what I thought just to keep the peace but this
Meredith was going to be true to herself and have her say. I really
didn't like the way he totally ignored how much effort Clem had put
into all the work. He deserved so much more credit than Russell
had given him last night and I was determined that he was going to
accept this today.

'Yes, that's right. You've both clearly worked hard and I'm sorry
if that didn't come across last night.'

'Yes, it's both of us who have done the work. Clem has been a
saint.'

I tilted my head as Russell rolled his eyes, but he very quickly
tried to cover it up, turning on that kilowatt smile.

'And what about the fact that you were trying to pressure me
into selling it? I haven't even considered that possibility and don't
want to right now. I just want to enjoy living there.'

'Oh God! I'm sorry about that too. I just remember you originally saying that you were buying it as a project and might sell it on.
I just wanted to let you know that you would make a considerable
amount of money.'

'Well, perhaps the way you went about it wasn't ideal. It made me feel uncomfortable and I didn't like it.'

'I'm sorry! Forgive me, please. In fact, come out for lunch with me today. Let me make it up to you.'

'It's fine, you don't have to do that.' I thought at this stage that I'd said my piece and that I'd made him grovel enough.

'I insist. Let me show you that I'm not that dickhead who came to your dinner party last night. You might even like me if you met the real me.' He lowered his eyes and looked at me from under his lashes, flirtatiously. 'I'll pick you up at twelve thirty and we can head out somewhere nice. Let me show you some places that I love around here that I think you'll like too. Go on, say yes. Please.'

He was like a child begging his parent for an ice cream. But I'd made him suffer enough. Lunch would be nice, but honestly, I really needed to stop eating all the time. My shopping list needed to be full of fruit and veg to make up for all the meals out I was having.

'OK, I'll see you then. Come on, Gladys. We need to get back.'

With that, I turned on my heel and began to walk away. To get back to Vi's, we went around the harbour, a route I chose with an ulterior motive. It just so happened that Clem lived there so if I saw him, then I could check and ask if he was OK.

As we approached *Penelope Plump*, I dithered, wondering whether to give the door a knock to see if he was around. Eventually, I told myself to stop dilly-dallying and just do it. I was just about to step on board, when, startled, I heard raised voices and footsteps from below deck.

'Well, you'll have to sort it out. I can't cope with all this secrecy.'

'That's why you have to help me, Clem.' It was a woman's voice. High-pitched, young sounding. 'I don't even know if I want to keep this baby and it's not going to be long before I'm showing.'

I gasped, wondering what on earth I was overhearing. My heart began pounding. I was rooted to the spot, not wanting to hear what was coming next but at the same time desperate to know.

'If we want people to accept us as a couple, we have a lot of work to do,' the woman said.

'I just don't know if I can do it, Soph.'

'I need your help now more than ever. You'd better grow a pair and help me get this situation sorted out.'

The tip-tap of footsteps was getting closer so I moved back, just in time to avoid getting hit by the door as it opened. I found myself looking into the prettiest of faces, framed by flowing white-blonde, poker-straight hair.

I just stood there with my mouth gaping open staring at her, taking in her slim waist and how glamorous she looked in tight white jeans. She had a red cashmere cardigan draped around her shoulders over a white strappy top. The woman – Soph – smiled at me sweetly and said good morning.

It was only then that I noticed the tiniest of bumps, which her hand was resting upon.

My heart felt like it had dropped out of my upper body into my feet. Who on earth was this woman who was clearly pregnant, and what was she doing coming out of Clem's boat?

I could hear footsteps approaching the stairs and starting to climb so I tugged on Gladys's lead and pulled her away.

Clem's voice called out to me. 'Mere, wait!'

But nothing was going to make me hang back to speak to him. I thought that even though he and I had never said we were anything more than good friends, there was something more there and, being totally honest with myself, I wanted there to be. But now I felt like such a complete and utter idiot. I'd obviously read the situation the wrong way and it seemed I had been the only one to do so. Clem had clearly got other irons in the fire – or maybe buns in the oven.

## 35

I was clearly flustered when I got back to Vi's. I knew that when I got myself in a state like this, I got all blotchy and hot and when she asked me what on earth was wrong, I could hardly speak. She led me to a chair in the lounge and went and made a cup of tea. The lounge overlooked the harbour, but luckily, I couldn't see all the way round to where Clem's boat was moored.

Outside, I heard the gate slam and there was a knock at the door. Muffled voices could be heard but it was almost like it was going on underwater because I couldn't focus on anything. My head was pounding.

Suddenly, a mug appeared on the table in front of me but it wasn't Vi who put it there.

'Mere. It's not what you think.'

I looked up into Clem's beautiful blue eyes. I waved him away and took a deep breath.

'It's nothing to do with me what you get up to in your spare time. I just didn't realise that you were seeing someone. And, to be honest, I don't think of you in that way anyway. We're just friends. We've already discussed this.'

'But, Mere, let me explain.'

'Nothing to explain, Clem. Now if you don't mind, Vi and I have got plans so could you leave now, please.'

'Mere.'

'Just go, please. I'm busy.'

He huffed as he backed away from me and then turned on his heel, leaving as quickly as he'd appeared. 'Suit yourself.'

I sipped at my tea and could hear him talking to Vi in the kitchen before the door slammed, quickly followed by the sound of the rattle of the gate latch outside.

'You should hear him out, you know.'

'I don't want to discuss it, Vi. I'm sorry and I really don't mean to be rude to you, but let's just crack on with this walking, shall we?'

'But—'

'Vi, I mean it. I'm not discussing it.'

'Well, don't say I didn't try. But you are a silly girl, you know.'

My lip wobbled but I held my shoulders back and filled my lungs with air, determined that a man would not make me cry again. I'd done enough crying when I was back in Staffordshire and one of the reasons for getting a new start in life was so that I didn't have to feel like this again. Dating was clearly not for me right now and maybe not ever and I just needed to accept it. Friends were all I needed and I had a good few of those. And Gabby would be here tomorrow.

I took another deep breath and composed myself, knocking back the last of my tea and plonking my mug down on the table.

'Come on, let's get you walking. I don't really fancy the harbour again this morning but how about we head up to the shops and see how far we get?'

Vi took my arm and folded her hand around it. I had calmed down somewhat and hopefully looked a whole lot better too.

We walked past Martin's shop where he insisted on coming out to say hello and tell us how delighted he was to see Vi out and about again. Gemma came out of the bakery too and asked if we wanted anything putting aside to pick up on the way back. I ordered a loaf and a pack of lemon doughnuts. They were my favourite and I had visions of holing up inside the lighthouse that afternoon and eating the whole pack to myself to drown my sorrows. Surely it was better to do that than to crack open a bottle of gin. Look what had happened the last time I got smashed on my own after a heartbreak. God only knows what I'd end up buying this time.

Vi ordered a Belgian bun, which made me smile, bringing forth a memory of Nana. We always used to call them a Belgian's bum after Nana took a fancy to a very handsome man called Yannick when we went to the Christmas markets in Brussels. Vi thought the story was most entertaining and vowed to call them the same from now on.

We made it as far as the mini-market, but by this point, Vi was looking a little tired. I asked her if she'd like to sit on the wall and wait for me while I popped in and picked up a couple of bits, which she readily agreed to. I checked that she was safely seated before entering the shop.

Dyllis seemed in surprisingly good spirits today, which was a shock, and then I noticed the blonde woman standing next to her.

'Good morning, Meredith. Have you met my daughter Sophie? She's a very good friend of Clement's.' She turned to Sophie. 'A very good friend, aren't you, my lovely girl?'

Crikey, so the woman escaping from Clem's boat this morning was Dyllis's daughter. That was a turn up for the books. But if her being around meant that Dyllis would be civil to me, then maybe that was a good thing.

'Nice to meet you, Sophie. And, er, congratulations.' I eyed up her bump again.

'Thank you. It's actually still a secret but I know that you overheard us talking this morning. I'd appreciate it if you might keep it quiet for the time being if it's not too much to ask.'

'Of course.'

Smiling nervously, I handed my money over to a smug Dyllis. I couldn't wait to get out. To think that Clem and Sophie were having a baby together and he hadn't thought to mention it in all the time that we'd spent together. It was honestly beyond me.

'Oh, wait, I'll walk out with you,' Sophie called to me. Great, that was all I needed. 'See you later, Mum.'

Outside, Sophie greeted Vi like an old friend but I didn't want to stick around to chat. I couldn't bear to hear her talking about Clem being a dad. I'm sure she was very nice and all but with the shock of the news, and added to that the fact that she was Dyllis's daughter – the woman who seemed to hate me – I just needed to get away from her.

Then it suddenly started to dawn on me why her mum had been acting the way she had. She must have known I had designs on Clem, when he was clearly fathering her future grandchild.

Vi could sense that I was feeling uncomfortable. 'Sophie, we must go before I piddle myself. My bladder isn't what it used to be.' I had to stop myself from laughing out loud at this. 'I just hope I don't sneeze too hard. It's hard to say what'll come out of where at my age.'

Sophie looked absolutely horrified at the thought and thankfully shuffled away up the street. Meanwhile, Vi and I meandered back down to her house via the bakery. She was clearly shattered but she'd done so well.

'Oh, I'm bloody knackered, Meredith, but I'm so proud of

myself. I can't wait to get up to that crocheting club next week. I'm going to have a little snooze now and get my energy back but thank you for your time. You are such a good 'un.' She patted my hand. 'And a word to the wise. Things aren't always what they seem. Don't forget, even salt looks like sugar!'

## 36

My plan for the rest of the afternoon was to turn off my phone, hunker down and watch cheesy romcoms on Netflix back to back. I had just turned on the first one and taken a huge bite into the lemon doughnut, though not estimating very well where the filling hole was, because I squirted it all down my chin, when there was a knock at the door. I ignored it, hoping that whoever it was would go away, but the persistent banging showed no sign of letting up.

I trudged down the stairs and reached the bottom, flinging the door open.

'Oh shit!' I let out the expletive before I could hold it back.

'Nice to see you too, Meredith. Your chariot awaits.' Russell waved his arm to the space behind him where a silver Mercedes convertible gleamed in the sunlight.

'Sorry, Russell, I had totally forgotten about lunch. I'm not even ready. I've had a bit of a morning. Can we do it another day?'

'Absolutely not. If you've had a crap morning then this is exactly what you need. Now go and wipe away whatever is dribbling down your chin before I'm tempted to lick it all off, grab a jacket and let's go.'

I frowned at him. I really wasn't in the mood for this.

'Chop-chop. You have five minutes and if you're not out by then, I'm coming in to get you.' He tilted his head to one side. 'Go on. Stop being a mardy arse. I have the perfect antidote for a bad day. Trust me. It'll be fun!'

Ten minutes later, we were tearing through the country lanes, heading away from Driftwood Bay with the wind in our hair and Meatloaf's 'Bat Out of Hell' playing at a ridiculously loud volume. Russell was absolutely right though. This did blow the cobwebs away along with my bad mood, and by the time the extended version of the song finished, after we'd sung the lyrics, which I already knew off by heart, at the top of our voices, I felt like a different person.

Russell was great company, which was just what I needed. He was slightly flirty, enough to make me feel good about myself, but not overly so to make me feel uncomfortable and he was the perfect gentleman. The restaurant he took me to initially looked like a beach shack but when you got inside turned out to be a fabulously classy bistro, nestled within its own private cove with the most spectacular coastal views. He asked lots of questions about the lighthouse and we did talk about whether I would sell. He reckoned that after doing all the additional things that I had plans for, I would have added £150,000 to the value. I nearly fell off my chair when he said this. I hadn't done the final sums completely but by the time I'd done everything I wanted to do, including getting the outside sorted, I reckon I would have spent probably £25,000, including Clem's labour costs.

A challenge was what he had promised me when I first agreed to buy Driftwood Bay Lighthouse and it was certainly what I'd got. I remembered back to that first day I arrived, and the fact that it was totally uninhabitable. I did take the opportunity to remind him that he should maybe have told me that, and he did have the good grace to be ashamed.

'I needed a quick sale, so I may have omitted some of the details. But anyway, I never thought that the mad bird on the end of the phone would actually buy a lighthouse that she'd never even seen. I had to snap your hand off before you changed your mind.'

'I know, what was I thinking? It's honestly the most spontaneous thing I've ever done in my life. And actually, I think possibly the best thing I've ever done too.'

He smiled at me and chinked his glass of sparkling water against my cold Pinot Grigio. And when I suggested splitting the bill, he said he would hear nothing of the sort.

It was late afternoon when we arrived back at Driftwood Bay. As we passed the pub, I could see Clem was walking up towards it. He glared at Russell and just smiled sadly at me. I had my sunglasses on, so he couldn't see that my eyes may have also looked sad, but I raised my hand in a small wave.

'Do you mind if I pop in to use your loo, Meredith?' Russell asked when we reached the lighthouse.

As I let him in and turned to close the front door, I saw Clem still standing there out on the road, watching us.

When it was time to say goodbye to Russell – I wanted to spend the evening on my own getting everything ready for Gabby's arrival tomorrow – I thanked him for a lovely afternoon, kissed him on the cheek and waved him off. Clem was no longer around so I presumed he'd gone up to the pub, probably to see the mother of his child, I thought a little bitterly.

I breathed deeply, stood up straight and headed back inside. It was none of my business what Clem got up to. We were just friends and I would just have to adjust to that way of thinking.

## 37

The sound of tyres on the gravel driveway had me running down the stairs to greet Gabby the minute she got out of the car.

'Gabs! Oh my God, am I pleased to see you?' I grabbed her and then hung on for dear life as we swayed from side to side.

'God, Meredith. You give the best hugs. I always did say it's because you have squishy boobs.' We laughed, still not letting go. It had only been a few weeks since we'd seen each other, but it felt like years.

'Right, get off me, you weirdo, and show me around this place. I can't wait any longer. I'll grab my bags later. It had better be worth the wait! I can't believe you wouldn't even send me any photos!'

'It would have spoilt the effect. Are you ready then?'

'You bet your life I am.'

We walked towards the front door and I couldn't stop grinning. Gabby held her phone up, showing the original picture and as she compared the photo to the real thing, I realised it really didn't look like the same place. The frame and actual door had both been sanded and painted so they looked brand new. Where there was a concrete base at the entrance before, there was now a small, paved

area with raised local slate semicircles, and buxus plants, wrapped
in fairy lights, in tall plant pots either side of the front door

Inside, Gabby gasped as she looked around.

I was literally grinning from ear to ear. The spare bedroom was
next and she oohed and aahed in all the right places when I showed
her where she'd be sleeping. She said that she adored my bedroom
and when we headed to the kitchen on the next floor she was
astounded by the views, wandering from one side to the other. She
was saying less and less the further up the lighthouse we went. I
hoped this was a good sign, but, at that particular moment, I
couldn't tell.

When we ascended the final staircase and she saw the lounge,
she headed over to the French doors and was literally lost for
words. I had been tidying the house all morning and it was immac-
ulate. I wanted it to look perfect for when she arrived. And to be
honest, I was using her as a trial run as, even though I'd been trying
to avoid looking at the calendar, next week was the week my
mother was coming to stay.

Gabby walked out onto the iron balcony and looked at the view;
to the right the sun was glistening on the sea over the sandy bay.
She turned her head to the left and saw boats in the harbour. The
gulls dived and soared across the sky, and there was that wind-
chime noise again of the boats' ropes jangling against the masts.
She turned to face me with the hugest of grins on her face.

'Meredith. It's absolutely perfect.'

I let out the breath I'd been holding in.

'You really think so?'

'I have never been more fucking proud of you in my life,
Meredith Robinson. Look at what you've done.' She extended her
arm around the room. 'I'm honestly bowled over. Not that I thought
you couldn't do it, of course. I knew all along that you had it within
you, but that you've done it so quickly and so bloody brilliantly and

beautifully has... I don't know how to express it. It's fabulous and you, my love, are incredible.' She paced across the room and wrapped me in her arms.

It felt good to feel some touch. While Gemma and Lucy were my friends, we didn't really know each other enough to be huggy. I had warmed to Gabby immediately, not realising that I was quite a touchy-feely person too until she had pointed it out.

'If you go back to graphic design, I may have to kill you. You must do something with this talent of yours. It's such a waste if you don't.'

'Well, I have some ideas in that area. I was going to chat to you about it while you are here, but what do you want to do first? I know you've had a long journey so you might want to freshen up and have a rest. Or do you fancy heading up to the local for a pub lunch? Or take a walk around the village, the beach, the harbour?' While my heart sank a little thinking of Clem and his boat in the harbour, I wanted to show her everywhere.

'I don't think I've ever seen you look so well, Mere.' She stood back to admire me. 'It suits you here, you look so chilled and at home. I want to do all of those things you've suggested, but yes, a quick shower and a cup of tea would be awesome and then maybe we can head out for some lunch. And then maybe you can tell me what's behind that tinge of sadness I can feel you have going on right now.'

'Oh, I'm fine. Come here. It's so good to see you.' I reached out to hug her again. She knew me so well.

I honestly think that female friendships are underestimated. This person in front of me, who was so important to me, gave me confidence, assurance, brought joy to my life just by being in it. I knew that no matter what I did, whether she thought I was right or wrong, she would always have my back and I knew that I'd always be able to depend on her. The best kind of friendships are those where you aggressively believe in each other and defend each other and know that with every beat of your heart that the other deserves the world and you would do anything to help them to achieve it.

I wondered whether putting distance between us would affect our friendship, but I knew the moment she stepped out of that car that, if anything, it might make our friendship stronger, that we wouldn't ever take our friendship for granted again. Truth be told, it was all feeling a bit overwhelming but in the best of ways.

\* \* \*

A couple of hours later, we were in the window seat at the pub, which had the best view in the building. They did a wicked Sunday lunch here and we'd both demolished the roast of the day as well as a glass of wine to wash it down with. We were just saying how stuffed we were when the door opened and in came Clem, followed by Sophie. They were laughing at something but when he locked eyes with me across the room he frowned and turned to the bar.

'Phwoar. Is that Clem? God he's even fitter in real life!' The pub was quite quiet for a Sunday lunchtime and her voice carried. I saw Clem's mouth twitch for a second.

'Keep your voice down, Gabs.'

'Well, he's the hottest bloke I've seen for months.'

'He's just the guy who has been doing up my lighthouse.'

Gabs raised a questioning eyebrow.

'Ok so he's a really nice bloke and he's been incredible at his work. We're just friends. Good friends. Nothing more. Just friends.'

She narrowed her eyes at me. 'OK, I hear you.' She peered at me and pursed her lips. 'OK.'

'OK what? That's it.'

'All right. Keep your knickers on.'

'It's a long story. I'll tell you later. Come on, let's go and walk this dinner off. I'll introduce you to Vi and Gladys.'

As we walked past the bar, Clem turned and nodded at me. I fake smiled and we shared a moment. Something that made me question what was in his gaze. I glanced across at Sophie and she smiled sadly at me as I whispered goodbye to no one in particular. What did all of this mean?

\* \* \*

Gabby and I headed out to the beach, stopping at Vi's first to pick up Gladys, and Gabby once again was lost for words when she saw how close I lived to the white sandy beach.

'Oh, Mere. How could you ever leave this place? It's just divine. I don't think even I will want to leave. What a little treasure you've stumbled across here. I've only been here a few hours and I feel more relaxed than I have in months. And I can tell already how it's working wonders for you.'

'I've never felt better to be honest. I feel alive. I feel full of hope and joy. I love it.'

'I can see how happy you are here. But I know you, Mere, and I know when you've got something on your mind. I might even have a clue as to who is behind it. Now, are you going to tell me what's going on with this Clem guy or not?'

Just as I was about to launch into the story, I heard a voice shout my name and saw Russell heading over towards us. Once again Gladys bounded over to Charlie and they played chase, covering a great deal of the beach.

'Bloody hell, another hottie. What's in the water around here?'

I grinned at her.

'Gabby meet Russell. Russell, this is my best friend in the whole world, Gabby. Russell is the estate agent who sold me the lighthouse.'

'Really? I thought you said the tosser who sold it to you had done a runner and you couldn't get hold of him?'

'Yes, I'm that tosser, I'm afraid. Nice to meet you.'

'Oh God. Sorry!' At least she had the decency to look mortified.

'Misunderstanding. Family bereavement that I had to attend to in a different part of the country. I try not to be a tosser if I can help it.' He smiled broadly and I realised that she was right; he was quite a hottie. And he was also so lovely on our day out yesterday...

I shook the thought away. Maybe I should stop thinking about the men in Driftwood Bay as potential partner material, and just stick to my friends-only vow. It would surely be far easier. But then when I looked at Russell and his eyes met mine, I did feel myself blushing.

'Charles, no! No! Stop!' We turned around to see what Russell was shouting at and watched, horrified, as Charles mounted Gladys from behind. He was clearly enjoying himself very much.

'Oh lord, stop him. Vi will kill me if she gets up the duff.'

Russell giggled at my panic.

'Go on, my son!' He laughed. 'Sorry, but please don't worry, I'm 99 per cent sure he's been done. He's just clearly fallen a little bit in love with your Gladys. And to be honest if I was a dog I would too. She's a beaut.'

Gabby raised an eyebrow and we laughed.

'Too much?' Russell asked.

'Way too much.' Gabby and I spoke as one voice.

'OK, I know when I'm being ganged up on. I shall take my trusty Labrador home and you can have the freedom of the beach again. I shall bid you good afternoon.' He held his hand up to his ear, making the phone gesture, and mouthed 'Call me!' Then he winked and walked away.

What was it with the men of Driftwood Bay? They sure were a funny breed.

## 38

'So, Gabby, what's young Meredith told you about the handsome Clem then?'

'Sadly, not much. Why? Do you have some gossip for me?'

'I am here you know!' I shouted through from the kitchen; however, you wouldn't have known it as Vi and Gabby continued their conversation regardless.

'Well, in a nutshell. She fancies the pants off him. He fancies the pants off her. She thinks that he's too young for her and now she thinks he's been having some "how's-your-father" with someone else and not told her. She won't listen when he tries to explain. And it's not getting anywhere. Yes. I think that's about the crux of it.'

Gabby looked towards me as I walked back into the room. 'I love her already.'

'Oh, you have noticed me then?'

'You know I'm right,' Vi continued. 'You can't keep your eyes off him.'

'And do you know about Russell too, Vi?' Gabby asked, eyes bright.

'Russell?'

'The estate agent. It seems that they've been on a date and he's got the hots for her too. I can tell these things. God, I let you move to a new place to get away from the dating scene and you're fighting the local men off with a shitty stick.'

'Stop it, the pair of you. I am not fighting anyone off. I'm just trying to make a new life for myself in a new village and meet new people and make new friends. That's all. It's hardly like they're duelling over me, is it? And if they're both gorgeous, whose fault is that?'

'Our Dennis said he thought you were a bit of all right too.'

'Oh, so there's Dennis to chuck into the mix too then? Tell me more, Vi.'

'You'll do no such thing. There is nothing to talk about. What are your plans for the rest of the day? Are we going for a spin round the village, or not?'

Maybe changing the subject might make the pair of them shut up about my love life, or in fact, lack of it.

'I'd love to,' Vi said. 'I was thinking, now I'm getting my stamina back, that one of the days, we could even walk as far as the pub. What do you think? Maybe even this evening. But I don't want to scupper any plans you two might have. I know you've only just arrived, my dear.'

'I think that's a marvellous idea. Now, are we cutting that cake or just looking at it?' Gabby grinned at Vi and I could see that they were already firm friends. It seemed that having a common thing to focus on was the basis of a good friendship.

'I thought you said you couldn't eat another thing?'

'I did, you're right but it must be the sea air giving me an appetite. Let's have some cake and then we can head back to the pub. Let's get Vi out on the pull. We might even get her a date if we play our cards right.'

'Oh lord. I'm too old and lazy these days for all that malarkey.

I'm not even entertaining the thought. All these things you have to do to get yourself a man and keep him isn't really up my street. Having to have all these Brazilian waxes and vajazzles on your fandango and wearing a thong up your arse. They can bugger right off.' She winked at me. 'I'd rather have a nice cup of tea.'

I literally spat my drink out and I thought Gabby was going to give herself a hernia. 'Oh, Vi, you are hilarious.'

'I am, aren't I? Come on, girls, let's go and get shit-faced at the pub!'

## 39

We had the most delightful couple of days. Gabby met Lucy and Gemma, and the three of them got on like a house on fire, just like I hoped they would. And Gabby was relieved, knowing that she was able to leave me in their capable hands.

Feeling sad and quite alone, I waved her off to head back to the Midlands and for me to face the next obstacle in my life. My mother. I had two days to make sure that the place was perfect.

In fairness, there wasn't much to do but she was one of those mothers who would come in and wipe her finger over the top of a door to see if there was dust, so I needed to clean the place to within an inch of its life. I didn't want to give her any room to criticise me. I wanted to show her what I'd done with my life and the skills I'd learned along the way. And, more than anything, I wanted to make her proud of me, or at least acknowledge what I'd achieved. Not that I had high expectations; where my mother was concerned, I was always left bitterly disappointed.

Clem was clearly keeping a low profile. I did bump into Martin, and he said that Clem was working on a new project at the top end of the village, and when I popped into the mini-market, Dyllis had great pleasure in telling me that this new project was the home Sophie was looking to move into.

'Are you coming along to the summer beach party next weekend?' she asked. 'Everyone will be there. Sophie. Clem too, I'm sure.' She locked her eyes onto mine, and it felt as if she was digging to see what my reaction was going to be.

'Wouldn't miss it for the world. My mother arrives in a couple of days, so she'll be here for it too. Sounds like it'll be a hoot.'

'It is. There'll be a big fire and a firework display. Everyone comes from the village and it's always a fabulous event. So, your mother is coming then? Where does she live?'

She really was a proper nosy old goat and I wasn't going to give her anything. Not when she'd been so unfriendly to me. She did seem to have thawed over the last couple of days, but maybe that was because her daughter was here and Clem was now working at hers instead of mine. But I didn't care. I was glad. I didn't want to have enemies in my new home. I'd never been the sort to fall out with people. I'm a lover not a fighter.

Wandering back to the lighthouse, my head was full of thoughts. My therapist told me that I was always overly nice to others because of my mother's behaviour towards me. That and the fact that I thought that it would make people like me. I tried so hard to be the perfect daughter however, my mother did use it to her advantage and manipulated situations so that I ended up pandering to her every whim. And then she would always bugger off and leave me with Nana anyway. I loved being with Nana, but she wasn't my mother, and I couldn't understand what I'd done to make her feel that way towards me. I was always trying to work out what I could do to make her love me more. I think that made me clingy and that made the problem even worse. A vicious circle, I suppose, but as a child I didn't really understand. Even as an adult it's hard to work out and I was just grateful that Nana was the person that she was and took me under her wing.

Vi was so like her, and it was nice to have an older person in my life again. Although Vi was continuously swearing and saying things to shock me, much more than Nana ever did.

It felt strange that Clem wasn't around every day, and I was missing his presence a great deal. The lighthouse seemed so quiet without him in it. Ever since I'd been there, he'd been there with me. We were a bit like a contented married couple. Without the sex.

I flushed as I wondered why I was thinking about Clem and sex in the same context once again.

'We've been in training for a while now. Do you think you're ready for this?'

'Just you try and stop me. Sorry, Gladys. You'll have to stay home alone for a couple of hours. I can't risk you getting excited and tripping me over again. Right then. I'm as ready as I'm ever going to be. Let's go.'

We started a slow and steady walk from Vi's house, reaching the bottom of the high street quicker than I thought we would, and Vi did well. She stopped to chat to people along the way whom she hadn't seen for a very long time. When she'd first become incapacitated they had come to visit her, but then apparently they had gone back to their normal lives. But I could see she held no resentment and everyone said how fabulous it was to see her back out and about.

'I'm sure you know by now that I'm a stubborn old bugger and I'll do this if it's the last thing I do. Even if I drop down dead when I reach the church hall.'

'Oh lord, don't let that happen, I haven't got the energy to deal with all of that today.' I winked at her, and she smiled back.

'While we're talking about that, there's something I'd like you to be aware of, if you don't mind. Dennis won't let me talk about anything to do with death, but it's inevitable that it's going to happen to me one day in the not-too-distant future and I wondered if I could tell you a few things I've organised, just in case. Then you can tell him for me if I'm not able to between now and then.'

'Do we really have to talk about this?'

'Yes, we do. It's important to me. Hear me out, please.'

'Oh, go on then. If I must.' I tried to make light of the heavy situation.

She patted my hand. 'You must.'

She turned to face me, her face suddenly very serious.

'I've left some papers in the bureau in the dining room. The password for my iPad is written in there and all my banking details too. At least that way it makes it easier for him to find my logins. I've written all my requests in another document and my will is there too. But above all, I want to know that you will make sure that Gladys goes to a good home. I know Dennis couldn't have her as he's out at work all day long and does a lot of travelling and I couldn't bear to think of her having to go to a dogs' home and sit in a pen waiting for someone to choose her.' A lone tear ran down her cheek. 'The thought of that breaks my heart.'

'I promise,' I said genuinely.

'Thank you, my dear girl. I honestly think that people come into your life for a reason. And I think you—' she reached out and patted my face '—came into mine to help me. Before I met you, I had resigned myself to a life of never leaving the house and that it was nearly the end of the road. Even the thought of venturing outside got my anxiety at an all-time high. It was the beginning of the end and I think I was giving up. I would have done if Dennis had insisted on Gladys going into a home. A month ago, I would never have dreamed that I'd be walking up this very high street to be joining a crocheting group. You are my fairy godmother, and I can't thank you enough!'

'Aw, Vi, be off with you. I have so much time on my hands, it's been a pleasure to have someone fabulous to spend it with. And taking Gladys out is good for my mental health too – and my belly! Living here and being surrounded by people who are feeders has meant that I'd be piling on the pounds if I wasn't out walking with Gladys every day.'

'Well, perhaps we're just perfect pals for each other then.'

'I'll drink to that! Well, I would if I had a drink. Now come on, let's get you inside that church hall and get you a cuppa and a chair.'

As we entered, a cheer went up. Dyllis, for all her faults, had told everyone that Vi was coming along and they all made such a huge fuss of her that she was practically whisked away from me the minute we arrived. I heard lots of offers of tea and cake and chatter and Vi looked like she was in her element.

Dyllis met my eye and nodded, and I smiled.

I walked away from the church hall with joy in my heart and I felt so very proud of what Vi had achieved. And really it was all under her own steam. I just motivated and encouraged her along the way.

Glancing at my watch, I realised that if I got a shimmy on, I'd got a good two hours to clean the lighthouse again before I returned to pick Vi up from her expedition. I needed to make sure the place was spotless before my mother arrived.

**41**

Ridiculously nervous, and after spending an hour preparing some of my mother's favourite food, I was pottering around tidying up in the garden room, when I heard an engine on the drive. I turned to see a taxi pull up and my mother unfold herself from the back seat. She barked orders to the driver to take her Louis Vuitton cases to the front door. She couldn't see me, but I could tell by the way she fleetingly raised her eyebrows and nodded to herself that she was impressed; an emotion I'd very rarely seen from her in my life.

Taking a deep breath, I pushed my shoulders back, braced myself, pasted a smile on my face and headed over.

'Oh, hello, Meredith. What an impr—interesting building.' She leaned across and air-kissed either side of my face.

'It is, isn't it? I can't wait to show you around.'

'I passed a pub on the way into the harbour. How about you take my luggage inside and then I'll take you out for an early lunch?'

'Well, I have got food in...'

'The pub looked nice; I think we'll go there if you don't mind.'

So much for my food plan then, but I didn't want to disappoint her as soon as she'd arrived, so, as usual, I agreed to keep the peace. I placed her cases just inside the hallway, locked the door behind me and we headed up to the pub.

Luckily, because we were early, the window seat was available, and Geoff came over to take our order. My mother chose a tomato juice – she was on a health kick – and I opted for my usual white coffee.

'Oh, darling,' she said, looking at me in that condescending way she did. 'You shouldn't have too much caffeine you know, it's not good for you.'

Geoff jumped to my rescue. 'Don't worry about that. Meredith always has decaf, don't you, my lovely?' He winked at me as he turned away. I had never asked for decaf in my life, but he could clearly pick up on a vibe.

We both picked a mango chicken salad although my mother tutted when I ordered a bowl of fries to accompany mine, despite going on to snaffle about half the bowl herself.

Over the years I'd discovered that the best way to endear yourself to my mother was to get her talking about herself so I asked her about the retreat she'd been on. She did seem a little less highly strung and less dramatic than normal, so hopefully it had been a great influence on her. When Geoff came over with the food, he asked if she was my sister and that clearly had a wonderful effect on her.

I watched her as she moved her hands around while she spoke to him and pondered. Why on earth did she create these feelings within me? Since living in Driftwood Bay, I'd felt like I had truly become me, but I couldn't be myself with her as I was still seeking her approval.

I took a moment to really look at her. She was such a truly attractive lady, maybe even pretty if she smiled more. She was clearly tanned from spending time in Bali, wore expensive, well-tailored clothes and her trademark Oscar de la Renta perfume lingered around her. She held herself tall and straight and her glossy dyed auburn locks fell perfectly onto her shoulders with the ends flicking out. Classy, Gabby always used to say, and she was right. She turned heads for sure but had always had this aloof quality about her, both to me and others.

I'm not sure why the memory flooded back to me now, but I was taken back to an evening when my nana was out and my mother and I were snuggled up together on the sofa, watching a film. I remember turning to her and seeing a tear roll down her cheek. She reached out to me, tucked a wayward strand of my hair behind my ear, and told me to never let anyone take advantage of me, no matter who they were and how much I loved them. Those words came back to me now, forgotten for all those years, and I wondered why she'd never really thawed again in all this time.

## 42

The village was buzzing with excitement for the annual beach party and I felt so lucky to be part of it. There had been a meeting of the planning committee a couple of days before at the pub when the final preparations were confirmed. It was a surprise to find out that Geoff had a catering trailer which he drove onto the beach each year, and which made life a whole lot easier for food and drink requirements.

All I had to do was to get myself ready and get down to the beach about half an hour before it started to help to put up the gazebos. Vi was beyond excited to be coming along and I'd arranged for Geoff to pick her up on the golf cart. He was also taking some of the more substantial but moveable pub furniture from the decking area for the older members of the community. I'd offered to take a load of throws along so people could put them over their knees, specifically thinking about Vi.

There had been no word from Clem for days. It felt so strange after all that time that we were working on the lighthouse together. Even when we weren't together, we had been constantly texting each other about the things that were going on. The silence felt sad, and I missed that constant contact with him. Oh well. We were clearly not meant to be best friends, or anything more, and no amount of dwelling on it would change that.

Nana always used to say that you can't change a situation, or another person. All you could do was to change your reaction to them, and I had to thank my blessings for the new life that had been offered to me down here in Cornwall.

I had enjoyed the renovation process, but I think probably because of Clem more than anything else. I had to have a real good think about whether I stayed or moved on. But if I did something similar in a new location, would I make good friends again? Had I got the energy to start all over a second time after I'd just got myself settled here? Maybe once was enough. It really had been hard work.

So much to think about but I had finally decided to trust the universe and hope that the answers would come to me rather than to force them. The future is not promised to anyone, so it was up to me to make the most of my life each day and put the joy into it daily. I seemed to have learned over the last few weeks that joy doesn't always have to be the big things. It can be lighting a scented candle, arranging fresh flowers, or even just sitting and watching the gentle waves of the sea lapping at the shore.

Sometimes I could lose hours just sitting and appreciating my surroundings, which was something very new to me. I always used to feel like I had to fill every moment of my time, but since I'd moved to Driftwood Bay, I had felt more at peace with myself and with life in general. I think it suited me and if that meant that I had to watch Clem and Sophie playing happy families then I would just have to get over it.

Mum and I were getting on so much better too. Her hard shell seemed to be cracking. She was softer than I'd ever known her to be and it had been a nice surprise to spend a pleasant evening in her company, although she seemed to be quite evasive when I asked her how long she was staying for and about her plans for the future. Maybe I'd see if the opportunity arose over the next day or so and approach her directly about it. While it was nice having company over all this time, first with Clem, then Gabby and now my mother, I'd hardly had any time to live truly on my own and enjoy my new life.

My outfit for the party was a pair of three-quarter length jeans and a bright paisley sleeveless blouse in various shades of reds and blues, topped off with a pair of sparkly flip-flops, When I looked in the mirror, I thought I looked OK. My freckles were in abundance from all the sunshine and my hair loosely flowed around my shoulders. I hadn't picked up my straighteners in days, and while a trim was probably overdue, it fell in its natural waves over my sun-kissed shoulders in a way that I found pleasing.

'Oh, Meredith. You look...' Mother looked me up and down.

'I look what? I'm not changing so it'll have to do.'

'I was going to say you look pretty actually. Please don't jump down my throat the minute I open my mouth.' She stepped towards me and tucked a wavy strand of hair behind my ear. 'Very pretty.'

This was the closest she had come to touching me since she'd arrived. I noticed that she hadn't been as critical of me as normal. Perhaps her time away on the retreat had done her good and maybe now I was more chilled too; we had become a better combination together.

'Thank you,' I said, not used to compliments from her. 'Will you come with me now, or later?'

'I just have a call to make and then I'll be along. Won't be far behind you. I can help you with anything you need when I arrive.'

Clem and Sophie were already there when I arrived, and I watched them from afar as she stretched up to fix the fairy lights to the top of the first gazebo. I noticed her bump seemed to be larger than before, although it was still small enough that other people might not actually even clock she was pregnant. She and Clem were laughing and as he reached up to take the lights from her – she was clearly not tall enough to reach – they shared a tender moment. It made me gulp. That was all I really needed to realise that he and I would never be 'a thing'. My fingers instinctively reached to fiddle with the charms on my bracelet.

I took a deep breath and approached them.

'What can I do to help?' I asked, forcing a jolly tone.

When Clem realised I was there, his face changed into a frown. He looked quickly at Sophie.

'Oh, thank you. Finally, someone sensible.' She grinned. 'You can help me with these blooming lights if you would. I'm sure two pairs of hands would be better than one and if Clem can put the gazebos up, then perhaps we can follow him with the bunting and lights. Does that sound OK?'

'Sure does.' She passed one end of the lights to me, and I showed her the folding stool I had brought. 'Oh my God. You're a genius. That will help so much.'

As we began to work, the stiffness in the air seemed to lessen but Clem still didn't speak.

'How are you enjoying life in Driftwood Bay then? I hear you've been working Clem quite hard.'

Looking away from her so that she couldn't see me blushing crimson red, I answered in a voice a little higher than normal for some unknown reason. 'Yes, he's been amazing. So clever and good with his hands... I mean, good at his job if you know what I mean.' I felt like I was really having to watch what I was saying so that I didn't drop Clem in it.

'Oh yes, he's always been good with his hands, haven't you, Penrose?' She ignored the glare he gave her and stopped hanging the lights to turn to me. She looked deep into my eyes, lowering her voice. 'He's a good man, Meredith. A really good man and there's not that many of those around. When you find one, you should really do all you can to hang on to them.'

I gulped. Was this her way of warning me away from him?

'Yes, I can tell that. He worked like a trooper on the lighthouse. If I hadn't been introduced to him, I don't think I'd ever have been able to live in it.'

'Well, it used to be in his family in the past so I think it was important to him. He's enjoyed every minute of it. I hear he's also taken you out on his boat and taught you to paddle-board too?'

She tilted her head, not taking her eyes away from mine.

I swallowed and turned back to unravel the bunting I was holding.

'Yes, he has. You'd think I'd know better at my age to be doing things like that. He's been very kind, introducing me to new things. I came here to get away from men, so it's been nice to know that men can be just friends. And good with us being so different in age too.' I said this pointedly, trying to pull her off the scent.

'It is, yes.' She turned back to hanging her lights but not before smirking at me. God, I hoped she didn't know how close we came to it being so much more. Surely, he wouldn't have said anything. He probably only told her about the boat trip and the paddle-boarding. If I only knew that one, he had a girlfriend and two, that she was pregnant, I wouldn't have dreamed of going anywhere near him. This was all a bit of a mess.

'Do you think you'll stick around a while?' she asked, offering her hand as I got down from my stool.

'Not sure to be honest. The lighthouse was only going to be a project, but I do love it here. It's all very well, enjoying the honeymoon period when visitors are around, and I've taken time away from work. I suppose I need to settle into a normal life and see how that feels.'

'Oh yes, I've been meaning to talk to you about work. Is there any chance you could come and have a look at my boat? After you've done Clem's, that is. I've heard that you've worked wonders on some old furniture that you got from Martin...'

'Oh, that's not my job. I'm a graphic designer by trade. The upholstery and interior design thing is just a hobby.'

Sophie continued to talk about the work she wanted doing but I had become distracted, seeing Russell standing nearby. He'd clearly been listening in and now that he'd clocked that I'd seen him he came over.

'I don't think you're planning on sticking around for too long. Are you? Remember how much I told you you'd be able to sell for. You'll be making a right good profit to move onto your next project.'

'Well, I did say that I haven't made my mind up what I'm going to do next.'

'If it was me, I'd be biting my hand off to sell. All your hard work would be well worth it when you looked at your bank account.'

There was that pressured feeling bearing down on me again, that feeling I got whenever Russell mentioned selling up.

'We'll see...'

Wanting to extricate myself from this conversation, I took the opportunity of Geoff having just arrived with the drinks trailer and decided to go help him set up. But as I walked over, I spotted my mother approaching. She was wearing a pair of oversized Prada sunglasses and had a gorgeous Michael Kors handbag over her arm, but she was frowning.

'All OK?' I asked as she reached me and perched her glasses on her head. She broke into a smile that didn't quite reach her eyes.

'Yes, darling. All fine, thank you. Is that bar open yet? I could murder a G & T.'

I laughed. 'That retreat sobriety has worn off?'

I thought of the amount of empty red wine bottles I'd put in the recycling bin that morning. Over the last couple of days, we'd polished off quite a few between us as we'd chatted – more amiably than ever before, even though I still got the impression she was guarding something, being positively shifty at times.

\* \* \*

The evening was going perfectly. Geoff had wired up some speakers around the gazebos and some slow contemporary music was playing. I recognised the words from popular songs being played acoustic style, which gave a really chilled-out vibe. The sun was still high in the sky and the drinks were flowing. James was continuously bringing beers for us all and Mother thought he was wonderful because he was keeping her required gin and tonic topped up, positively pandering to her. While it made me happy that she clearly approved of my new friends, it made me a little sad to think that she never looked at me that way. However, I would accept that she seemed happy here in my world and that was a first. She even flirted a little with Geoff when he came round with burgers and pulled-pork baps.

While I was over at the public toilets at the edge of the beach, I heard hushed raised voices coming from behind the building.

I gasped when I heard a conversation that clearly wasn't meant for my ears.

'I'm going ahead with this pregnancy with or without you. I'm not getting rid of it. But you really do need to stop flirting with Meredith. It's driving me insane.' Sophie's voice had a distinct wobble to it.

I couldn't believe the next words.

'For god's sake. Surely you know she's not my type. All that girly wholesomeness. She gets right on my tits. I'm just trying to butter her up.'

My heart was pounding.

What a cruel thing for him to say, he was clearly not the person I thought he was. And she even told me he was a good man. Maybe we were both wrong.

'I actually really like her. I can see the attraction.' I quietly thanked Sophie for sticking up for me.

Then the next sentence made my blood turn cold.

'For fuck's sake, Sophie. If I can just persuade her to sell the lighthouse, I'll make a fortune and then I can pay off my debts. And if you're still insistent on having this baby, you can make a plan for its future.'

This wasn't Clem's voice but Russell's. So, he was only being nice to me so that I sold up and he made loads in commission. The double-crossing git.

'What's all the shouting?' Now this was Clem's voice.

'Oh, here he comes, bloody Perfect Penrose. I don't know why you're poking your nose into mine and Sophie's business. Why don't you just fuck off and leave us alone?'

I could see them through the gap. Clem turned towards Sophie. 'You deserve better than him and your baby deserves a better father than him.'

I gasped out loud. So, Russell was the father of the baby, not Clem? What a muddle. Why did Clem let me think it was him?

'Because you're so chivalrous, aren't you, Clement?' he continued. 'Maybe you should have told Miss Prissy Pants that the only reason you were helping her with the lighthouse was because she outbid you and pissed you off. Now you've got it how you want it, you can buy it back into your family, even though you have to pay more for it than you ever wanted to.'

I could not believe what I was hearing. Did I continue to stand here and listen to them slagging me off, or did I move away and let them get on with it? My nosy nature decided on the former.

Movement through the gap in the fence alerted me to the fact that Clem was squaring up to Russell.

'You're a shit. You always were and you always will be and she—' he pointed towards Sophie '—deserves a million times better than you.'

'Yeah well, you always did have designs on her, didn't you? Jealous much?'

Russell sneered. He was right in Clem's face.

'I've known Sophie all my life. She's like a little sister to me and all I'm doing is looking out for her. I've kept your secret for long enough now. If she can't see that the father of her child is a complete and utter twat, then so be it. I can't do any more. I hope you'll be very happy together but, Sophie, I'm done. Don't come crying to me again when it all goes tits up. Because you know it will.'

He stormed away but to my horror that meant that he was going to pass me. There was literally nowhere for me to go. I just hoped that maybe he'd be so furious that he wouldn't notice me. Not a chance of that though.

'Oh, great. So now you heard all of that. Well, at least now you know that I'm not the shit that you think I am.' I went to speak but he cut me off. 'I honestly can't believe you think so little of me that I'd be spending time with you knowing that my girlfriend – who isn't actually my girlfriend by the way, just someone I've known all my life – was up the duff with my child. Thanks a lot, Meredith. Clearly the time we spent getting to know each other meant nothing to you at all.'

'But, Clem—'

He stomped past me, raising his palm. 'Not interested. Save your breath.'

## 43

The others were still standing near the gazebo and, flustered, I walked up to the group. Gemma looked at me and tilted her head, knowing immediately that something was up. I shook my head, silently willing her to leave it. She nodded in acknowledgement but as I tried to talk to the rest of the group normally she kept looking at me out of the corner of her eye. I necked two ice-cold beers quite quickly, wanting to numb some of the guilt I was feeling at jumping to conclusions.

Dyllis came over to me. Distracted with my thoughts, when she asked if she could have a word, I agreed.

'I owe you an apology. I've not been very nice to you since you've arrived. I thought you would take Clem away from my Sophie, but now I realise that they were never more than friends. I wanted them to be more, but it wasn't what they wanted. It appears that she's been keeping quite a lot from me over the last few years. I'm sorry. I hope we can put this behind us.'

I looked across and saw Clem wandering across the beach.

'Yes. Fine. Sorry, I need to...'

I strode over to my rock where he sat hunched over, just staring out at the sea. I coughed as I approached, and he looked up and sighed deeply.

'May I?'

'Suit yourself.'

We sat in silence. I knew that the words I spoke next were some of the most important of my life.

'I'm sorry. I misjudged the situation. I should have known you better.'

'Yes, you should. I've been nothing but straight with you since we met, and I really thought... hoped... that what I was feeling wasn't one-sided. I know that there's an age gap between us and that it bothered you but it never once bothered me. I thought that we had something special between us.'

I touched his shoulder. 'We have.' I looked into his big blue beautiful eyes and drank him in. How could I ever have thought that he was capable of lying like that?

'We had.' He shook my hand off. 'I don't think I can get over this. Did you really think I could do something like that? If you did, then you just don't know me at all.'

He stood and walked away without even a glance back.

I could feel tears streaming down my face, and I curled my knees up to my chest and that was how my mother found me a few minutes later. She sat next to me and put her arm around my shoulders. 'Whatever is the matter?'

'What isn't the matter? I've just upset the one person in my life that I thought really liked me for who I really am.'

'Not the only person surely. I do.'

'No, you don't. You never have.' I unfolded myself and stood to my full height. 'You have never loved me the way a mother should love her daughter. You've kept me at arm's length all my life. Nothing I ever did was good enough for you.'

'But that's not—'

'True? I think you'll find it is.' The rage of many years was rising in my body as I finally faced her, something I should have done a long time ago. 'Have I ever been the daughter you wanted me to be? Have I ever been able to do anything right for you? You left me, Mum. You went off to live in America and you left me behind.'

'It was the best thing for you.' She almost whispered those words and at least she had the decency to look ashamed.

'The best thing for you, you mean. What mother would leave her daughter and go and live literally the other side of the world rather than be with her?'

'But—'

'But what? What can you possibly say that could make this better? All that time I've known you never wanted me enough to stay. That I, your own flesh and blood, wasn't enough. That you would rather be in America without me than you would be in England with me. And since then, you've spent years belittling me, telling me how I could do everything better, nothing was ever good enough for you, even though I broke my back trying.'

Once I started telling her exactly how she'd hurt me, years of pent-up emotion came tumbling out and the sentences seemed to just roll into each other as she stared back at me.

'I spent night after night breaking my heart because you'd abandoned me. Then I thought that you'd come back for me, so I did everything I could to be the best that I could for you. Behaving for Nana, so that you would finally get your perfect daughter. But even that wasn't enough. And you never came back for me. You broke my heart and it's never been the same since.'

I turned to walk away, almost feeling the same hurt from her leaving years ago come flooding right back, but this time I had the gumption to speak up.

I turned back. 'It's no wonder I find it hard to love people, isn't it? I just think they're never going to love me quite enough to stay. No wonder my marriage fell apart. Thanks for nothing.'

'That's simply not true, Meredith,' she said sharply. 'Your nana told me that you were absolutely fine with me going. In fact, it was her who told me to go.'

I sank to my knees and cried, for all that had been lost, for everything that had come out tonight. I cried and, without realising it, the cries quickly turned to sobs, all that I had been suppressing. Mother came to my side and took me in her arms, rocking me from side to side, in a way that I'd wanted her to do so many times before.

'Nana wouldn't have done that. She wouldn't. I know it.' My words came out snatched.

'I think you and I need to have a proper talk, don't we? Something we probably should have done many years ago.'

I nodded, and she helped me to get up. We walked back across the beach and when we reached the others she explained that I wasn't feeling well and she was taking me home.

Russell stood in my path, choosing the worst possible moment to ask me about the lighthouse. He clearly didn't know that I'd overheard everything he'd said earlier.

'Have you had any more thoughts about selling up?'

'Yes, I have,' I said bitingly. 'I should have realised this place could never be a home.' There was a collective gasp from my friends around me. 'Go ahead. Put the lighthouse back up for sale. I'm leaving.'

**44**

When I woke the following morning, I could smell coffee and as the events of the night before came back to me, for the first time since I'd been here, I didn't want to get out of bed. I was tired and my eyes felt sore. However, I knew that the only way to resolve what I'd started was to plough straight in. I needed to finish the conversation I'd started with Mother, so I grabbed my dressing gown from the hook on the back of my bedroom door and headed up to the kitchen where she was sat on a stool at the breakfast bar, flicking through a magazine.

'Morning, darling. Coffee?'

I nodded nervously, feeling like the insecure little girl I became whenever she came back to the UK for a visit, not knowing what the right thing was to say or do, and hoping that maybe it would be the time that, if I behaved properly, she might come back to stay or even take me back with her.

We went up to the top floor to drink our coffees, looking out over the harbour. The weather today was overcast and a bit gloomy, very much like the mood inside.

She put a tray down on the coffee table and sat opposite me in one of the armchairs I'd reupholstered.

'I really do love this chair, Meredith,' she said, stroking the fabric on the arm. 'You are so talented.'

'Thank you, I enjoy doing it.'

'Yes, I can see that.' There was total silence as I picked up my mug and took a sip.

'So...' she whispered.

I whispered back, 'So...'

'Do you want to go first or shall I?'

'Go ahead, Mother.'

'I do wish you'd call me Mum. You make me sound so old.'

'You said that you wanted me to call you Mother?'

'Whenever did I say that? I really dislike it. It makes us sound like we're so distant.'

I raised my eyebrows.

'OK, I get it. I've messed up in the past,' she said, softer. 'So many times, and regretfully, I can't change what's done. But I'm hoping that after this talk, we'll have more of a bearing on whether we have a future and I hope to God that we have.' She paused, as if collecting her thoughts. 'I'm sorry that I've never been the parent you wanted me to be. I've been doing some real soul searching on the retreat and digging right back into my past. I believe that I owe you many huge apologies.'

I didn't speak. I wasn't going to make this particularly easy for her.

'I have things I'd like to talk about,' she continued. 'Some of them aren't going to be easy to say, and some of them might not be easy to hear. But they're all important and I feel like the time has come to get everything out in the open. No stone unturned, as they say. That OK?'

I nodded back at her and she smiled sadly, taking a deep breath. I never really appreciated that this might be hard for her too.

'Feel free to chip in as I go along or wait until I've said everything, but I would like today to be about trying to put the past behind us, if we can both allow that to happen, and hopefully we can forge a good future for us both.'

I took another sip of my drink, needing to do something.

She took my silence as approval to continue.

'As I've told you before, I met your father at a friend's party. I was going through a rebellious stage and your nana and I clashed about everything. What I haven't ever told you was that he was part of a gang. They weren't even invited, and I'd had way too much to drink and felt ill. I genuinely thought he was taking me into a bedroom so I could sit and gather myself, but he thought differently and I was...' she took an even deeper breath '...taken advantage of. I didn't even know his name and I was so ashamed of myself. My own stupid fault and I should have known better, but I didn't. When I became pregnant with you, I didn't tell anybody. I kept it a secret for so long that the only alternatives I had were to become a mother or have you adopted, and I didn't want to do the latter. So, instead of going to St Andrews University as planned, I ended up in a crappy job to make ends meet, and when I wasn't doing that, I was changing nappies, wiping up snot and going to baby groups instead of nightclubs with my friends.

'Your nana was amazing. She did everything she could to help me. She adored you and loved spending time with you, but for me... I just couldn't. I had – what I now know, since talking to counsellors at the retreat, to be – post-natal depression. It wasn't really a thing in those days. I remember going to the doctor's once and being told that I was being a silly little girl, to pull my socks up and just get on with it. Can you imagine that happening these days?'

'I'm sorry Moth—Mum. I didn't know.'

'Nobody did, darling. I kept it hidden. I was already ashamed of being a single mother and then I felt like I couldn't cope. I don't know how your nana managed it, but she held down a full-time job, and looked after you and me too. But still I rebelled. I knew that she'd take care of you, so I used to just take off and leave you with her. She never really reprimanded me, and I wanted to punish her and myself and let myself get in with a crowd who weren't good for me, drinking and doing drugs.'

I couldn't believe that the person she was talking about was herself. I couldn't imagine for one minute my mother doing any of these things.

'One night I was taken into hospital and had to have my stomach pumped and they called your nana to tell her. She had to confide in a neighbour because she needed them to look after you while she came to fetch me. And she was so angry; she told me that I had to get myself together somehow, that she couldn't stand by and let me destroy your life, even if I wanted to destroy my own. That was hard to hear.

'I rallied round. Got myself a job, broke away from the gang and that's when I met Phil who was over here on a work trip. We had a whirlwind romance and for the first time in my life, I felt like I had a future. He offered me, well, us actually, a new life in America but I felt that I was such an awful mother to you, that it would be better for us both if I left you behind, just to start with. I was going to pull myself together, get a job and get settled and then I was going to bring you over. Your nana could visit too and see how well I was doing for myself.'

She smiled at me through damp eyes.

'But we never went. What happened?'

She took a deep breath. 'I discovered I was pregnant.'

My eyes widened. 'Are you telling me I have siblings I've never met?'

She shook her head and laid her hand on her stomach. Another deep breath followed.

'My baby died when I was seven months pregnant.'

'Oh, Mum.' A single tear trickled down my cheek to match the one that was trickling down hers.

'I had to give birth to him. It was horrendous. Even though there was no baby, the post-natal depression came back, this time along with grief. I was heartbroken. I had painted a picture of the perfect family life. Giving that baby everything that I should have given you, and you finally being part of our lives too. And then it was all snatched away.' The tears were flowing now for both of us. 'When I told your nana what had happened, she said that she felt that you were better where you were, that you were loved and looked after and didn't want for anything. And that made me feel worse. You never needed me.'

At this point, she put her head in her hands and I heard a muffled sob. I moved across to her, perched on the arm of the chair and put my arm around her shoulders, pulling her in tight. She turned and tucked herself into my body and she wept.

Stroking her hair and rocking her gently seemed to soothe her and eventually she pulled away slightly.

'I'm so very sorry, Meredith,' she croaked. 'I should have told you before.'

'Oh, Mum. I'm so sorry you had to go through this. This really does explain a lot. Thank you for finally feeling up to sharing it with me.'

There was part of me that wished this had happened years earlier. Why had it taken for me to get to nearly fifty before we could have this very honest conversation? And what happened now? Was I supposed to just forgive her because she'd talked about it? I honestly didn't know if I would ever be able to.

'The retreat taught me that I can't continue to bottle up these feelings and put on a hard front when inside I've been hurting for so long. I think that's why I've had so many husbands, going from one to the next, just fixing the problem temporarily with things and people that made me happy in each moment. But I've always hated myself, Meredith, for what I did to you, and I'll never be able to forgive myself. Well, I suppose you know everything now. No more secrets.'

It wasn't often that I was stuck for words but right then I was.

'I don't know what to say. I wish you'd told me sooner, but you didn't, and we can't change that.' I stood and walked over to the French windows and looked at the view.

'You look at peace here, Meredith,' she said. 'You've never really been that before. I know you weren't happy with David, that you fitted in with what he wanted rather than have an opinion yourself, and it broke my heart to see you that way. To see that I had affected your life so much as an adult. So I kept away. I felt that it was the right thing to do for you. How could I interfere in your life, when I had no right?

'You seem so very different here. So calm and relaxed and you fit. I hope that me sharing this with you, while it may be very upsetting now, may help you to understand. Then maybe we can look at our relationship and see if it can be repaired.'

I closed my eyes, trying to take it all in. My ears started to buzz and my head began to pound and I could feel the walls closing in around me. These revelations were making me feel suffocated and I needed to escape.

'I need to go for a walk. I'll be back soon.'

She nodded, and as I went to go downstairs to change, she shouted after me. 'Meredith?'

I turned and looked her way.

'I know it might be difficult for you to understand but I do love you and I always have in my own way.'

How on earth was I supposed to respond to that? Did it even need an answer? I didn't know what to say, so I said nothing and ran away.

*　*　*

Even a walk on the beach didn't clear my head so I found myself walking towards Vi's house. When she asked me how I was, I burst into tears.

Through my sobs, as I sat on the pouffe next to her chair, the whole story tumbled out and she listened without saying a word. I cried for the years of sadness and grief for what could have been. When I was spent, she went to the kitchen, returning with a tray of tea and biscuits.

'Nothing in the world that can't be sorted out with a cup of tea and a Hobnob, you know.' I smiled and Gladys came over and licked my salty tear-streamed cheeks.

'First time she's moved in a couple of days. She's not herself at the moment. She was a little bit sick this morning. I was going to ring you and ask you to come and see her. I couldn't bear it if anything happened to her.' Vi's voice trembled as she spoke.

'Ah, Gladys sweetheart. Are you feeling a little under the weather?' She had plonked herself back on her bed and looked at me forlornly from across the room. 'Keep an eye on her, Vi, and if she's no better tomorrow, I can nip her to the vet's. She may have eaten something funny on a walk maybe.'

'Thank you, dear. And I can't stop thinking about your poor mum and everything she went through. What an ordeal for her.'

As if I'd needed to hear it from someone else, I suddenly found myself understanding. For the first time in what felt like forever, instead of feeling sorry for myself, I began to feel sorry for Mum. It must have taken some real courage for her to tell me everything. I wanted to go back and see how she was.

'I can see you are itching to get away, but what are we going to do with you? I saw you and Clement talking last night and his storming off. What is going on with you two? I feel like banging your blooming heads together!'

'Oh, Vi, it's like every relationship I have I mess up. I do wonder whether I do it so I can bugger it up before the other person does. At least that way I'm in control.'

'Oh yes, you really look like you're in control right now.' She smiled. 'Clement brought me home last night, Meredith, and he didn't stop talking about you. I think you and he should clear the air.'

'I'm not sure there's anything left to say. I let him down. And now the work is done on the lighthouse, I don't think there's any point in me staying here any more. You're on the mend and will soon be out and about on your own. Clem hates me.' I saw her mouth twitch. 'I think it's best if I finish the renovation, sell the lighthouse to him because that's clearly what he wanted all along, then Russell gets his commission. And then I can look for something else, somewhere else. No one needs me here.'

'People might not need you, my dear, but it doesn't mean that they don't want you. Two very different things. Don't think too hard about it all, Meredith. A wise man once said to me that all the answers will come to you when they are meant to.' She patted my hand and took another Hobnob from the packet.

Gladys didn't even lift her head.

## 45

Hearing myself retell my mother's story to Vi had actually helped me to get it more into perspective and I finally realised that she'd not had an easy time at all. She probably deserved more compassion from me rather than me walking away from her when it was all difficult to hear.

Movement from the guest room made me knock on the door first, and a muffled 'Come in,' told me to enter.

'Mum, what are you doing?'

I wasn't sure why I was even asking because it was perfectly clear that she was packing.

'I thought I'd get out of your way, darling. There's a room at the B & B I thought I'd move into and give you some space. When you work out what you want for yourself and are ready, then perhaps we can talk. And do make things up with that lovely man, Clem. I can see how you feel about him by the way you look at him. I know you've protected yourself as much as you can by putting up a shell around you, but sometimes you have to take a chance on love. True love doesn't come into your life very often and you should grasp it with both hands when it does. Whether it works out or not, it's part of life and love is too special not to have it in your life.'

'Oh, I don't know, Mum,' I said bashfully, not trying to deny the feelings I had for Clem. 'If you don't love, you don't get hurt.'

'But if you never know love—' she reached across and tucked a stray hair behind my ear '—you are missing out on so much. You know the saying, "It's better to have loved and lost than never to have loved at all." Just think about it. Promise me that at the very least.'

I nodded, speechless.

A horn hooted from outside.

'That'll be my taxi. You know where I am if and when you are ready to talk. James said that he'll come and collect the rest of my bags later.' She kissed my cheek and walked away. I slumped down onto the bed and felt like I was going to weep all over again.

* * *

I knew I had some issues that needed dealing with, with both my mother and Clem, but kept myself to myself while I worked out how, when and what to say. A few times there was a knock at the front door, but I ignored it and put my head back under the duvet. I couldn't be bothered to do anything, not even eat. All I wanted to do was to forget everything and sleep – although my sleep was restless.

'Right, lady, time you got out of your pit.' I looked up and saw Gemma standing over me with her arms folded. 'You can't hide away for ever.'

'Yes, I can.' I pulled the duvet back over my head only to have it whisked off me completely two seconds later.

'No! You! Can't!'

I groaned.

'Get yourself in that shower and I want to see you upstairs in fifteen minutes, dressed. Don't let me down. I do not want to see you looking like...' she circled her finger and pointed at me '...that!'

I glanced back at the duvet as she made to walk out of the room, and she smirked.

'Don't even think about it, lady. In fact...'

She grabbed the duvet and pillows from the bed and tucked them under her arms, carrying them out of the room with her. Then I heard her footsteps clomping up the stairs. I didn't even know how she'd got into the lighthouse. As far as I knew the only other person apart from me who had a key was...

Ah. Clem. She must have got it from him.

* * *

The hot water flowed over me, and I was grateful that I'd decided on the high-pressure rainfall shower head. That and the grapefruit shower gel stimulated all my senses and I began to feel more awake than I had in days. I washed and conditioned my hair and after I'd stepped out of the shower and wrapped myself in the huge soft bath sheet, I felt a million times better. A quick blast of the hairdryer, a clean pair of cut-off denim shorts and a T-shirt from the wardrobe, and I really did feel like a new woman. Bless Gemma for knowing what I needed.

'Well, you definitely look a bit more human than you did when I arrived.' I fake smiled at her. 'How are you feeling on the inside? Your mum told me everything, by the way. She was in a bit of a state when she arrived.'

'I bet she was. Having to hang on to those secrets for that many years must have been just awful for her.'

I still didn't know in my own mind if I would ever be able to forgive her totally, even though I now knew her reasons for behaving the way she did and felt dreadfully sorry for her. Surely you have choices to make in life, and you can choose to make the best of a situation or the worst. Instead of fighting for the child that she did have, she chose to spend her life mourning the one that she didn't. But I knew too well that mental illness took no prisoners, especially in that day and age. Today it could have been a whole different scenario.

'I thought we could grab Gladys and take her for a walk on the beach. Fresh air will do you good.'

I nodded, although I didn't feel like I had any energy. However, after a few deep breaths of Driftwood Bay air, I was definitely feeling more up to it, if not fully up to speed.

When we reached the edge of the harbour, to my surprise, Lucy and James appeared and fell into step with us too.

'How's things? How are you feeling? Your mum really is sorry, you know.'

'God, Lucy,' I said. 'It's a good job I didn't want this kept a secret.'

'Your mum is stopping with us, Meredith, so she thought it was only fair to keep us in the picture.'

'Well, she should really have checked with me before blabbing our story around.'

Lucy squeezed my hand. 'We're your friends, Meredith. And friends don't judge.'

They waited outside while I went into Vi's house.

Vi stood to greet me and gave me a little hug which was exactly what I needed right then and I gave out a little sigh.

'How are you my dear? I've heard you've been under the weather the last couple of days. You must be coming out in sympathy with Gladys who has been feeling the same. How are you coping?'

'I'll be fine in time. I'm still processing everything to be honest. How are those legs doing?'

'They're doing great. I got my steps up again yesterday and even managed to walk to the harbour wall and back. I got chatting with the lovely Martin from the bric-a-brac shop. Nice man. Handsome old fox. I bet I could give him a run for his money when I'm fully back on form.'

'Oh, Vi, you are a tonic. I hope I'm like you when I'm your age.'

'Well, life is for living, my dear. You've taught me that along with the fact that we all deserve a second chance. Maybe it's time that you and your mother got yours.'

'Who knows, eh?' I turned my attention to Gladys, who was lying at Vi's feet looking despondent. 'Come on, girl, are you feeling better?'

'She's still not right but does seem a little brighter. I'll have to put her on a diet, she's getting a right podge on her. We'll have to stop all those treats.'

'Well, we'll go for a nice big walk today and she can run around after the ball.'

Vi patted my hand. 'Thank you for all you've done. I hope you find your peace.'

I smiled and turned to leave before I started to cry. The one thing that people who are feeling delicate do not need is someone being nice to them. That's a sure-fire way to dissolve into tears.

Gemma, Lucy and James and I walked along the harbour in silence until it turned into beach. I let Gladys off, but she stayed close by. She didn't seem to fancy a run even when I threw the ball for her. Maybe she still wasn't feeling 100 per cent.

We walked towards my rock and, to my surprise, there sat upon it was my mother and – of all people – Clem. He raised his big blue eyes and locked them onto mine. God, I'd missed those eyes. Mum was sitting next to him, and when I looked at her, she looked back at me forlornly.

Lucy's hand reached down to mine.

'Here, let me take Gladys's lead and we'll walk her down the beach and back. Leave you to it.'

It was hitting me now that this was a complete set-up and not the coincidence that I originally thought it was. I took a big sigh.

'So...'

'Please may I go first?'

I nodded at Mum, and she took in a deep breath before she spoke.

'I know I've never been the mother to you that I should have been. I know that I should have behaved differently and put your feelings ahead of my own. But I couldn't see it at the time because of the depression. That's not an excuse by the way, but it is a reason. If you will give me a chance now, moving forward, to be the mother that you deserve, I will spend the rest of my life making it up to you and making you feel like the most loved daughter in the world. I'm asking you, Meredith, to please give me that chance.'

'How will you do that? Where will you live?'

'Well, that all depends on you, my darling. Wherever you are, I want to be nearby, if you'll have me.'

I inhaled the hugest of breaths and flicked my eyes towards Clem, who was looking at the floor. I exhaled. What was he even doing here?

'I'm not sure there's anything here for me any more,' I said tentatively.

He lifted his head and his eyes met mine. 'It's my turn now. I have something to say.'

I nodded, not trusting myself to speak.

'When I saw you in that supermarket car park, the very first time we met, I was having the crappiest day. I'd loved Driftwood Bay Lighthouse for years and always said that I'd like to buy it, but Russell was messing me around big time and was sitting on my offer. I'd just come off the phone from him and he'd told me that it was a done deal and that someone was moving in that day. I wasn't concentrating and this fiery, bad-tempered woman started shouting at me and pissed me right off. I drove away wondering what had got her all riled up and, try as I might, I couldn't get her out of my mind. Those beautiful blue eyes and soft, golden ramrod straight hair that I would have loved to run my fingers through. Then I found out that it was the same person who gazumped me in trying to buy the lighthouse. Russell told me that it was a couple from London who were minted, said they had literally offered an amount he couldn't refuse. And that really pissed me off. Then I discovered that you were on your own, and weren't filthy rich, and that he'd lied about that.'

He didn't take his eyes off mine as he spoke.

'I already knew at that point that Sophie was pregnant,' he continued, 'and Russell was messing her around, saying one minute he wanted her to get rid of the baby and the next he wanted them to be a family. And then he began to get jealous of me and Sophie. Sophie and I have literally been best mates since we were little, I'm like a big brother to her, nothing more than that, but he thought there was more. So that's why he's been acting up and that's why he was flirting with you, because he knew it would wind me up. I also suspect it's because he wanted you to sell, once we'd done all the work on the lighthouse. It turns out that he's got some huge debts and saw you as a cash cow.'

'So, I just became stuck in the middle?'

'Pretty much. And even though you kept telling me about the crap dating scene you'd escaped and that you wanted to be on your own, I just got the feeling that it maybe could be more, even though you thought I was too young for you...'

'But you were giving me signs that you weren't interested. That's why I said that. So you didn't feel bad...' I paused as I remembered what had happened so soon after. 'But that day when you nearly kissed me...'

'God, I wanted to kiss you so much, Mere.'

'Oh, you pair! What are you like?' My mum had piped up, cutting through the magic of the moment. 'Hope you don't mind but I'm going to excuse myself from this. It's getting a bit personal. I'll be with the others on the dog walk.' She touched my arm and kissed my cheek. 'He's a good man. You seem to be giving me a second chance. Give him one too.' She winked. 'Second chance I meant.'

Clem patted the now vacant space next to him and I sat, taking everything in.

'So, you do like me then?'

'Like you? You silly arse. I'm bloody crazy about you. I think about you night and day and I can't bear the thought of you leaving. You being here feels so right. You've fitted in perfectly and become part of the community. Look what you've done for Vi.'

'Dyllis hates me though. She thinks I'm way too old for you.'

'Dyllis thought that you were coming between me and Sophie. She's been put right on that score now, I can assure you. And what's age got to do with anything?'

'Oh, so can I just check again? You do like me?'

He gently cupped my cheek with his hand. 'Like you? I'm head over heels in love with you. You're fiercely independent, kind and absolutely gorgeous. Even if you are a demon when you're hangry! Stay, Meredith. Please. Give us a chance. No one knows what the future holds but we could take it slowly and face it together. What do you think?'

'Are you sure you don't just want me for my lighthouse?'

'Well, that is obviously the icing on the cake, but even if you do decide to sell, I will still feel exactly the same about you as I do right now. Please stay.'

'What if things don't work out between us?'

'But what if they do?'

I shifted across the rock and we turned to each other. I couldn't have got closer if I'd tried. Warmth flooded my body as I lifted my head to his, and as my hands weaved into the hair at the nape of his neck, his lips met mine and we kissed. We kissed like we'd never been kissed before and a million fireworks exploded in my heart.

We broke away with a laugh to a round of applause and cheers from further down the beach.

And then we kissed again.

Maybe it was OK not to know what the future held.

Maybe the fun was in the finding out.

# EPILOGUE

'Gabby, I have news.'

'Spill. You know I love a bit of juicy gossip.'

'Clem and me, well... we're a couple.' It sounded strange saying it out loud but good too. I held the phone away from my ear as she screeched down the line.

'Woohoo! That's brilliant news. I knew it! I want to know all the details.'

'Well, I'll tell you some of it, but maybe not all the details.'

'Obviously those are the bits that I want to hear, you saucy minx. I'm so happy for you, Mere. At our age, we can't hang about you know. When you get a chance of happiness you have to grab it with both hands.'

'We're certainly nowhere near that stage but we are together and we're taking it slowly. I still need to work on me some more. Being down here is a good start but that's what I'm concentrating on now. Oh, and Mum is staying around for a bit too. She's looking to rent somewhere close by.'

'Well, that's a turn-up for the books. You've forgiven her for being a shit mum all her life then?'

I knew that Gabby was just being protective of me. She was only too aware of how hurt I'd been in the past.

'Maybe living here in Driftwood Bay is stopping me from living in the past and is encouraging me to live in the present. The old Meredith is gone. And she's taken all that shit she's been carrying around in her head with her.'

'You do know that talking about yourself in the third person is the first sign of going mad, don't you, mate?'

I laughed. 'It's a way of dealing with it for me. That Meredith is a different person now. This is the new me.'

'Well, I'm liking the new you. I'm so happy for you, Mere. For what it's worth, from what you've said about Clem, and in the brief time that I met him, I think you're perfect for each other. And let's hope your mum has had her own epiphany and she really has turned over a new leaf. I can't wait till we can come down and see you. I'm going to smoosh you so hard. Do you want us to book into the B & B? We don't want to be gooseberries when you and your toy boy are having rampant sex everywhere in the lighthouse.'

'I don't have the energy for rampant sex these days, Gab. I'm nearly fifty, don't you know. And Clem doesn't stay over every night anyway. Sometimes I stay on the boat with him. Sometimes we're on our own. We just see how each day takes us.'

'Look at the new you. I like her. In fact, I love her! I'm so looking forward to seeing you.'

'Me too. Can't wait. Right, got to dash. I've just had a text from Clem to say that we're needed. There's a new addition to Driftwood Bay about to make an appearance. Love you, Gabs.'

'You too, Mere. Love you too.'

* * *

'Oh my God! I can see the head. Come on, girl, you've got this. Now one final push.'

Clem held my hand and smiled. 'We've got this.'

'Woohoo! It's out. Is it a boy or a girl?'

'It's just a little slimy fur ball.'

Gladys turned round and licked her puppy. When we saw the vet earlier that week for her final scan, they said she had just one puppy in her belly. Unusual but not unheard of.

'Oh, my darling girl.' Tears streamed down Vi's cheeks as she reached down and tickled Gladys gently behind her ear. Then she turned to me. 'There's your new puppy, Meredith. Remember, I told you that if my Gladys got up the duff, it was all your fault and you'd have to have it.'

Clem and I laughed as he squeezed my hand. 'I can't see a willy so it must be a girl. What are we going to call her?'

'Welcome to the world, little one,' I whispered as I slowly moved closer. Gladys rested her head on my knee. She was clearly exhausted. 'You're such a clever girl.'

I touched the puppy gently on her snout. I instantly knew that I was going to name her after my nana.

'Welcome to the world, Alice.'

# ACKNOWLEDGMENTS

To Mark Fisher, who has had to put up with my ridiculous Facebook messages for two books now, asking about boats and what their parts are called, and what would happen in the middle of the ocean if an engine dropped and how you get Wi-Fi on a boat... Thank you for your patience and your answers x

As always to my sister Lisa, my biggest supporter and cheerleader. Love you x

To the incredible friends who inspire me to write about characters who have wonderful friendships. I am so very lucky to have amazing people like you in my life. Thank you x

To all the writers, the bloggers and to my readers. The book community is one of the most supportive I've ever known. You keep me going every single day with your messages, reviews, quips, social media posts. Thank you for everything. You'll never know how much of a difference that you make.

To Helen Rolfe, for always being available, and for letting me be totally myself with the most inappropriate message chain that no one else could ever see. Thank you x

To Jessica Redland, for being the kindest, most supportive and inspiring writer friend, and for championing me and my writing. I can't wait to sit in the same room as you and put the world to rights with a gin in our hands. And I'm buying!

And last and absolutely not least to my son Ollie, who makes me proud and laugh every single day. As you grow up, I love you more each day which I never thought was possible. Thank you for everything, for putting up with me as your mom and for being proud of me and my books x

# MORE FROM KIM NASH

We hope you enjoyed reading *Hopeful Hearts at the Cornish Cove*. If you did, please leave a review.

If you'd like to gift a copy, this book is also available as an ebook, large print, hardback, digital audio download and audiobook CD.

Sign up to Kim Nash's mailing list for news, competitions and updates on future books.

https://bit.ly/KimNashNews

# ABOUT THE AUTHOR

**Kim Nash** is an author of uplifting, romantic, feel-good fiction, having wanted to write books since she was a little girl. She works as both Digital Publicity Director for publisher Bookouture and a book blogger at www.kimthebookworm.co.uk. She lives in Staffordshire with her son Ollie and English Setter rescue dog Roni. When she's not working or writing, Kim can be found walking her dog and reading, as well as running a book club in Staffordshire and organising local and national reader/author events.

Visit Kim's website: www.kimthebookworm.co.uk

Follow Kim on social media:

 twitter.com/kimthebookworm

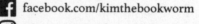 facebook.com/kimthebookworm

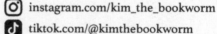 instagram.com/kim_the_bookworm

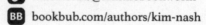 tiktok.com/@kimthebookworm

BB bookbub.com/authors/kim-nash

# Boldwo*od*

Boldwood Books is an award-winning fiction publishing company seeking out the best stories from around the world.

Find out more at www.boldwoodbooks.com

Join our reader community for brilliant books, competitions and offers!

Follow us
@BoldwoodBooks
@BookandTonic

Sign up to our weekly
deals newsletter

https://bit.ly/BoldwoodBNewsletter

9 781805 494638